MW01679384

lost boy lost girl

BY PETER STRAUB

Novels

Marriages
Under Venus
Julia
If You Could See Me Now
Ghost Story
Shadowland
Floating Dragon
The Talisman (with Stephen King)
Koko
Mystery
Mrs God
The Throat
The Hellfire Club
Mr X
Black House (with Stephen King)
lost boy lost girl

Poetry

Open Air
Leeson Park & Belsize Square

Collections

Wild Animals
Houses Without Doors
Peter Straub's Ghosts (editor)
Magic Terror

PETER STRAUB

lost boy lost girl

HarperCollinsPublishers

This is a work of fiction. All incidents and dialogue, and all characters, with the exception of some well-known historical and public figures, are products of the author's imagination and are not to be construed as real. Where real-life historical figures and public figures appear, the situations, incidents and dialogues concerning those persons are entirely fictional and are not intended to depict actual events or to change the entirely fictional nature of the work. In all other respects, any resemblance to persons living or dead is entirely coincidental.

HarperCollins*Publishers*
77–85 Fulham Palace Road,
Hammersmith, London W6 8JB

www.harpercollins.co.uk

This paperback edition 2004
1

First published in Great Britain by
HarperCollins*Publishers* 2003

First published in the USA by
Random House 2003

ISBN 978-0-00-789668-4

Typeset in Sabon by Palimpsest Book Production Limited,
Polmont, Stirlingshire

Printed and bound in Great Britain by
Clays Limited, St Ives plc

PETER STRAUB

Peter Straub was born in Milwaukee, Wisconsin. His bestselling novels and story collections have been translated into more than twenty languages. He has won the British Fantasy Award, two Bram Stoker Awards and two World Fantasy Awards. For a decade he lived in Ireland and England, and he now lives in New York City with his wife, Susan, the director of Project Read to Me.

Black House, his recent collaboration with Stephen King, was a massive worldwide success, a No 1 bestseller in both the *Sunday Times* and *New York Times*.

Lost Boy Lost Girl

'*Lost Boy Lost Girl* is intense and yet measured, serious and melancholy at times, but also humorous. Straub's prose has a tart clarity that allows him to delineate the muddiness of life with great economy and richness. He has a superb ear for dialogue, both spoken and silent. He is adept, too, with ambiguity, the emotional blur of the real world, of our tentative and ambivalent responses to each other and the things we do. These qualities create an atmosphere that lingers like the novel's own ghost, and Straub achieves this invisibly, in the background. He doesn't insist you notice how intelligent and subtle the novel is, and you don't: you merely appreciate how good a time you're having, and that you don't want it to stop.'

MICHAEL MARSHALL, *Guardian*

'Stephen King's mate and co-author puts the monster master into the shade. This'll have you anxiously contemplating the shadows' *Mirror*

'Mr Straub's latest is an unusually taut, dynamic, spooky display of horror expertise, and its story is deftly told.' *New York Times*

'*Lost Boy Lost Girl* operates on many levels and is skilfully told through the lives of its many characters. Part thriller, part chiller, this one is hard to put down' *Irish Examiner*

'The chilling presence of evil permeates every page of this Straub classic and takes horror to new heights. Straub has long been a master of the dark fantastic. He has co-written with Stephen King and could be ready now to take his crown.' *Northern Echo*

For Charles Bernstein and Susan Bee

There was set before me a mighty hill
And long days I climbed
Through regions of snow.
When I had before me the summit-view,
It seemed that my labours
Had been to see gardens
Lying at impossible distances.

– STEPHEN CRANE

What was at stake here, he thought,
was the solidity of the world.

– TIMOTHY UNDERHILL, *The Divided Man*

Contents

Part One

THE DEAD MOTHER

1

NANCY UNDERHILL'S DEATH had been unexpected, abrupt – a death like a slap in the face. Tim, her husband's older brother, knew nothing more. He could scarcely be said really to have known Nancy. On examination, Timothy Underhill's memories of his sister-in-law shrank into a tiny collection of snapshots. Here was Nancy's dark, fragile smile as she knelt beside her two-year-old son, Mark, in 1990; here she was, in another moment from that same visit, snatching up little Mark, both of them in tears, from his baby seat and rushing from the dim unadorned dining room. Philip, whose morose carping had driven his wife from the room, sat glaring at the dried-out pot roast, deliberately ignoring his brother's presence. When at last he looked up, Philip said, 'What?'

Ah Philip, you were ever a wonder. *The kid can't help being a turd*, Pop said once. *It seems to be one of the few things that make him feel good.*

One more of cruel memory's snapshots, this from an odd, eventful visit Tim had paid to Millhaven in 1993, when he flew the two and a half hours from La Guardia on the same carrier, and from all available evidence also the same craft, as this day: Nancy seen through the screen door of the little house on Superior Street, beaming as she hurried Tim-ward down the unlighted hallway, her face alight with the surprise and pleasure given her by the unexpected arrival on her doorstep of her brother-in-law ('famous' brother-in-law, she would have said). She had, simply, *liked* him, Nancy had, to an extent he'd understood only at that moment.

That quietly stressed out little woman, often (Tim thought) made wretched by her husband and sewn into her marriage by what seemed determination more than love, as if the preparation of many thousands of daily meals and a succession of household 'projects' provided most of the satisfaction she needed to keep her in place. Of course Mark must have been essential; and maybe her marriage had been happier than Tim imagined. For both their sakes, he hoped it had been.

Philip's behavior over the next few days would

give him all the answers he was likely to get. And with Philip, *interpretation* was always necessary. Philip Underhill had cultivated an attitude of discontent ever since he had concluded that his older brother, whose flaws shone with a lurid radiance, had apparently seized from birth most of the advantages available to a member of the Underhill clan. From early in his life, nothing Philip could get or achieve was quite as good as it would have been but for the mocking, superior presence of his older brother. (In all honesty, Tim did not doubt that he had tended to lord it over his little brother. Was there ever an older brother who did not?) During all of Philip's adult life, his grudging discontent had been like a role perfectly inhabited by an actor with a gift for the part: somewhere inside, Tim wanted to believe, the real Philip must have lived on, capable of joy, warmth, generosity, selflessness. It was this inner, more genuine self that was going to be needed in the wake of Nancy's mysterious death. Philip would need it for his own sake if he were to face his grief head-on, as grief had to be faced; but more than that, he would need it for his son. It would be terrible for Mark if his father somehow tried to treat his mother's death as yet another typical inconvenience different from the rest only by means of its severity.

From what Tim had seen on his infrequent

returns to Millhaven, Mark seemed a bit troubled, though he did not wish to think of his nephew in the terms suggested by the word 'troubled.' Unhappy, yes; restless; unfocused; afflicted with both a budding arrogance and what Tim had perceived was a good and tender heart. A combination so conflicted lent itself naturally to restlessness and lack of focus. So, as far as Tim remembered, did being fifteen years old. The boy was trim and compact, physically more like his mother than his father: dark-haired and dark-eyed – though presently his hair was clipped so short its color was merely some indeterminate shade of darkness – with a broad forehead and a narrow, decisive chin. Two steel rings rode the outer ridges of his right ear. He slopped around in big T-shirts and oversized jeans, alternately grimacing and grinning at the music earphoned into his head from an improbably tiny device, an iPod or an MP3 player. Mark was devoted to a strange cross section of contemporary music: Wilco, the Magnetic Fields, the White Stripes, the Strokes, Yo La Tengo, Spiritualized, and the Shins, but also Bruce Springsteen, Jimmy LaFave, and Eminem, whom he seemed to appreciate in an ironic spirit. His 'pin-up girl,' he had informed his uncle in an e-mail, was Karen O of the Yeah Yeah Yeahs.

In the past sixteen months, Mark had e-mailed

his uncle four times, not so briefly as to conceal a tone Tim found refreshing for being sidelong, sweet, and free of rhetorical overkill. Mark's first and longest e-mail used the excuse of a request for advice, Tim thought, as a way to open communications between them.

From: munderhill697@aol.com

To: tunderhill@nyc.rr.com

Sent: Sunday, February 3, 2002 4:06 PM

Subject: speak, o wise one

hi de ho

this is your nephew mark in case u couldn't decipher the from line. so I was having this lil disagreement with my father, and I wanted 2 ask your advice. after all u managed 2 get out of this burg & travel around & u write books & u live in nyc & all that means u shd have a pretty open mind. I hope it does.

bcuz u & u alone will decide what i do next. my dad sez he will go along with u no matter what. I dunno maybe he doesn't want 2 have 2 decide. (mom sez, quote, don't ask me, I don't want to hear abt it, unquote. that's what mom sez.)

i turn 14 next month and 2 celebrate my bday I'd like 2 get a tongue piercing. 1 of my friends has a pierced tongue and he sez it isn't 2 painful at all and its over in a jiff. I'd really like 2 do this. don't u think 14 is the rite age 2 go out and do something dumb, provided u do think it is dumb to pierce your tongue, which I obviously do not? in a year or 2 I'll take it out & go back 2 being boring & normal. or what d'you say, move up 2 a cool tat?

waiting 2 hear from the famous unk
m

From: tunderhill@nyc.rr.com
To: munderhill697@aol.com
Sent: Sunday, February 3, 2002 6:32 PM
Subject: Re: speak, o wise one

Dear Mark,
First of all, it is wonderful to hear from you! Let's do this more often. I like the idea of our being in touch.

I've been thinking about your question. To begin with, I'm flattered that you thought to ask my opinion on such a personal matter. I'm also flattered that your father placed the decision in my hands, but I suppose he really did not want to think about his son having his tongue pierced! If I had a son, I wouldn't want to think about it, either.

bcuz, as u wld say, the idea of tongue piercings makes me feel a bit queasy. I like your earrings and I think they look good on you, but whenever I see some young person with a metal ball riding on top of his/her tongue, I begin to fret about the discomfort of such an arrangement. Doesn't it complicate the whole eating business? I almost hate to admit this to you, but to me tongue piercings really do seem like weird self-mutilation. So you are far ahead of me in this regard.

This is not the answer you were expecting, I'm sure. I'm sorry to stand in the way of you getting what you want, but you asked and I had to answer you truthfully. I'd rather think of you without a metal ball in your mouth than with one. Sorry, kiddo, but I love you anyhow.

Is there anything special you'd like me to get for your birthday? Maybe I can make up for being so boring and middle-class.

Uncle Tim

The next day two messages from his family turned up in his Inbox.

From: munderhill697@aol.com
To: tunderhill@nyc.rr.com
Sent: Monday, February 4, 2002 7:32 AM
Subject: Re: speak, o wise one

TYim, this is nme Philip using Mark's computyer. Hje showed me what you wrote him. I hadf the feeling you'd do the right thing for once. So, well, thanks. IO hate that crap too.

From: munderhill697@aol.com
To: tunderhill@nyc.rr.com
Sent: Monday, February 4, 2002 5:31 PM
Subject: Re: speak, o wise one

>Is there anything special you'd like me to get for your birthday? now that you mention it, yep. ordnance. :)
m

For once, as his brother would put it, Tim was grateful for the Internet's assumption that its users were incapable of perceiving a joke unaccompanied by a nudge in the ribs. Philip's error-riddled message contained a different kind of reassurance – that of its having been sent at all.

During Pop's life, the brothers had come together – meaning that Tim flew to Millhaven from New York – once or twice a year; in the five years since his death, they had scarcely spoken. Pop had come to New York once, as a widower of two years in his late seventies, saying that he wanted to see what all the fuss was about, and he had stayed in Tim's loft at 55 Grand Street, which he had found awkward and discomfiting. His knees made the trek up and down three flights of stairs difficult, and Tim had overheard him complain to dear Michael Poole, who lived one floor up with the amazing and equally dear Maggie Lah, that he had imagined his son was at least rich enough to put in an elevator. ('I used to run an elevator, you know,' he told Michael. 'At the famous St Alwyn Hotel, right there in Pigtown. All the big musicians stayed there, niggers included.') The next day, at an informal little get-together Tim put together with Maggie Lah, Michael Poole, and Vinh Tran, who with Maggie owned and operated Saigon, the Vietnamese restaurant on the ground floor of 55 Grand Street, Pop turned to Michael and said, 'You know something, Doctor? As far as I'm concerned, the whole world can blow up right soon's I die, and I wouldn't give a damn. Why should I?'

'Doesn't Tim's brother have a son?' Michael asked. 'Don't you care what happens to your grandchild?'

'Not a hell of a lot.'

'You a tough ol' coot, aren't you?' Maggie said.

Pop grinned at her. Vodka had loosened him up to the point where he supposed this stunning Chinese woman could see through the cobwebby disguise of old age to the seductive rascal he was at heart. 'I'm glad someone down here in New York City is smart enough to understand me,' he said.

Tim realized he had read through three pages of the new George Pelecanos novel without registering anything more than individual words. He looked up the aisle to discover that the flight attendants handing out the wrapped lunches were only two rows in front of him. On Midwest Air, a one-class airline noted for its wide seats and attentive service, the approach of the in-flight meal could still arouse some interest.

A blond woman with a Smithsonian-quality Millhaven accent handed him a wrapped chicken Caesar salad, more than acceptable by airline standards, and a minute later her twin sister filled his Midwest Air wine glass a quarter of an inch above the line with a decent cabernet, and when he had taken a sip and let it slide down his throat, it came to Tim Underhill that for the past twenty minutes, when he was supposed to be enjoying George Pelecanos as a kind of palate cleanser before making notes for his new and highly uncharacteristic project, he had been engaged in the fruitless task of obsessing about his brother.

If he actually did intend to accomplish any work during this trip, which in spite of everything he hoped he might, he was going to have to stop brooding about his brother and dedicate at least some of his attention to a surprisingly little known figure in American life, Dr Herman Mudgett, a.k.a. H. H. Holmes. Probably the country's first serial killer and undoubtedly one of its most prolific, Mudgett had adopted the surname of a famous fictional detective and constructed in Chicago a monstrous murder palace in the form of a hotel just in time to siphon off young women in town to attend the 1893 Columbian Exposition. In his vast hotel, he killed almost every woman who became involved with him to a degree greater than serving him breakfast in a local restaurant or selling him collars and cravats at the haberdashery. LD Bechtel, a young musician of Tim's acquaintance, had suggested that they collaborate on a chamber opera about Holmes, and for the past two months this project had occupied a portion of his thoughts.

He knew when he had first begun to see his own access into it. The moment had been the result of various unrelated objects producing a small but vital electrical pulse when accidentally joined together. He had gone out to loaf through the St Mark's Bookshop and pick up a cup of coffee at Starbucks, and the first element of his inspiration had been an odd slogan stenciled atop a high, rounded Spring Street gutter passed on his eastward trek. The stencil had just been applied, and the ink glistened. It consisted of four words, all lowercase: *lost boy lost girl.* Downtown indie-rock bands sometimes advertised themselves by stenciling their names on sidewalks, and Tim had known of a couple of small presses that did the same with titles of books they did not have the money otherwise to promote. He supposed that somewhere, someone had done it with a movie title. Whatever it was, he liked the phrase and hoped he would remember to notice where it might crop up again.

In St Mark's Bookshop, he cruised the New Fiction tables and pulled a copy of John Ashbery's *Chinese Whispers* from a poetry shelf. Any new book by John Ashbery was an automatic purchase. At a big table stacked with oversized art books, he picked up a jumbo-sized collection of Magritte paintings, opened it at random, and found himself looking for maybe the hundredth time at a painting called *Not to Be Reproduced*, in which a young man with a fine head of hair stands, his back to the painter and the viewer, looking into a mirror that reproduces, instead of his face, the back of his head. He is looking at an image of himself that looks away from him. Because his face is not visible, the young man has no face.

Then it happened: Tim felt the unmistakable tingle of the little electrical pulse and told himself that he was looking at a portrait of H. H. Holmes. His access, his way in, was a kind of feel, a kind of tone – the feeling aroused in him by the Magritte painting. As a painting, it was a virtual Chinese whisper, or could be seen that way, always leaning toward a further misprision. It was one of the *creepiest* of all surrealist paintings, and the feelings it awakened in him had all to do with dread. Tim could see their H. H. Holmes, his and LD's, before the furnace in which he had incinerated his victims, his back to the audience, singing his lungs out and posed more like an icon than a man. The image contained a kind of splendor that all but brought its music into audibility. With his inner ear, Tim could hear their little orchestra hammering and beating away, and it sounded gorgeous. *We're going to do this*, he said to himself.

When he passed Spring Street on his way home, he looked down to see the enigmatic *lost boy lost girl*, but the slogan had disappeared, as though the fresh ink had melted into the smooth concrete of the curb. *Impossible*, he thought, *I'm on the wrong corner*. It was not the wrong corner, he knew, but for three or four blocks he kept looking at the curb, and abandoned the search only when he began to feel foolish.

Now it came to him that he was going back to a city perfectly attuned to his project. Millhaven had struck him as essentially surreal ever since he had left it for the first time. Nancy Underhill would have had no appetite for the surreal. She had been required to stand up to Philip for the decade and a half when they had skulked from neighborhood to neighborhood until returning to within two blocks of the house on Auer Avenue where Timothy and Philip were born to Mom and Pop Underhill. Had something in the scruffy old part of the city once known as Pigtown, with its two-story houses burdened with dark, suspicious-looking porches, its tiny sloping lawns and narrow alleyways, the ugly rows of liquor stores, diners, and cheap clothing outlets on its avenues, reached out for funny little Nancy Underhill and taken her life? Had some *person* from that world killed her?

His next thought shamed Tim even as it formed itself into coherence: his brother's wife had seemed almost too self-effacing, you could say too unimportant, to get murdered.

Forty minutes before the plane set down, the rich, delicious smell of chocolate-chip cookies baking golden brown filled the cabin. Midwest Air served freshly baked chocolate-chip cookies on every flight long enough to include a meal. Ten minutes later, the flight attendant leaned toward him and, winking, handed over a paper napkin holding three warm cookies, one more than the usual ration. She smiled at him.

'Do you know who was in your seat on yesterday's flight?'

He shook his head.

'That actor who was in *Family Ties*.'

'Michael J. Fox?'

'No, the one who played his father.' She looked away for a second. 'He must be really old by now. He still looks pretty good, though.'

Tim raised the first cookie to his mouth. Its wonderful fragrance seemed to move directly into the center of his head, making him ravenous. What was the name of that actor, anyhow? Michael somebody: he'd had a nice quality, like Alan Alda without the smarm. The cryptic phrase stenciled on a Spring Street curb came back to him. *lost boy lost girl.*

How on earth, he wondered, had Nancy died?

[illegible] handed him a paper napkin holding three [illegible] care more than the usual [illegible]. She watched him.

[illegible]

[illegible]

He [illegible] his [illegible]

[illegible]

[illegible]

[illegible]

He still feels pretty good, though.

[illegible] into the centre of his head, [illegible] was the [illegible]

[illegible]

[illegible]

2

THE OBITUARY NOTICE in that morning's *Ledger* told him nothing but Nancy's age, family details, and funeral information. There was no photograph. For Nancy's sake, Tim felt grateful. He had known his sister-in-law at least well enough to feel sure that she would have hated having the only photograph of her to appear in the city newspaper run after her death. Tim looked again at the obituary's few column inches and realized that it had been published four days after Nancy's death. Wasn't that later than usual? Perhaps not. And it contained nothing about the cause of death but the words 'without warning.' *Without warning* Nancy Kalendar Underhill, wife to Philip, mother to Mark, a resident of 3324 North Superior Street in Millhaven's Sherman Park district, had been taken from her devoted family and loving friends. Without warning had she laid down her spatula and mixing bowl, stripped off her comely apron, straightened her arms by her sides, and zoomed away from the surface of the earth at a nice, sharp forty-five-degree angle.

Tim experienced a peculiar tumult in the region of his heart. Yes, that was exactly what Nancy had done. The shock of the recognition made him go to the edge of the bed and sit down, fast. Of her own volition had Nancy shot rocketlike off the planet. Philip's wife and Mark's mother had killed herself. Now Tim understood how he could have failed to grasp the situation from the beginning. Philip's voice, Philip's words had thwarted him. The voice sounded tamped down, flattened out to stifle any emotion that might shine through: Philip with someone standing on his throat. That had been Philip, standing on his own throat. Philip would be happiest if Tim were never to learn that Nancy had not died in her sleep. He would feel that the knowledge meant a personal loss, that some degree of power had been transferred into his brother's hands. The tight, stepped-on voice therefore had divulged as little information as possible. *I thought you should know that Nancy unexpectedly passed away yesterday afternoon. It happened very suddenly, and I guess you could say I'm in shock. In shock. Probably will be for a while, huh? You don't have to tell me right away, but let me know if you want to come here for the viewing on Friday and the funeral and all that on Saturday afternoon.*

Philip might as well have been speaking to an answering machine.

I don't suppose you'll want to stay here, will you? When did you ever want to stay here?

Tim's heart trembled at the thought of what Mark must be going through.

He found that he was holding his hands clamped down over the top of his head, as if to keep this new information from bouncing around the hotel room, spattering blood as it went. Feeling like Philip, he lowered his hands and for a moment concentrated on his breathing. What could he say to his brother?

With this question came a great, dirty tide of misery and despair, at its center a piercing bolt of pain for Nancy Underhill, for how she must have felt in the weeks and days before. That was monstrous, obscene. Tim made up his mind on the spot: he would not leave Millhaven without knowing why Nancy had killed herself. It was as though she herself had given him the charge.

From Timothy Underhill's journal, 12 June 2003

I'm checked into the Pforzheimer, and just to make sure I realize that I am once again back in my hometown, Millhaven voices are rolling through my head. My nephew Mark's sweet e-mail voice; Philip's dour rumble. Even Pop's smoky rasp. In the midst of all these voices, why not listen to Nancy's, too?

Nancy's voice was soft, tennis-ball fuzzy. She once asked me, *How do you write a book, anyhow?* Heart in mouth, I said. She gave me a lovely laugh, her eyes half-closed. Nancy handled customer complaints for the Millhaven Gas Company. Philip, the vice principal of John Quincy Adams Junior High and High School ('Quincy'), wanted her to quit. He thought that having people yell at his wife all day was beneath him, though when you came down to it, the nuts and bolts of his job weren't all that different. That Nancy could be funny about her job annoyed Philip. If she was going to insist on going to that office every day, at least she could have the decency to show its cost; that was Philip's point of view. *All day long, these ignorant black dumbbells are calling her 'mother-fucker,'* Philip had once stage-whispered to him. *Tell me you could take that every day.*

Philip, she had said, *they're not ignorant, they're not dumb, and they're certainly not all black. They're just afraid they'll freeze to death if they lose their gas. We work out a little deal, that's all.*

Do white people ever get that deal? Philip wanted to know.

That gas company job must have been difficult more often than not, but she kept showing up. At night, she cooked for Philip and Mark. Obviously, she did all the housework. A woman with two jobs then, and I bet she seldom complained. To a girl from Pigtown, Philip had seemed a good enough catch. A budding educator, he already wore a jacket and tie every day. Probably, Philip had opened up to her back then, probably showed her a little flash, a little soul, enough to convince her it would still be there in the years to come. Think of the long marriage afterward, think of how she endured the person he became. I remember the light in her eye as she hurried down the hall toward me, a glow I could see right through the screen door. A great capacity for feeling, then, starved, unused, except for her son.

I want to know why you killed yourself.

A fatal disease? Philip would have told me. A love affair gone wrong? Nancy was not so romantic, not so foolish. Some overwhelming shame? If not shame, then a deep guilt? Guilt for what? For something undone, some action unperformed – that felt like Nancy's brand of guilt.

Brave, steadfast, resigned, disappointed, true of heart, Nancy was all of these things. Poisoned by an old guilt – when she could have intervened, when she was needed, she stepped back, and the disaster happened. What else? Somewhere, I think, there's a lot of fear, a big *old* fear. She feared the cause of her guilt: she feared what had made her needed. Some person, some man, loomed back there in Nancy's life. He was terrifying.

This is where we locate Nancy's story: I can feel it stir.

I'm reminded of what sometimes happened to me in Bangkok during the late seventies – I sensed death, actual Death, capering behind me on the crowded street, sending before him as his sign or sigil a naked Vietnamese girl running through the Patpong circus, a girl showing her bloody palms to the world.

It's so tempting to give Nancy a history similar to mine. A grim creature peering in from just offstage; and with her we have someone she failed to rescue from the hideous Death-figure.

. . . For me, the naked Vietnamese girl represented a kind of salvation, the reawakening of my imagination; for her, it was only dread.

I'm not sure what I think about this. It feels right, but looked at objectively it seems too much a by-product of my own story. Not to mention my imagination.

Nancy's story – I wonder if I'll ever really get inside it, ever really *see* the beast that perched on her shoulder. But this is a start, maybe.

From this window on the fourth floor of the Pforzheimer's original building, Tim Underhill and Michael Poole once had looked down on wintry Jefferson Street as an infuriated motorist with a snowed-in car whipped his tire iron against the side of a bus moving slowly toward Cathedral Square. At the time, what they were looking at seemed like pure Millhaven.

The sparse traffic on Jefferson Street swam through the hot, languid air. Directly below, a Pforzheimer valet in a short-sleeved brown uniform lounged against a parking meter. Across the street, a hunched old man in a seersucker suit, a bow tie, and a straw hat, the image of prosperous old-school midwestern propriety, picked his way down the red stone steps of the Millhaven Athletic Club.

Some retired judge or doctor going home after a bowl of tomato soup and a turkey club. At his back, the weathered red brick facade of the athletic club was sturdy, peaceful, traditional; although less sturdy, the old man looked much the same. Tim watched him ease himself off the last step and down onto the sidewalk. He wondered where the doctor had parked his car. All the spaces in front of the club were empty.

Working his elbows as if in a hurry, the old party in the jaunty hat and the spiffy bow tie proceeded directly across the sidewalk. He glanced quickly from side to side, then hitched up his shoulders and stepped down into Jefferson Street. To Tim, he no longer looked so peaceful. For an old guy who had just finished lunch, he was moving with an awkward, herky-jerky haste.

Like a hideous dream-chariot, a long black car of antique design came rushing up the middle of Jefferson Street, heading straight toward the old man. Tim froze at his window; the retired doctor had more presence of mind. After a moment's hesitation, he backpedaled toward the curb, keeping an eye on the car racing toward him. The car corrected for his change of position. 'Get out of there, old man!' Tim said aloud, still unable to believe that he was watching an attempted murder. 'Go! *Move!*'

As the black car swung left toward the curb, the old man vaulted across three feet of roadway, came down on his toes, and started to run. The Pforzheimer's parking valet had disappeared. The black car slithered forward and sideways with the speed of a mongoose charging a cobra, and a straw hat sailed into the air. *'No!'* Underhill shouted, and rapped his forehead against the cool window. A seersucker shoulder and a white-haired head slid out of sight beneath the car.

Tim's breath misted the window.

Inexorably, the car ground over the roadbed. After a horrifically long second or two, it picked up speed and rolled toward Grand Avenue. The old man lay still on the concrete, his long legs drawn up and one arm outstretched. Tim tried unsuccessfully to catch the car's license number.

Hadn't anyone else seen the murder? Tim spun toward the telephone in his room, then moved back to check the scene again. Now the street was filled with people. Two men in loose-fitting jackets, one a dusty red, the other navy blue, stood by the driver's side of the car. The man in the navy blouson wore a long-billed black cap that covered half his face. Another man and a young woman had run up to the old man in the seersucker suit, and as Tim watched, they held out their hands, and the victim, not dead, not even injured, pulled himself upright. A young woman wearing a headset trotted through the little crowd with the straw hat in her hand. A man in a fedora and a pin-striped suit got out of the car, pointed back down the street, and nodded at something said by the man in the long-billed cap. He, too, wore a headset.

Tim pushed up the window and leaned out. The man in the seersucker suit, no longer quite so old, settled the boater back on his head and laughed at something said by the young woman. Most of the people on the street had begun to retreat to their positions. The black car was backing down Jefferson Street, where a bare-chested man in shorts rode sidesaddle beside an enormous camera set on miniature railroad tracks.

A visiting film company had transformed Jefferson Street into a movie set.

Tim watched the actor in the seersucker suit trot up the red stone steps of the Millhaven Athletic Club and duck into the doorway to await the next take. Once again, the street looked empty. In a couple of minutes the old man would reappear on the red steps, the long car would begin rolling, the man and the car would come into conjunction, and what looked like murder would again take place; this would happen over and over again until the light changed.

Tim closed the window and went to the telephone beside his journal on the busy writing table. When the desk clerk answered, he asked what was going on outside. 'I mean, is it a movie or a television episode?'

'A movie. Big-budget job. The director's somebody like Scorsese or Coppola, someone like that. The crew will be outside there another two days, and then they'll be shooting at a location down in the warehouse district.'

Tim remembered the warehouse district, a few blocks south of Grand, from when it still had warehouses and nobody called it anything at all. He also remembered a time when desk clerks at the Pforzheimer would mean something entirely different when they used the word 'shooting.' 'Ah,' he said. 'Gas lamps and cobblestones. What is it, a Golden Days of the Mafia story?'

'Gangsters and tommy guns,' said the clerk. 'Whenever they want to set a movie in old-time Chicago, they come to Millhaven.'

Tim moved back to the window. Here came the actor in his retired doctor getup, jerking his shoulders and elbows as he hitched himself off the curb; here was that impression of haste. Now the black dream-mobile, which had running boards and a spare-tire well on the trunk, gathered speed as it cruised southward on Jefferson Street, which would not be Jefferson now but a street in Chicago,

South Dearborn or South Clark. The actor froze, glided backward, broad-jumped forward; the car twitched like a living thing, and the straw boater sailed off. The actor disappeared beneath the antique car. This time, Tim was able to see the second camera dollying in, accompanied by the man in the long-billed black cap. This, too, had happened the first time, but Tim had seen none of it.

Idly, his gaze drifted northward to the trim little park beyond the club's parking lot. Angled paths intersected at a concrete circle with a wooden bench and a dead fountain. Beech trees cast angular shadows on the grass. An old woman scattered bread crumbs to several families of combative sparrows. At the top of the square, digital bells in the cathedral's tower tolled three times, sending out a dull *clang clang clang* that hung like bronze smoke in the bright air. Then an argument between two teenage boys proceeding toward the bottom of the square snagged his attention. The floppiness of their clothing, as alike as the dress of twins clothed by their parents – baggy jeans, oversized short-sleeved T-shirts (pale blue and navy blue) worn over oversized long-sleeved T-shirts (light yellow and dirty white) – heightened the vehemence of their gestures. At the bottom of the square they turned right and began moving toward the Pforzheimer, on the far side of Jefferson.

The taller of the two had cropped dark hair and shoulders so broad his arms seemed to swing at a distance greater than usual from his slim body. He was walking backward and waving his arms. The smaller boy, wider, rounder, and with long, sandy-reddish hair, had the resigned, rubbery face of a comedian, but Tim saw that his instinctive equanimity was strained to the breaking point. He kept slowing the pace, jamming his hands into the deep, low pockets of his capacious jeans, then raising them in a gesture that said, *What can I do? Sorry, I can't help you.* Dancing before him, the dark-haired boy seemed to be saying, *Man, I need you with me on this. Give me a break!* A pair of mimes could not have drawn the poles of their disagreement any more clearly, nor the passion of one and the resistance of the other. The tall boy stopped moving and clutched the sides of his head. Tim knew he was cursing and hoped he was not trying to coax his red-haired friend into some illegality. It did not look like that kind of dispute, exactly. Something crucial was at stake, but probably an advanced form of mischief, not a criminal charge. *Come on, we'll have a blast, it'll be great* versus *Give it up, there's no way I'm doing that, and I don't think you should do it, either.*

Tim thought he heard a wail of frustration and outrage.

The red-haired boy dodged around his gesticulating friend and continued up the sidewalk. The taller boy ran up to him and clouted his shoulder. Looking extraordinarily graceful in his pale blue and light yellow shirts, he shot out an arm and pointed at, or very near to, Tim Underhill's window. Instinctively, Tim stepped back. Almost immediately, he moved forward again, drawn by an unexpected recognition. The taller of the two boys was strikingly handsome, even beautiful, in a dark-browed, clean-featured manner. A second later, Tim Underhill's recognition system at last yielded the information that he was looking at his nephew, Mark. By a kind of generational enhancement, features that passed for pleasing but unremarkable in his mother emerged, virtually unchanged, as beautiful in her son. In all likelihood, Mark had no idea of how attractive he was.

The next message that came bubbling into consciousness was that just then Mark could have been speaking of him to his red-haired friend. Philip had probably mentioned that he would be in town for the funeral, and it would be like Philip to throw in a sneering reference to the Pforzheimer. That Mark was probably speaking of him meant that Tim had some role in the dispute between the two boys. What sort of role, he wondered: advice, direction, decision?

Whatever his point had been, Mark – for it really *was* Mark, Tim saw – had decided to save his powder for another day's battle. That this was a truce, not surrender, was evident in his loping slouch, the ease of his stride, the wry set of his mouth. The red-haired boy spoke to him, and he shrugged in feigned indifference.

It almost hurt, that Mark should have become so beautiful – the world at large had already begun to conspire against the straightforward destiny that would otherwise have been his. Would you just look at him, down there on the sidewalk? He's pretending to be too tough to be wounded by his mother's death.

Both boys stopped moving to watch the man in the seersucker suit and straw hat once again come hitching down the red steps of the MAC. There was always something horrible about catching an actor at work, suddenly becoming aware that he was after all merely playing a role.

From Timothy Underhill's journal, 20 June 2003

Eight days after my last entry, and I must go back to Millhaven again. Philip told me that

Mark has been missing for a couple of days, and he only called me *because he thought I might have been hiding him in my loft!* Really, he was furious, barely able to contain it. And though I resent his attitude, in all honesty I can't be angry with him or even really blame him very much for what he's been thinking.

From what I could make of Philip's rant, Mark vanished sometime in the evening of, I think, the 18th. Philip waited up for him until two in the morning, then retired in the reasonable certainty that before long Mark would be in his bed. In the morning, Mark's bed was still empty. Philip called the police, who informed him of what he already knew, that two other boys recently had disappeared from that part of town, but added that he ought not jump to any conclusions. They added that most teenage runaways come back home within twenty-four hours and recommended patience. Philip drew on his capacity for patience and discovered that he possessed a limited supply. By noon he was calling the police again, with the same result. He had of course walked up the block to confront Jimbo Monaghan, Mark's best friend, but Jimbo either knew nothing about the disappearance or pretended he knew nothing. Thinking he smelled complicity, Philip accused the boy of lying. Jimbo's mother, Margo, ordered him out of the house – threw him out, really. For a couple of hours, Philip drove around Millhaven, looking for his son everywhere he thought his son might be, every place he had heard Mark speak of. He knew it was a hopeless effort, but he was unable to keep himself from cruising past playgrounds his son had not visited in years, staring in the windows of fast-food restaurants, driving around and around Sherman Park. He felt so desperate he wept. In the space of ten days, he had lost both wife and son.

Grimly, Philip bounced back and forth between two equally fearful notions: that Mark had been abducted by the 'Sherman Park Killer,' who had already claimed two boys his age; and that Mark had killed himself, possibly in imitation of his mother, even more possibly out of the mixture of horror and despair set loose within him by what he had been obliged to witness. The police, being police, were concentrating on the first of these alternatives. They walked through the parks and searched the wooded areas in Millhaven but failed to uncover a body. They also checked the records at the airport, the train and bus stations; they, too, questioned Jimbo Monaghan, his parents, and other teenagers and parents Mark had known. When none of this yielded as much as a suggestion of the boy's whereabouts, the police released Mark's information and requested the assistance of the city's residents. A none-too-recent photograph was sent to the FBI and to police departments across the country. There, for all practical purposes, the matter rested.

Except of course for Philip, who at this pre-Dewey Dell stage could face none of the possibilities aroused by his son's disappearance: that a psychopath had kidnapped and probably murdered him; that he had killed himself in some location yet to be found; or that he had simply run off without a word. When Philip found himself face to face with this unacceptable series of choices, another occurred to him, and he called his overprivileged, never quite to be trusted brother in New York.

'All right, you can tell me now,' he said. 'I never thought you'd be capable of doing a thing like this to your own brother, but I'm sure you had your reasons. He must have told you a hell of a story.'

'Philip, you'd better start at the beginning. What can I tell you now, and what do you think I did to you?'

'What *did* he tell you, exactly? How bad is

it? Did I beat the crap out of him every night? Was I psychologically abusive?'

'Are you talking about Mark?'

'Gee, do you think? Why would I be asking you about Mark, I wonder? If my son happens to be there with you, Tim, I'm asking you to let me talk to him. No, I'm not asking. I'm begging.'

'Jesus, Philip, Mark left home? What happened?'

'What happened? My son hasn't been here for three days, that's what. So if he's staying in that fucked-up circus of yours on Grand Street, goddamn you, I'm on my knees here. Put him on. Do whatever you have to, all right?'

It took a while, but I did manage to convince Philip that his son was not hiding in my loft, and that I'd had nothing to do with his disappearance. I felt silenced, stunned, baffled.

'Why didn't you call me before this?'

'Because it didn't occur to me that he might be in New York until about an hour ago.'

Seen one way, Philip and I are alone in the world. We have no other siblings, no cousins or second cousins, no grandparents, no aunts or uncles, no living parents.

I asked him if there was anything I could do for him.

'Isn't one of your best friends Tom Pasmore? I want you to talk to him – get him to help me.'

Tom Pasmore, I add for posterity's sake, is an old Millhaven friend of mine who solves crimes for a living, not that he needs the money. He's like Sherlock Holmes or Nero Wolfe, except that he is a real person, not a fictional one. His (biological) father was the same way. He solved crimes in city after city, chiefly by going over all the records and documents in sight and making connections everyone else missed, connections you more or less have to be a genius to see. Tom inherited his methods along with his talents and his wardrobe. As far as I'm concerned, Tom Pasmore is the best private investigator in the world, but he only works on cases he chooses by himself. Back in '94 he helped me work out a terrible puzzle that my collaborator and I later turned into a novel.

I told Philip I would get to Millhaven as quickly as possible and added that I'd do my best to get Tom Pasmore to think about the boy's disappearance.

'Think about it? That's all?'

'In most cases, that's what Tom does. Think about things.'

'Okay, talk to the guy for me, will you?'

'As soon as I can,' I said. I didn't want to

explain Tom Pasmore's schedule to my brother, who has the old-time schoolmaster's suspicion of anyone who does not arise at 7:00 and hit the hay before midnight. Tom Pasmore usually turns off his reading light around 4:00 A.M. and seldom gets up before 2:00 P.M. He likes single-malt whiskey, another matter best unmentioned to Philip, who had responded to Pop's alcohol intake by becoming a moralistic, narrow-minded teetotaler.

After I arranged for my tickets, I waited another hour and called Tom. He picked up as soon as he heard my voice on his answering machine. I described what had happened, and Tom asked me if I wanted him to check around, look at the records, see what he might be able to turn up. 'Looking at the records' was most of his method, for he seldom left the house and performed his miracles by sifting through newspapers, public records on-line and off, and all kinds of databases. Over the past decade he had become dangerously expert at using his computers to get into places where ordinary citizens were not allowed.

Tom said that you never knew what you could learn from a couple of hours' work, but that if the boy didn't turn up in the next day or two, he and I might be able to accomplish something together. In the meantime, he would 'scout around.' But – he wanted me to know – in all likelihood, as much as he hated to say it, my nephew had fallen victim to the monster who earlier probably had abducted and murdered two boys from the same part of town.

'I can't think about that, and neither can my brother,' I said. (I was wrong about the latter, I was to learn.)

Forty-five minutes later, Tom called me with some startling news. Had I known that my late sister-in-law had been related to Millhaven's first serial killer?

'Who was that?' I asked.

'A sweetheart named Joseph Kalendar.'

The name seemed familiar, but I could not remember why.

'Kalendar became public property in 1979 and 1980, when you were misbehaving in Samarkand, or wherever it was.'

He knew exactly where I had been in 1979 and 1980. 'Bangkok,' I said. 'And by 1980 I was hardly misbehaving at all. What did Kalendar do?'

Joseph Kalendar, a master carpenter, had begun by breaking into women's houses and raping them. After the third rape, he began bringing his fourteen-year-old son along with him. Soon after, he decided it would be prudent to murder the women after he and his son raped them. A couple of months later, he got even crazier. During his third-to-last foray, on the verbal orders of a persuasive deity, he had killed, then decapitated his son and left the boy's headless body sprawled beside their mutual victim's bed. God thanked him for his faithfulness and in a mighty voice sang that henceforth he, lowly Joseph Kalendar, family man, master carpenter, and Beloved Favorite of Jehovah, was charged with the erasure of the entire female gender worldwide, or at least as many as he could get around to exterminating before the police brought a close to the sacred project. In 1979 Kalendar was at last arrested. In 1980 he went on trial, was found not guilty by reason of insanity, and was sentenced to the Downstate Hospital for the Criminally Insane, where three years later he was strangled by a fellow inmate who objected wholeheartedly to Kalendar's attempt to wash him in the blood of the Lamb and deliver him posthaste into the arms of his Savior.

'This florid madman was related to Nancy Underhill?'

'They were first cousins,' Tom said.

'I guess that explains something my brother told me after the funeral,' I said.

'Can you think of one reason your nephew would have taken off?'

'Well,' I said, 'I can certainly think of one.'

3

NOT LONG AFTER he had read Nancy's obituary in the paper and seen Mark through his hotel room's window, Tim got into his rented Town Car and set out on an eccentric course to his brother's house. Even allowing for one or two episodes of backtracking, the drive from the Pforzheimer to Superior Street should have taken Tim no longer than twenty to twenty-five minutes. If he had chosen to get on the expressway, the trip would have been five minutes shorter, but because he had not been in his hometown for nearly five years, Tim decided to drive north from downtown, then turn west on Capital Drive and keep going until he hit Teutonia Avenue's six wide lanes, jog southwest on a diagonal and drive until he saw Sherman Park, Sherman Boulevard, Burleigh, or any of the little web of streets backed by alleys he had known in childhood. He knew where his brother lived. Assuming that its essential makeup had not changed significantly beyond a nice economic updrift, Philip had moved back into the neighborhood of his childhood. And as far as they went and no further, his assumptions had proved correct: adjusted for inflation, the average household income in the neighborhood made up of Superior, Michigan, Townsend, Auer, and Forty-fourth Street had probably quadrupled from the days of Tim's and Philip's childhood. However, other aspects, ones Philip had not taken into account, had changed along with income levels.

Tim had no trouble getting on Capital Drive and rolling west to Teutonia Avenue's wide swath through a landscape of shopping centers and three-story office buildings separated by taverns. Everything looked like a cleaner, brighter, more prosperous version of the Millhaven of old, exactly what his earlier visits had led him to expect. He saw the Burleigh sign from a block away and turned into a more residential area. Identical four-story apartment buildings of cream-colored brick marched along side by side, the narrow concrete strips to their entrances standing out against the grass like a row of neckties.

Half a mile on, he saw a sign for Sherman Drive

and turned left. It was not Sherman Park or Sherman Boulevard, but it had to be in the same general area. Sherman Drive dead-ended in front of a windowless bunker of poured concrete called the Municipal Records Annex. Tim doubled back and turned left again onto a narrow one-way street called Sherman Annex Way, and this came to an end at the southwest corner of Sherman Park itself, where Pops had now and then escorted little Tim and little Philip to the magnificent wading pool, the jouncing teeter-totter, the high-flying swing set, and the little realm given to the sleeping tigers and ponderous elephants of its stupendous, now long-vanished zoo.

He drove completely around the park without quite figuring out where to go next. On his second spin around the perimeter, he noticed the sign for Sherman Boulevard, turned onto it, and was instantly rewarded by the appearance on the left side of the street in remembered or shadow form of a great, ambiguous landmark of his childhood, the Beldame Oriental Theater, presently the tabernacle of a sanctified Protestant sect.

But when he turned into the old network of alleys and intersections, Tim drove twice past his brother's house without being absolutely positive he had found it. The first time, he said to himself, *I don't think that's it*; the second time, *That isn't it, is it*? That, of course, was Philip's house, a combination of brick and fieldstone with a steeply pitched roof and an ugly little porch only slightly wider than the front door. Screwed into the screen door's wooden surround were the numerals 3324. With no further excuse for delaying, Tim parked his ostentatious but entirely comfortable vehicle a short way down the block and walked back through the humid sunlight. Where enormous elms had once arched their boughs over the street, the dry leaves of plane trees clung to their branches a modest distance above their pale, patchy trunks. Tim reached the walkway before his brother's house and checked his watch: the twenty-five-minute journey had taken him forty-five.

Tim pushed the buzzer. Far back in the house, a tiny bell rang. Footsteps plodded toward the door; a smudgy face ducked into, then out of, the narrow glass strips set high in the dark wood; the door swung back; and Philip stood before him, scowling through the gray scrim of the screen door. 'Decided to show up, after all,' he said.

'Nice to see you, too,' Tim said. 'How are you doing, Philip?'

With the air of one performing an act of charity, his brother stepped back to let him in. He looked a decade older that he had the last time Tim had seen him. His thinning hair was combed straight back from his forehead, revealing strips of scalp the same pinkish-gray as his deeply seamed face. Rimless spectacles with thin metal bows sat on his high-prowed nose. Above his soft, expansive belly, a silver tie tack anchored a shiny claret necktie to his cheap white shirt. He was still doing his utmost, Tim thought, to look exactly like what he was, a midlevel administrator of a thoroughly bureaucratic enterprise. A vice principalship was the kind of job Philip had spent all of his earlier life struggling to attain: unassailably respectable, tedious unto stupefaction, impervious to the whims of the economy, tied into a small but palpable degree of power, fodder for endless complaints.

'I'm still ambulatory,' Philip said. 'How the hell do you think I should be?' He moved the few steps that took him from the little foyer into the living room, and Tim followed. Nancy, it seemed, was not to be mentioned until Philip's sense of ritual had been satisfied.

'Sorry. Dumb question.'

'I guess it was nice of you to come all this way, anyhow. Sit down, rest up. After being in New York, you probably appreciate our famous midwestern peace and quiet.'

Having been given all the thanks he was likely to get, Tim walked across the living room and placed himself in an upholstered armchair that had come into Philip's household after Nancy's arrival. Philip stayed on his feet, watching him like a hotel detective. Philip's gray suit was too heavy for the weather, and he tugged a wrinkled handkerchief from his pocket and dabbed his forehead. From overhead came the ongoing rhythmic pulse of an electric bass.

'There's a lot of action around the Pforzheimer,' Tim said. 'Some big-time director is shooting a movie on Jefferson Street.'

'Don't tell Mark. He'll just want to go.'

'He's already been there. I saw him from my window. He and a red-haired kid came out of Cathedral Square and walked down the street to watch them filming a scene. They were right beneath me.'

'That was Jimbo Monaghan, his best buddy. Hell, his one and only buddy. You see one, the other one's right behind him. Jimbo's not a bad kid, for a dodo. Went through junior high at Quincy without any more than a half dozen demerits. Most kids rack up twice that.'

'Did Mark?'

'I had to be a little extra hard on Mark. The kids would have made his life hell if I'd shown any favoritism. Do you remember what kids are like? Find a weakness, they home in like sharks. Little bastards are barely human.'

Philip thought giving his son demerits proved that he was a stern and responsible father, but the truth was that it had given him pleasure.

'I got Cokes, root beer, ginger ale. You want beer or anything stronger, you can supply it yourself.'

'Ginger ale, if you're having something.'

Philip ducked into the kitchen, and Tim took his usual cursory inspection of the living room. As ever, it contained the same peculiar mixture of furniture Philip had shifted from house to house before settling back in the old neighborhood. All of it seemed a bit more worn than it had been on Tim's previous visits: the long green corduroy sofa, black recliner, highboy, and octagonal glass coffee table from Mom and Pop sharing space with the blond wooden furniture from some now-bankrupt 'Scandinavian' furniture store. Tim could remember Mom sitting in the rocking chair beside Pop's 'davenport,' the fat needle working as she hooked thick, interwoven knots of the rug that covered three-fourths of Philip's living room floor. Fifty years ago, it had been a lot brighter: now, it was just a rag to keep your shoes from touching the floor.

Philip came back into the room holding two glasses beaded with condensation. He passed one to Tim and dropped onto the far end of the davenport. His gray suit bunched up around his hips and shoulders.

'Philip, with apologies for my earlier question, how are you doing these days? How are you handling it?'

Philip took a long pull at his ginger ale and sagged against the worn cushions. He seemed to be staring at something akin to a large insect moving up the half-wall leading to the dining room and kitchen.

'With apologies, huh? That's nice. It should be Nancy who apologizes to me, not you.' He fixed Tim with a cold, brown-eyed glare. The rimless spectacles slightly magnified his eyes. 'We're getting into a strange, strange topic here. It is *truly* strange, this topic. I have to say, it surpasseth comprehension. Do you know what I mean, or do I have to explain it to you?'

'I think I understand. I read the obituary in today's *Ledger*. When I saw the words "without warning," I thought –'

'You thought?'

'I thought Nancy probably killed herself.'

'Is that what you thought? Well, guess what? Big brother rings the bell.'

'Would you prefer it if I didn't understand?'

'*I* don't know what I'd prefer.' Philip's face twisted, and everything below his nose seemed to collapse like a punctured paper bag. 'Nobody asked me for my opinion about anything.' He snatched off his glasses and passed a hand over his eyes. 'No, they just go ahead and do whatever they feel like.' He emitted a shaky sigh.

'Do you think she should have asked your permission before she killed herself?'

Philip aimed an index finger at him. 'There, that's a great question, I mean it. A *great* fucking question.'

Tim swallowed cold ginger ale and forced himself to remain silent.

'Yes,' Philip said. 'I do think so. I would have said, *You selfish bitch, you can't kill yourself. You have a husband and a son. Are you crazy*?'

'It was selfish – a selfish act.'

'All suicides are selfish.' He considered that proposition. 'Unless the person is in tremendous pain, or dying, or whatever.'

'Was she feeling depressed lately?'

'What are you, a shrink? I don't know. Nancy usually seemed a little depressed, if you ask me.' He shot Tim a wary look. 'Are you asking if I *noticed* that she seemed depressed lately?'

'I'm not accusing you of anything, Philip.'

'Keep it that way. I'm not to blame for what happened. Nancy and I got along all right. Why she did it is a mystery to me. Maybe she had some kind of secret existence. Maybe I didn't know what was going on in her life. If she didn't tell me, how the hell could I?'

'How is Mark handling all this?'

Philip shook his head. 'The kid keeps his feelings all wrapped up inside. He's been hit hard, though. Keeps to himself, except for when he's with Jimbo, the knucklehead you saw today. We'll see how he gets through tonight and tomorrow and the next couple of weeks. If he looks like he needs it, I'll get him some counseling or therapy, or whatever.'

Tim said that sounded like a good idea.

'Sure it does, to you. You live in New York, where everybody sees a shrink. For you people, a shrink is a status symbol. Out here in the real world, it's different. Plenty of people see it as an admission that something is wrong with you.'

'You wouldn't have to tell anybody. Neither would Mark.'

'Word gets out,' Philip said. 'Vice principal's wife commits suicide, his son starts seeing a head-shrinker. How do you suppose that plays out? What kind of effect do you think it would have on my career? On top of that, those appointments don't come cheap. Excuse me, elder brother, but I'm a humble educator in the public school system, not a millionaire.'

'Philip, if Mark could benefit from therapy, and you'd have trouble paying for it, I'd be happy to take care of it.'

'Things aren't quite that dire,' Philip said. 'But thanks for the offer.'

'Do you really think your job is going to be affected by what Nancy did?'

'One way or another, yeah. Subtly, in most ways. But what do you think my odds are of moving into a principal's office anytime soon? I was on track before this. Now, who knows? It could hold me back for years. But you want to know the worst part of this whole deal?'

'Sure,' Tim said.

'Whenever anybody looks at me, they're going to say to themselves, *There's Underhill. His wife killed herself.* And two-thirds, three-fourths of them are going to think I had something to do with it. She did it because of me, they'll think. Goddamn it, I never thought I'd hate her, but I'm getting there. Fuck her. *Fuck* her.'

Tim decided to say nothing and let him roll on.

Philip glared at him. 'I have a role in this community. I have a certain *position.* Maybe you don't know what that means. Maybe you don't care. But it is of very, very great importance to me. And when I think that stupid woman did her best, out of no reason at all but her own private unhappiness, to tear down everything I've worked for all my life – yes, I'm angry, yes I am. She had no right to do this to me.'

At least one thing was clear to Tim Underhill as he watched his brother chewing an ice cube from the bottom of his empty glass: Philip was going to be of no use at all.

'What's our schedule?' he asked.

'For tonight?'

'For everything.'

'We go to the Trott Brothers Funeral Home from six to seven for the viewing, or the visitation, or whatever it's called. The funeral is at one tomorrow afternoon, out at Sunnyside.' Sunnyside, a large cemetery on the Far West Side of the city, was still segregated into separate areas for Protestants, Catholics, and Jews. There were no African-Americans in Sunnyside. When you drove past it on the expressway, it went on for mile after mile of flat green earth and headstones in long rows.

'Philip,' Tim said, 'I don't even know how Nancy died. If it isn't too painful for you, could you tell me about it?'

'Oh, boy. I guess you *wouldn't* know, would you? It's not exactly public information, thanks be to God. Well, well. Yes. I can tell you how she did it. You've earned it, haven't you? Coming out here all the way from New York City. All right, you want to know what someone does when she's going to kill herself and really wants to make sure there are no ifs, ands, or buts about it? If she wants to hit that nail right square on the head? What she does is, she basically kills herself three different ways, all at the same time.'

He tried to grin. The attempt was a hideous failure. 'I had this bottle of sleeping pills left over from a couple of years ago. Not long after I left for work that morning, Nancy swallowed most of the pills – twenty of them, more or less. Then she ran a nice hot tub. She put a plastic bag over her head and fastened it around her neck. After that, she got in the tub and picked up a knife and cut open both of her forearms. Lengthwise, not those pussy sideways cuts people make when they're faking it. She was serious, I'll say that for her.'

The bass notes booming through the ceiling wavered in the air like butterflies.

Through the windows came the sound of cicadas, but Superior Street had never seen a cicada. Something else, Tim thought – what? Overhead, a door slammed. Two pairs of footsteps moved toward the top of the staircase.

'Enter the son and heir, accompanied by el side-kick-o faithful-o.'

Tim looked toward the staircase and saw descending the steps a pair of legs in baggy blue jeans, closely followed by its twin. A hand slid lightly down the railing; another hand shadowed it. Loose yellow sleeves, then loose navy sleeves. Then Mark Underhill's face moved into view, all eyebrows, cheekbones, and decisive mouth; just above it floated Jimbo Monaghan's round face, struggling for neutrality.

Mark kept his gaze downward until he reached the bottom of the staircase and had walked two steps forward. Then he raised his eyes to meet Tim's. In those eyes Tim saw a complex mixture of curiousity, anger, and secrecy. The boy was hiding something from his father, and he would continue to hide it; Tim wondered what would happen if he managed to get Mark into a private conversation.

No guile on Jimbo's part – he stared at Tim from the moment his face became visible.

'Looky here, it's Uncle Tim,' Philip said. 'Tim – you know Mark, and his best buddy-roo, Jimbo Monaghan.'

Reverting to an earlier stage of adolescence, the boys shuffled forward and muttered their greetings. Tim sent his brother a silent curse; now both boys felt insulted or mocked, and it would take Mark that much longer to open up.

He knows more than Philip about his mother's suicide, Tim thought. The boy glanced at him again, and Tim saw some locked-up knowledge surface in his eyes, then retreat.

'This guy look familiar to you, Tim?' Philip asked him.

'Yes, he does,' Tim said. 'Mark, I saw you from my window at the Pforzheimer early this afternoon. You and your friend here were walking toward the movie setup on Jefferson Street. Did you stay there long?'

A startled, wary glance from Mark; Jimbo opened and closed his mouth.

'Only a little while,' Mark said. 'They were doing the same thing over and over. Your room was on that side of the hotel?'

'I saw you, didn't I?'

Mark's face jerked into what may have been a smile but was gone too soon to tell. He edged sideways and pulled at Jimbo's sleeve.

'Aren't you going to stay?' his father asked.

Mark nodded, swallowing and rocking back on his heels while looking down at his scuffed sneakers. 'We'll be back soon.'

'But where are you going?' Philip asked. 'In about an hour, we have to be at the funeral home.'

'Yeah, yeah, don't worry.' Mark's eyes were sliding from his father to the front door and back again. 'We're just going out.'

He was in a nervous uproar, Tim saw. His engine was racing, and he was doing everything in his power to conceal it. Mark's body wanted to behave exactly as it had on Jefferson Street: it wanted to wave its arms and leap around. In front of his father these extravagant gestures had to be compressed into the most minimal versions of themselves. The energy of misery was potent as a drug. Tim had seen men uncaringly risk their lives under its influence, as if they had been doing speed. The boy was aching to get through the door; Jimbo would soon have to resist more high-pressure pleading. Tim hoped he could stand up to it; whatever Mark had in mind almost had to be reckless, half crazy.

'I hate this deliberate vagueness,' Philip said. 'What's *out*? Where is it?'

Mark sighed. 'Out is just out, Dad. We got tired of sitting in my room, and now we want to walk around the block or something.'

'Yo, that's all,' Jimbo said, focusing on a spot in the air above Philip's head. 'Walk around the block.'

'Okay, walk around the block,' Philip said. 'But be back here by quarter to seven. Or before. I'm serious, Mark.'

'I'm serious, too!' Mark shouted. 'I'm just going outside, I'm not running away!'

His face was a bright pink. Philip backed off, waving his hands before him.

Mark glanced at Tim for a moment, his handsome face clamped into an expression of frustration and contempt. Tim's heart filled with sorrow for him.

Mark pivoted away, clumped to the door, and was gone, taking Jimbo with him. The screen door slammed shut.

'Good God,' Philip said, looking at the door. 'He does blame me, the little ingrate.'

'He has to blame someone,' Tim said.

'I know who it should be,' Philip said. 'Killed herself three times, didn't she?'

Nodding meaninglessly, Tim went toward the big front window. Mark and Jimbo were moving north along the sidewalk much as they had proceeded down Jefferson Street. Mark was leaning toward his friend, speaking rapidly and waving his hands. His face was still a feverish pink.

'You see them?'

'Yep.'

'What are they doing?'

'Philip, I think they're walking around the block.'

'Didn't Mark seem awfully tense to you?'

'Kind of, yes.'

'It's the viewing and the funeral service,' Philip said. 'Once they're history, he can start getting back to normal.'

Tim kept his mouth shut. He doubted that Philip's concept of 'normal' would have any real meaning to his son.

On the grounds that the overall roominess more than made up for the added cost, whenever possible Tim Underhill rented Lincoln Town Cars. At a quarter to seven, the boys having returned from their walk in good time, he volunteered to drive everyone to Highland Avenue. They were standing on the sidewalk in the heat. Philip looked at the long black car with distaste.

'You never got over the need to show off, did you?'

'Philip, in this car I don't feel like I've been squeezed into a tin can.'

'Come on, Dad,' put in Mark, who was looking at the car as if he wanted to caress it.

'Not on your life,' Philip said. 'I'd feel like I was pretending to be something I'm not. Tim, you're welcome to ride along with us in my Volvo if you don't think you'd feel too confined.'

Philip's twelve-year-old Volvo station wagon,

the color of a rusty leaf, stood ten feet farther up the curb, as humble and patient as a mule.

'After you, Alphonse,' Tim said, and was pleased to hear Mark chuckle.

The Trott Brothers Funeral Home occupied the crest of a hill on Highland Avenue, and to those who looked up at it from the street after they left their vehicles – as did the four men young and old who left the leaf-colored Volvo – it looked as grand and dignified as a great English country house. Quarried stone, mullioned windows, a round turret – a place, you would say, where the loudest sounds would be the whispers of attendants, the rustle of memorial pamphlets, and some quiet weeping. Mark and Jimbo trailed behind as the little group walked toward the imposing building.

A languid man with a drastic combover waved them toward a muted hallway and a door marked TRANQUILLITY PARLOR. On a stand beside the door was a fat white placard.

Mrs Nancy K. Underhill
Viewing: 6:00–7:00 P.M.
Loving Wife and Mother

There, in the Tranquillity Parlor, lay the mortal remains of Nancy K. Underhill within a gleaming bronze coffin, the top half of its lid opened wide as a taxi door. The soft, buttoned interior of the coffin was a creamy off-white; Nancy K. Underhill's peaceful, empty face and folded hands had been painted and powdered to an only slightly unrealistic shade of pink. None of the four people who entered the small, dimly lighted chamber approached the coffin. Philip and Tim drifted separately to the back of the room and picked up the laminated cards prepared by the funeral home. On one side was a lurid depiction of a sunset over rippling water and a flawless beach; on the other, the Lord's Prayer printed beneath Nancy's name and dates. Philip took another of the cards from the stack and handed it to Mark, who had slipped into a seat next to Jimbo in the last row of chairs.

Mark snatched the card from his father's hand without a word.

When Jimbo looked around for a card of his own, Tim passed one to him. Both boys were deep in contemplation of the Pacific sunset when a brisk, rotund little woman bustled into the room. Joyce Brophy was the daughter of the last, now-deceased, of the Trott Brothers.

'Well, here we are, Mr Underhill, isn't that right?

It's a pleasure to see you, sir, and to welcome you back to our humble establishment, despite the sadness of the circumstances. I think we can all say that what we're doing is the best we can, wouldn't you agree, Mr Underhill?'

'Um,' Philip said.

She turned a brisk, meaningless smile upon Tim. 'And a heartfelt welcome to you, sir. Are you a member of the family circle?'

'He's my brother,' Philip said. 'From New York.'

'New York, New York? Well, that's wonderful.' Tim feared that she would take his hand, but she merely patted his arm. 'The hubby and I had a lovely weekend in New York City, oh, it was nine – ten years ago now. We saw *Les Mis*, and the next day we saw *Cats*. You New Yorkers never run out of things to do and places to go, do you? Must be like living in an anthill, ants ants ants, all running running running.'

Having disposed of Tim, she transferred her hand to Philip's arm. 'Feeling a little bit shy, are we? You'd be surprised how many of our people feel that exact same way, but the minute you go up and commune with your late missus, you'll understand there's no need at all for that sort of thing.'

She placed her free hand on his elbow and piloted him down the aisle between the rows of empty chairs. Loyally, Tim came along behind.

'Now, see, Mr Underhill? Your little bride looks every bit as peaceful and beautiful as you could ever want to remember her.'

Philip stared down at the effigy in the coffin. So did Tim. Nancy appeared to have been dead since birth.

In a strangled voice, Philip said, 'Thank you for all you've done.'

'And if you will take the advice of someone who is pretty much an expert in this sort of thing,' Joyce Brophy whispered close to Philip's ear, 'you make sure that handsome boy of yours comes up here and communes with his mama, because believe you me, if he misses this chance he'll never have another and he'll regret it all the rest of his life.'

'Excellent advice,' said Philip.

With a neighborly pat of his wrist, she bustled out of the room.

'Mark, this is your last chance to see your mother,' Philip said, speaking in the general direction of his left shoulder.

Mark mumbled something that sounded unpleasant.

'It's the reason we're here, son.' He turned all the way around and kept his voice low and reasonable. 'Jimbo, you can come up or not, as you wish, but Mark has to say good-bye to his mother.'

Both boys stood up, looking anywhere but at the coffin, then moved awkwardly into the center aisle. Tim drifted away to the side of the room. Halfway to the coffin, Mark looked directly at his mother, instantly glanced away, swallowed, and looked back. Jimbo whispered something to him and settled himself into an aisle chair. When Mark stood before the coffin, frozen-faced, Philip nodded at him with what seemed a schoolmaster's approval of a cooperative student. For a moment only, father and son remained together at the head of the room; then Philip lightly settled a hand on Mark's shoulder, removed it, and without another glance turned away and joined Tim at the side of the room. In wordless agreement, the two men returned to their earlier station next to the dark, polished table and the stacks of memorial cards. A few other people had entered the room.

Slowly, Jimbo rose to his feet and walked up the aisle to stand beside his friend.

'You have to feel sorry for the poor kid,' Philip said softly. 'Terrible shock.'

'You had a terrible shock yourself,' Tim said. At Philip's questioning glance, he added, 'When you found the body. Found Nancy like that.'

‘The first time I saw Nancy’s body, she was all wrapped up, and they were taking her out of the house.’

‘Well, who . . .’ A dreadful recognition stopped his throat.

‘Mark found her that afternoon – came home from God knows where, went into the bathroom, and there she was. He called me, and I told him to dial 911 and then go outside. By the time I got home, they were taking her to the ambulance.’

‘Oh, no,’ Tim breathed out. He looked down the aisle at the boy, locked into unreadable emotions before his mother’s casket.

Inside his brother’s house on the following afternoon, after the sad little funeral, a good number of the neighbors, many more than Tim had anticipated, were sitting on the furniture or standing around with soft drinks in their hands. (Most of them held soft drinks, anyhow. Since his arrival at the gathering, Jimbo’s father, Jackie Monaghan, whose ruddy, good-humored face was the template for his son’s, had acquired a dull shine in his eyes and a band of red across his cheekbones. These were probably less the product of grief than of the contents of the flask outlined in his hip pocket.

Tim had witnessed two of the other attendees quietly stepping out of the room with good old Jackie.)

Jimbo's mother, Margo Monaghan, had startled Tim by revealing that she had read one of his books. Even more startling was her extraordinary natural beauty. Without a trace of makeup Margo Monaghan looked like two or three famous actresses but did not really resemble any of them. She looked the way the actresses would look if you rang their bell and caught them unprepared at three o'clock on an ordinary afternoon. Amazingly, the other men in the room paid no attention to her. If anything, they acted as though she were obscurely disfigured and they felt sorry for her.

Part of the reason Tim had expected no more than three or four people to gather at his brother's house was Philip's personality; the remainder concerned the tiny number of mourners at the grave site in Sunnyside Cemetery. The pitiless sunlight had fallen on the husband, son, and brother-in-law of the deceased; on the Rent-a-minister; on Jimbo, Jackie, and Margo; on Florence, Shirley, and Mack, Nancy's gas company friends; on Laura and Ted Shillington, the Underhills' next-door neighbors to the right, and Linda and Hank Taft, the next-door neighbors to the left. The Rent-a-minister had awaited the arrival of additional mourners until the delay became almost embarrassing. A grim nod from Philip had finally set him in motion, and his harmless observations on motherhood, unexpected death, and the hope of salvation lasted approximately eight endless minutes and were followed by a brief prayer and the mechanical descent of the casket into the grave. Philip, Mark, and Tim picked up clayey brown clods from beside the open grave and dropped them onto the lid of the coffin; after a second, Jimbo Monaghan did the same, giving inspiration to the other mourners, who followed suit.

Back on Superior Street, Laura Shillington and Linda Taft stopped off to pick up the tuna casseroles, Jell-O and marshmallow salad, ambrosia, and coffee cake they had prepared. Florence, Shirley, and Mack partook of the banquet and the Kool-Aid and left soon after. Their departure had an insignificant effect on the assemblage, which by that time had grown to something like thirty. Tim wondered if so many people had ever before been in Philip's house at the same time. Whatever his experience as a host, Philip now moved easily through the various groups, talking softly to his neighbors and the other guests. The Rochenkos, a pair of young elementary school teachers incongruous in matching polo shirts and khaki trousers, showed up, and so did a sour-looking old man in a plaid shirt who introduced himself to Tim as 'Omar Hillyard, the neighborhood pest' and seldom moved out of the corner from which he eyed the action.

Four people from John Quincy Adams arrived. After his colleagues turned up, Philip spent most of his time with them. Their little group settled at the far end of the dining room, within easy striking distance of the table.

Tim was introduced to Linda and Hank, Laura and Ted, the Monaghans, and a few other neighbors whose names he did not remember. When Philip attempted to reintroduce him to Omar Hillyard, the old man held up his hands and retreated deeper into his corner. 'Neighborhood pest,' Philip whispered. In the dining room, Tim shook the hands of Philip's coworkers, Fred and Tupper and Chuck (the guidance counselor, the school secretary, and the administrative secretary) and Mr Battley, the principal, a man set apart from the others by the dignity of his office. Philip seemed perfectly comfortable with this group, despite his evident concern for Mr Battley's ongoing comfort. Like Philip, his superior wore a slightly oversized suit, a white shirt, and a tie with a tie tack. Mr Battley's rimless eyeglasses were identical to Philip's. And like Philip, Fred, Tupper, and Chuck, Mr Battley quietly suggested that they owned a higher, nobler calling than the salesmen, factory foremen, clerks, and mechanics around them.

Almost always flanked by Jimbo Monaghan, Mark filtered through the little crowd, now and then stopping to say something or be spoken to. Men settled their hands on his shoulder, women pecked him on the cheek. Not for a moment did he seem at ease or even at home. What you saw when you looked at Mark was a young man who longed desperately to be elsewhere. He concealed it as well as he could, which is to say not very successfully. Tim was not sure how much of what was said to him Mark actually took in. His face had never quite lost the frozen, locked-up expression that had overtaken it in the Tranquillity Parlor. He nodded, now and again offered his handsome smile, but behind these gestures he remained untouched and apart; remained also, Tim thought, under the sway of the amped-up energy, that inflammatory recklessness, which had made him leap up and spin around when he was alone on the sidewalk with his red-haired friend.

This was the quality that most made Tim hope that Philip would find it in himself to aid his son.

He was afraid of what Mark might do if left to himself. The boy could not bear what he had seen, and without sensitive adult help, he would break under its fearful weight.

Spotting Mark for once standing by himself near the living room window, Tim pushed his way through the crowd and sidled next to him. 'I think you should come to New York and stay with me for a week or so. Maybe in August?'

Mark's pleasure at this suggestion gave him hope.

'Sure, I'd love that. Did you say anything to Dad?'

'I will later,' Tim said, and went back across the room.

While being introduced to Philip's principal, Tim glanced again at Mark, and saw him shrug away from a wet-eyed elderly couple and cut through the crowd toward Jimbo. Whispering vehemently, Mark nudged Jimbo toward the dining room.

'I understand you're a writer of some sort,' said Mr Battley.

'That's right.'

Polite smile. 'Who do you write for?'

'Me, I guess.'

'Ah.' Mr Battley wrestled with this concept.

'I write novels. Short stories, too, but novels, mostly.'

Mr Battley found that he had another question after all. 'Has any of your stuff been published?'

'All of it's been published. Eight novels and two short-story collections.'

Now at least a fraction of the principal's attention had been snagged.

'Would I know any of your work?'

'Of course not,' Tim said. 'You wouldn't like it at all.'

Mr Battley's mouth slid into an uneasy smile, and his eyes cut away toward his underlings. In a second he was gone. On the other side of the space he had occupied, Philip Underhill and Jackie Monaghan stood deep in conversation, their backs to their sons. The boys were a couple of feet closer to them than Tim, but even Tim could hear every word their fathers said.

'Wasn't Nancy related to this weird guy who used to live around here? Somebody said something about it once, I don't remember who.'

'Should have kept his mouth shut, whoever he was,' Philip said.

'A murderer? That's what I heard. Only, there was a time when people called him a hero, because he risked his life to save some kids.'

Mark swiveled his head toward them.

'I heard they were black, those kids. Must have been one of the first black families around here.

It was back when they weren't accepted the way they are now.'

Tim waited for his brother to say something revolting about acceptance. At the time he'd sold his house in the suburbs and bought, at what seemed a bargain price, the place on Superior Street, Philip had been unaware that the former Pigtown was now something like 25 percent black. This had simply escaped his notice. It was Philip's assumption that the neighborhood would have remained as it had been in his boyhood – respectable, inexpensive, and as white as a Boy Scout meeting in Aberdeen. When the realization came, it outraged him. Adding to his wrath was the presence of a great many interracial couples, generally black men with white wives. When Philip saw such a couple on the sidewalk, the force of his emotions often drove him across the street. No black people of either gender had bothered to drop in for the 'reception,' as Tim had overheard Philip describing the gathering.

'I'd say we're still working on that acceptance business,' Philip said. 'To be accepted, you have to prove you're worthy of acceptance. Are we in agreement?'

'Absolutely.'

'When I have my vice principal's hat on, I am scrupulously fair. I have to be. I never make any decision based on race. Here in the privacy of my own home, I believe I am entitled to my own opinion, however unpopular it may be.'

'Absolutely,' Jackie repeated. 'I'm with you one hundred percent. Don't say any of this stuff to my wife.'

Their sons looked at each other and began to back away.

'But whatever you hear about my wife's family – my *late* wife's family – take it with a grain of salt. Those people were as crazy as bedbugs. I should have known better than to marry into a bunch of screwballs like that.'

His face white, Mark silently glided around the two men and vanished into the kitchen. Jimbo followed, looking stricken. The men never noticed.

When Tim flew back to New York the next day, it was with the sour, unpleasant feeling that Philip might after all have driven Nancy to suicide.

Half an hour before they landed at La Guardia, a delicious aroma filled the cabin, and the flight attendants came down the aisle handing out the chocolate-chip cookies. Tim wondered what Mark was doing and how he felt. Philip was incapable of doing what was right – the boy might as well have been all alone. Tim's growing anxiety made him feel like hijacking the plane and making it return to Millhaven. He promised himself to send the boy an e-mail the minute he got home; then he promised himself to get Mark to New York as soon as possible.

Part Two

THE HOUSE ON MICHIGAN STREET

4

A WEEK BEFORE Tim Underhill's initial flight to Millhaven, his nephew, Mark, began to realize that something was wrong with his mother. It was nothing that he could quite pin down, nothing obvious. Unless her constant air of worried distraction had a physical origin, she did not appear to be ill. Mark's mother had never been an upbeat person, exactly, but he did not think that she had ever before been so out of it for so long. As she went through the motions of preparing dinner and washing dishes, she seemed only half present. The half of her taking care of things was pretending to be whole, but the other half of Nancy Underhill was in some weird, anxious daze. Mark thought his mother looked as though all of a sudden she had been given some huge new problem, and whenever she allowed herself to think about it, the problem scared the hell out of her.

On a recent night, he had come home shortly before eleven P.M. after being out with Jimbo Monaghan – 'being out' a euphemism for the one activity that had compelled him during these past days – hoping not to be punished for having missed his curfew by twenty minutes or so. Ten-thirty was a ridiculously early hour for a fifteen-year-old to have to be home, anyhow. In he had come, twenty minutes past his curfew, expecting to be interrogated longer than he had been AWOL and ordered into bed. However, Mark did not take off his shoes or tiptoe to the stairs. Some unacknowledged part of him regretted that the living room was dark except for the dim light leaking in from the kitchen, and that neither of his parents was ensconced on the davenport, tapping the crystal of a wristwatch.

From the foyer he could see a light burning at the top of the stairs. That would be for both his benefit and his parents' peace of mind: if they woke up to see that the hallway was dark, they would know he had come home, and they could perfect the scolding he would get in the morning. The dim yellow haze in the living room probably meant that either his father or his mother had grown sick of lying in bed and gone downstairs to wait for their errant son.

He moved into the living room and looked through to the kitchen. Curiouser and curiouser. The kitchen did not appear to be the source of the light. The floor tiles and the sink were touched by a faint illumination leaking in from the side, which meant that the overhead light in the downstairs bathroom was on.

Riddle: since the upstairs bathroom is right across the hall from their bedroom, why would one of his parents come downstairs for a nocturnal pee?

Answer: because she was downstairs already, dummy, waiting to give you hell.

That light spilled into the kitchen meant that the bathroom door was either completely or partially open, thereby presenting Mark with a problem. He made a little more noise than was necessary on his journey across the dining room. He coughed. When he heard nothing from the region in question, he said, 'Mom? Are you up?'

There was no answer.

'I'm sorry I'm late. We forgot what time it was.' Emboldened, he took another step forward. 'I don't know why my curfew's so early anyhow. Almost everybody in my class . . .'

The silence continued. He hoped his mother had not fallen asleep in the bathroom. A less embarrassing possibility was that she had gone upstairs without switching off the light.

Mark braced himself for whatever he might see, went into the kitchen, and looked at the bathroom. The door hung half open. Through the gap between the door and the frame, he could see a vertical section of his mother. She was seated on the edge of the bathtub in a white nightgown, and on her face was an expression of dazed incomprehension, shot through with what he thought was fear. It was the expression of one who awakens from a nightmare and does not yet fully realize that nothing she had seen was real.

'Mom,' he said.

She failed to register his presence. A chill slithered from the bottom of his spine all the way up his back.

'Mom,' he said, 'wake up. What are you doing?'

His mother continued to stare with empty eyes at something that was nowhere in front of her. Folded tightly together, her hands rested on the tops of her clamped knees. Her shoulders slumped, and her hair looked dull and rumpled. Mark wondered if she could actually see anything at all; he wondered if she had drifted downstairs in her sleep. He came within a foot of the bathroom door and gently pulled it all the way open.

'Do you need help, Mom?'

To his relief, increments of consciousness slowly returned to his mother's face. Her hands released each other, and she wiped her palms on the fabric spread across her knees. She blinked, then blinked again, as if deliberately. A tentative hand rose to her cheek, and awareness dimly appeared in her eyes. Very slowly, she lifted her head and met his gaze.

'Mark.'

'Are you okay, Mom?'

She swallowed and again lightly stroked her cheek.

'I'm fine,' she told him.

5

NOT FINE, SHE was emerging from the aftereffects of a profound shock. Just now, a girl of five or six in ripped, dirty coveralls had materialized in front of her, simply come into being, like an eerily solid hologram. The child was inconsolable, her weeping would never stop, so great, so crushing, were the injuries this child had endured. Frightened and dismayed, Nancy had thought to reach out and stroke her hair. But before she was able to raise her hand, the sobbing child turned her head and gave Nancy a glance of concentrated ill will that struck her like a blow. Pure vindictive animosity streamed from her, directed entirely at Nancy. This *happened*. Having happened, it spoke of a ferocious guilt, as ferocious as the child herself.

Yes I am here, yes I was real. You denied me.

Nancy found she was trembling violently and was incapable of speech. She had nothing to say anyhow. Back in the shabby little suburban house in Carrollton Gardens, she could have spoken, but then she had remained silent. Terror rooted her to the side of the tub. Why had she come in here in the first place?

Having communicated, the little girl vanished, leaving Nancy in shock. She had never seen that child before, but she knew who she was, yes she did. And she knew her name. Finally, Lily had come searching for her, after all.

6

'ARE YOU SURE?' Mark asked.

'I'm just . . . you surprised me.'

'Why are you sitting here?'

Nancy raised her left arm and looked at her bare wrist. 'You're late.'

'Mom, you're not wearing your watch.'

She lowered her arm. 'What time is it?'

'About eleven. I was with Jimbo. I guess we forgot about the time.'

'What do you and Jimbo do at night hour after hour?'

'Hang out,' he said. 'You know.' He changed the subject. 'What are you doing down here?'

'Well,' she said, collecting herself a bit more successfully. 'I was worried because you hadn't come home. So I went downstairs . . . I guess I dozed off.'

‘You looked funny,’ he said.

Nancy wiped her eyes with the heels of her hands, her mouth flickering between mirth and despair. ‘Get yourself to bed, young man. I won’t say anything to your father, but this is the last time, understand?’

Mark understood. He was not to say anything to his father, either.

7

MARK'S OBSESSION HAD begun quietly and unobtrusively, as simple curiosity, with no hint of the urgency it would so quickly acquire. He and Jimbo had been out with their skateboards, trying simultaneously to improve their skills, look at least faintly impressive, and irritate a few neighbors. Over and over they had seen it proved that the average adult cannot abide the sight of a teenage boy on a skateboard. Something about the combination of baggy jeans, bent knees, a backward baseball cap, and a fiberglass board rattling along on two sets of wheels made the average adult male hyperventilate. The longer the run, the angrier they got. If you fell down, they yelled, 'Hurt yourself, kid?'

Unsurprisingly, the city of Millhaven offered no

skateboarding venues with half-pipes, bowls, and purpose-built ramps. What it had instead were parking lots, the steps of municipal buildings, construction sites, and a few hills. The best parking lots tended to be dominated by older kids who had no patience with newbies like Mark and Jimbo and tended either to mock their equipment or to try to steal it from them. They did have amazingly good equipment. Mark had seen a *Ledger* classified ad placed by a dreadlocked twenty-year-old hippie named Jeffie Matusczak who was giving up the sport to pursue his spiritual life in India and was willing to sell his two boards for fifty dollars apiece. They went on the Internet and spent the last of their money on DC Manteca shoes. Their outfits looked great, but their skills were drastically under par. Because they wished to avoid ridicule and humiliation, they did some of their skateboarding in the playground at Quincy; some on the front steps of the county museum, far downtown; but most of it on the streets around their houses, especially Michigan Street, one block west.

On the day Mark's obsession began, he had pushed himself past the entrance to the alley, rolled up to Michigan Street, and given the board a good kick so that he could do the corner in style, slightly bent over, his arms extended. Michigan Street had a much steeper pitch than Superior Street, and its blunt curves had donated a number of daredevil bruises to the forearms and calves of both boys. With Jimbo twenty or thirty feet behind him, Mark swung around the corner in exemplary style. Then it took place, the transforming event. Mark saw something he had never really, never quite *taken in* before, although it had undoubtedly been at its present location through all the years he had been living around the corner. It was a little house, nondescript in every way, except for the lifeless, almost hollowed-out look of a building that had long stood empty.

Knowing that he must have looked at that house a thousand times or more, Mark wondered why he had never truly noticed it. His eyes had passed over its surface without pausing to register it. Until now, the building had receded into the unremarkable background. He found this so extraordinary that he stepped backward off his board, pushed sharply down on its tail, and booted it up off the street. For once, this stunt worked exactly as it was supposed to, and the nose of the skateboard's deck flew up into his waiting hand. Jimbo rumbled up beside him and braked to a halt by planting one foot on the ground.

'Stellar,' Jimbo said. 'So why did you stop, yo?'

Mark said nothing.

'What're you looking at?'

‘That house up there.’ Mark pointed.

‘What about it?’

‘You ever seen that place before? I mean, really *seen* it?’

‘It hasn’t gone anywhere, dude,’ Jimbo said. He took a few steps forward, and Mark followed. ‘Yeah, I’ve seen it. So have you. We run past that stupid place every time we come down this street.’

‘I swear to you, I have never, ever seen that house before. In my whole life.’

‘Bullshit.’ Jimbo stalked about fifteen feet ahead, then turned around and feigned boredom and weariness.

Irritated, Mark flared out at him. ‘Why would I bullshit you about something like this? Fuck you, Jimbo.’

‘Fuck you, too, Marky-Mark.’

‘Don’t call me that.’

‘Then stop bullshitting me. It’s stupid, anyhow. I suppose you never saw that cement wall behind it either, huh?’

‘Cement wall?’ Mark trudged up beside his friend.

‘The one behind your house. On the other side of the alley from your sorry-ass back fence.’

The wooden fence Philip Underhill had years ago nailed into place around a latched gate at the far end of their little backyard sagged so far over that it nearly touched the ground.

'Oh, yeah,' Mark said. 'The wall thing, with the barbed wire on top. What about it?'

'It's in back of this place, dummy. That's the house right behind yours.'

'Oh, yeah,' Mark said. 'Right you are.' He squinted uphill. 'Does that place have numbers on it?'

Rust-brown holes pocked the discolored strip of the frame where the numerals had been.

'Somebody pried 'em off. Doesn't matter. Check out the numbers on the other side. What are they?'

Mark glanced at the house closest to him. 'Thirty-three twenty-one.' He looked at Jimbo, then carried his skateboard up the low hill until he was standing in front of the abandoned building and read off the numbered address of the next house in line. 'Thirty-three twenty-five.'

'So what's the address of this one?'

'Thirty-three twenty-three,' Mark said. 'Really, I never saw this place before.' He began to giggle at the sheer absurdity of what he had said.

Jimbo grinned and shook his head. 'Now we got that out of the way –'

'They had a fire,' Mark said. 'Check out the porch.'

'Huh,' Jimbo said. The wooden floor of the porch and the four feet of brick below the right front window had been scorched black. These signs of an old fire resembled a fading bruise, not a wound. The place had assimilated the dead fire into its being.

'Looks like someone tried to burn it down,' Jimbo said.

Mark could see the flames traveling along the porch, running up the bricks, then subsiding, growing fainter, dying. 'Place wouldn't burn,' he said. 'You can see that, can't you? The fire just went out.' He stepped forward, but not far enough to place a foot on the first rectangular stone of the walkway. There was a bemused, abstracted expression on his face. 'It's empty, right? Nobody lives there.'

'Duh,' said Jimbo.

'You don't think that's a little unusual?'

'I think you're a little unusual.'

'Come on, think about it. Do you see any other empty houses around Sherman Park? Have you ever heard of one?'

'No, but I've seen this one. Unlike you.'

'But why is it empty? These houses must be a pretty good deal, if you're not completely racist, like my dad.'

'Don't leave Jackie out,' Jimbo said. 'He'd be insulted.'

A well-known foe of skateboards, Skip, old Omar Hillyard's even more ancient, big-nosed dog, pushed itself to its feet and uttered a sonorous bark completely empty of threat.

'I mean,' Jimbo went on, 'it's not one of those places with whaddyacallems, parapets, like the Munster house. It's just like all the other houses in this neighborhood. Especially yours.'

It was true, Mark saw. Except for the narrowness of the porch and the beetle-browed look of the roofline, the building greatly resembled the Underhill house.

'How long do you think it's been empty?'

'A long time,' Jimbo said.

Tiles had blown off the roof, and paint was flaking off the window frames. Despite the sunlight, the windows looked dark, even opaque. A hesitation, some delicacy of feeling, kept Mark from going up the walkway, jumping the steps onto the porch, and peering through those blank windows. Whatever lay beyond the unwelcoming windows had earned its peace. He did not want to set his feet upon those stones or to stand on that porch. How strange; it worked both ways. All at once, Mark felt that the house's very emptiness and abandonment made up a force field that extended to the edge of the sidewalk. The air itself would reject his presence and push him back.

And yet . . .

'I don't get it. How could I miss seeing this

place before today?' He thought the house looked like a clenched fist.

Jimbo and Mark spent the next two hours rolling down Michigan Street, sweeping into curved arcs, leaping from the street onto the sidewalk, jumping off the curb back into the street. They made nearly as much noise as a pair of motorcyclists, but no one stepped outside to complain. Whenever Mark eyed the empty house, he half-expected it to have dissolved again back into its old opacity, but it kept presenting itself with the same surprising clarity it had shown when he'd first rolled around the corner. The house at 3323 North Michigan had declared itself, and now it was here to stay. His obsession, which in the manner of obsessions would change everything in his life, had taken hold.

During dinner that evening, Mark noticed that his mother seemed a bit more distracted than usual. She had prepared meat loaf, which both he and his father considered a gourmet treat. After asking the customary perfunctory questions about how his day had gone and receiving his customary perfunctory evasions, Philip was free to concentrate on impersonal matters. Instead of recounting tales of intrigue and heroism from the front line of the gas company's customer relations office, his mother seemed to be attending to an offstage conversation only she could hear. Mark's thoughts returned again and again to the house on Michigan Street.

Now he wished that he had after all walked up to the place, climbed onto the porch, and looked in the window. What he remembered of the feelings he had experienced in front of the house boiled down to a weird kind of politeness, as if his approach would have been a violation. A violation of what? Its privacy? Abandoned buildings had no sense of privacy. Yet . . . he remembered feeling that the building had *wanted to keep him away* and erected a shield to hold him back. So *the building* had kept him from going up the stone walkway? That was ridiculous. *Mark* had kept Mark from leaving the sidewalk. He knew why, too, though he did not want to admit it. The house had spooked him.

'Pretty quiet tonight, Mark,' said his father.

'Don't pick on him. Mark's fine,' his mother said in a lifeless voice.

'Am I picking on him? Am I picking on you?'

'I don't know. Are you?' He watched his mother shaving tiny slices off her meat loaf and sliding them to the side of her plate.

His father was getting ready to call him on his

insubordination. Mark rushed through the verbal formula for exiting the dining room and said, 'Jimbo's waiting for me.'

'God forbid you should keep Jimbo waiting. What are you going to do that's so important?'

'Nothing.'

'When it begins to get dark, I don't want to hear the sounds of those skateboards. Hear me?'

'Sure, fine,' he said, and carried his plate into the kitchen before his father remembered that his irritation had a cause more specific than its usual source, his son's adolescence.

After losing the yolky look of the afternoon, the sunlight had muted itself to a dispersed, fleeting shade of yellow that struck Mark Underhill with the force of a strong fragrance or a rich chord from a guitar. Departure, beautiful in itself, spoke from the newly shorn grass and infolding hollyhocks in the Shillingtons' backyard. He thought he heard the scraping of an insect; then the sound ceased. He rushed toward his destination.

Beyond the defeated fence Jimbo had remarked lay eight feet of dusty alley, and beyond the alley rose the cement-block wall also remarked by Jimbo. If the wall fell over and remained intact, it would blanket fourteen feet of the alley with concrete blocks; and the triple strands of barbed wire running along the top of the wall would nearly touch Philip Underhill's ruined fence.

Eight feet tall, fourteen feet long, and mounted with coils of barbed wire – Mark had certainly noticed the wall before, but until this moment it had seemed no less ordinary than the Tafts' empty doghouse and the telephone wires strung overhead, ugly and unremarkable. Now he saw that while it was undoubtedly ugly, the wall was anything but unremarkable. Someone had actually gone to the trouble to build this monstrosity. The only function it could possibly have had was to conceal the rear of the house and to discourage burglars or other invaders from sneaking onto the property from the alley.

Both ends of the wall disappeared into a thick mass of weeds and vines that had engulfed wooden fences six feet high walling in the backyard on both sides like false, drastically overgrown hedges. From the alley, this vegetation looked impenetrably dense. In mid-summer, it oozed out a heavy vegetal odor mingling fertility and rot. Mark could catch a hint of that odor now, fermenting itself up at the heart of the weedy thicket. He had never been able to decide if it was one of the best smells he knew, or one of the worst.

That he could not see the house from the alley made him want to look at it again all the more.

It was a desire as strong as thirst or hunger – a desire that dug a needle into him.

He ran up the narrow alley until he reached the Monaghans' backyard, vaulted over their three feet of brick wall, and trotted over the parched, clay-colored earth softened by islands of grass to their back door, which he opened a crack.

'Yo, Jimbo!' he called through the opening. 'Can you come out?'

'He's on his way, Marky,' came the voice of Jimbo's mother. 'Why are you back there?'

'I felt like coming up the alley.'

She appeared in the arch to the kitchen, coming toward him with an unsettling smile. Margo Monaghan's smile was not her only unsettling feature. She was easily the most beautiful woman Mark had ever seen, in movies or out of them. Her watercolor red hair fell softly to just above her neck, and she combed it with her fingers. In summer, she usually wore T-shirts and shorts or blue jeans, and the body in these yielding, informal clothes sometimes made him feel like swooning. The woman smiling at Mark now as she walked to the screen door seemed not only to have no idea of how stunning she was, but to have no personal vanity at all. She was friendly in a half-maternal way, slopping around in her old clothes. Apart from her amazing looks, she fit into the neighborhood perfectly. His mother was the only person Mark had ever heard speak of Mrs Monaghan's beauty. She opened the door and leaned against the frame. Instantly, Mark's penis began to thicken and grow. He shoved his hands into his pockets, grateful for the roominess of his jeans. She made the situation infinitely worse by reaching out and stroking the top of his head with the palm of her hand.

'I wish Jimbo would get one of those haircuts,' she said. 'He looks like a silly hippie. Yours is so much cooler.'

Mark needed a moment to realize that she was talking about body temperature.

'What adventures are the homeboys getting into tonight?'

'Nothing much.'

'I keep asking Jimbo to show me what he can do on that skateboard, but he never does!'

'We have a way to go before we're ready for the public,' Mark said.

She had the whitest, purest skin he had ever seen, more translucent than a young girl's; it seemed that he could look down through layers, getting closer and closer to her inner light. The blue of her irises leaked out in a perfect circle into the whites, another suggestion of gauzy filminess contradicted by the luxuriance of the shape beneath the black T-shirt, which bore the slogan: 69 LOVE SONGS. It was one of his, borrowed weeks ago by Jimbo. His shirt, hugging Margo Monaghan's shoulders, Margo Monaghan's chest. Oh God oh God.

'You're a handsome kid,' she said. 'Wait till those high school vixens get their mitts on you.'

His face had become as hot as a glowing electrical coil.

'Oh, honey, I'm sorry I embarrassed you,' she said, rendering his embarrassment complete. 'I'm such a klutz, honest –'

'*Mo-om*,' Jimbo bellowed, sidling past and nearly pushing her aside. 'I told you, stop picking on my friends!'

'I wasn't picking on Mark, sweetie, I –'

If you wanted to drive yourself crazy you could remind yourself that fifteen years ago, Jimbo had crawled out from between Margo Monaghan's columnar legs.

Jimbo said, 'All right, Mom,' and jumped down the steps to the backyard. Mark pressed a hand to a burning cheek and glanced at his friend's mother.

'Go,' she said.

He jumped off the steps and caught up to Jimbo on the other side of the low brick wall.

'I hate it when she does that,' Jimbo said.

'Does what?'

'Talks to my friends. It's creepy. It's like she's trying to get *information*.'

'I don't mind, honest.'

'Well, I do. So what do you want to do?'

'Check out that house some more.'

'Yeah, let's go to the dump and shoot rats.'

This was an allusion to a Woody Allen movie they had seen a couple of years before in which, faced with any amount of empty time, a brilliant guitarist played by Sean Penn could think to fill it only by shooting rats at the local dump. For Mark and Jimbo, the phrase had come to stand for any dumb, repeated activity.

Jimbo smiled and cast him a sideways look. 'Only I was thinking we could go over to the park, see what's happening over there, you know?'

On summer nights, high school students and hangers-on from all parts of town congregated around the fountain in Sherman Park. Depending on who was there, it could be fun or a little scary, but it was never boring. Ordinarily, the two boys would have walked to the park almost without discussion, understanding that they would see what was going on and take it from there.

'Humor me, all right?' Mark said, startled by the bright pain raised in his heart by the thought of not immediately going back down the alley. 'Come on, look at something with me.'

'This is such bullshit,' Jimbo said. 'But okay, do your thing.'

Mark was already moving down the alley. 'You've seen it a thousand times before, but this time I want you to *think* about it, okay?'

'Yo, I can remember when you used to be sort of fun to hang with,' Jimbo said.

'Yo, I can remember when you still had an open mind.'

'*Fuck* you.'

'No, fuck *you*.'

Feeling obscurely improved by this exchange, they walked down the alley to the point between Mark's backyard and the concrete wall.

'Look at that thing. Just *look* at it.'

'It's a concrete wall, with barbed wire on top.'

'What else?'

Jimbo shrugged. Mark gestured toward the tangle of vines and leaves erupting from the sides of the wall.

'Plus all that crap,' Jimbo said. 'And lots of plants around the sides.'

'Yeah, the sides. What's on the sides?'

'Like fences, or big hedges.'

'What's all this stuff for? Why was it put here?'

'Why? To keep other people off his property.'

'Take a look at the other houses on this block. What's different about this one?'

'You can't get in there without a hell of a lot of grief.'

'You can't even see in,' Mark said. 'This is the only house in this whole neighborhood that you can't see from the alley. Does that tell you anything?'

'Not really.'

'The guy who put this up, whoever he was, didn't want anyone looking at his backyard. That's what all this stuff is for, to keep people from seeing it.'

'You've been thinking about this way too much,' Jimbo said.

'He was hiding something. Look at that humongous wall! Don't you wonder what his secret was?'

Jimbo stepped backward, his eyes round with disbelief. 'You're like the world champion of bullshit. Unfortunately, to you everything you say makes sense. Can we go to the park now?'

In silence, the boys left the northern end of the alley and turned east on Auer Avenue, not an avenue at all but merely another residential street lined with houses and parked cars. Down Auer they proceeded for a single block that offered for their consideration two interracial couples sitting on their respective porches, a sight that so forcefully brought to the boys' minds what their fathers would have to say about this spectacle that they themselves maintained their silence throughout their turn onto Sherman Boulevard and the one-block trek past the diner, the liquor stores, and the discount outlets to the corner of West Burleigh. Without waiting for the light, they ran across the busy street and continued on into the little park.

A substantial crowd of people milled aimlessly around the dry twenty-foot basin of the fountain. The competing sounds of Phish and Eminem drifted out of two facing boom boxes. Together, Mark and Jimbo noticed the uniformed officer leaning against the patrol car parked off to the side.

As soon as they saw the cop, their way of walking became more self-conscious and mannered. Indicating their indifference to official observation, they dipped their knees, dropped one shoulder, and tilted their heads.

'Yo, little homeboys,' the policeman called.

They pretended to take in his presence for the first time. Smiling, the cop waved them forward. 'Come here, you guys. I want you to look at something.'

The boys lounged toward him. It was like a magic trick: one second the officer's hands were empty, the next they held up an eight-by-ten black-and-white photograph of a stoner metalhead. 'Do you know this guy?'

'Who is he?' Jimbo asked. 'He's in trouble, right?'

'How about you?' the cop asked Mark.

'I don't know him,' Mark said.

The cop moved the stoner's photograph closer to their faces. 'Have either of you ever seen him here at night? Does he look familiar to you guys?'

They shook their heads. 'Who is he?' Jimbo asked again.

The policeman lowered the photograph. 'This kid's name is Shane Auslander. He's sixteen years old.'

'Where does he go to school?' Jimbo asked.

'Holy Name,' the cop said.

That explained a lot. For Mark and Jimbo, the boys who went to Holy Name fell into three basic categories: squeaky-clean nerds who were secret lushes; bullies and/or jocks who had a tendency to get in car wrecks from which they emerged pretty much unscathed; and, on the bottom rung, potheads struggling with the question of Mary's virginity. Members of the third category often failed to complete high school.

'What'd he do, break into a drugstore and steal all the OxyContin?' Jimbo asked.

'He didn't do anything,' the cop said. 'Except four days ago, he went missing.'

'Went missing?' Jimbo asked.

'Vanished,' the cop said. 'Disappeared.'

'He ran away, believe me,' Jimbo said. 'Just look at this guy! His parents drop-kicked him into Catholic school, and he couldn't stand the place.'

'Shane Auslander,' Mark said, looking at the boy in the photograph. 'What do you think happened to him, Officer?'

'Thank you for your time.' The photograph had already disappeared into the manila envelope in the officer's right hand.

'Do you think he's still alive?' Mark asked.

'We appreciate your cooperation, sir,' the cop said.

As they moved away, the officer beckoned to a couple of girls who were whispering to each other a little way down the path. Soon the boys were on the edge of the crowd.

'Look, there's another cop!' Mark said. 'They come in, like, dyads.'

The second police officer, who was tall, slender, and blond, was showing Shane Auslander's photograph to four seniors from Madison High.

'Shit,' Jimbo said. 'That's Raver, Sparkman, Tillinger, and Beaney Jacobs. Don't let them see us.'

'Someone ought to snatch one of those assholes, them and their stupid hemp necklaces,' Mark said, moving toward the other side of the fountain. 'Hey!

I bet that's what happened!'

'What?' Jimbo was keeping one eye on Raver, Sparkman, Tillinger, and Jacobs. Horrible individually, collectively they were a nightmare.

'Someone grabbed that kid right here. Or they met him here and led him away, you know, to their car, or to their house, whatever.'

'It's not going to be a whole lot of fun around here tonight,' Jimbo said.

'Well,' said Mark, 'if you feel like leaving, I can think of somewhere to go.'

8

FOR THE NEXT two days, Mark felt as though he were balancing two opposed forces, the house on Michigan Street and his mother. Both of these forces demanded great quantities of his time and attention, the house overtly, his mother passively. As if in thrall to some insidious disease, Nancy Underhill crept out of the house in the morning, crept back in at night, and did strikingly little in between. She 'rested,' which meant disappearing for hours behind the closed bedroom door. According to Philip Underhill, a highly regarded expert on the mental and physical peculiarities of the contemporary American female, especially as represented by his wife, Mark's mother was undergoing a long-anticipated and long-delayed spiritual backlash from the abuse she suffered daily on behalf of the gas company, not to mention the symptoms common to women experiencing a certain inevitable physical-hormonal milestone. In other words, she got into bed and, with luck, slept through her hot flashes. To Mark, she looked as though she hardly slept at all, nor did he think she was menopausal. From what he had learned in a compulsory sex-education class, women undergoing menopause could be emotionally overwrought. His mother was nothing like that. He would have preferred it if she were. Better a hot-tempered scold than a dispirited wraith.

Mark's father seemed almost relieved by the change in his wife. Now that she had at last succumbed to the indignities inflicted upon her by the gas company, she needed to rest up before reaching the next stage, that of realizing that she ought to quit her crummy job. He had never liked the idea of her working; he had adjusted to it when they needed her salary to meet the mortgage and car payments, but ever since his move up into the vice principal's office at Quincy, he had merely tolerated it.

Philip was pleased that Nancy came home from work worn and exhausted; he was pleased by the very things that distressed Mark. Mark thought that his mother was grateful for the distractions provided by indigent or irate consumers, and also for the gossipy company afforded by Florence, Shirley, and Mack. She did not meet her new problem at the office; she carried it around with her, like the consciousness of an illness. The problem frightened her. *That* frightened Mark. He had never considered his mother a fearful person, and now she looked as though some particular terror had stopped her in her tracks.

And while she either could not or refused to talk about the particularities of that terror, his mother expressed it in another way, by focusing on her son. She acted as though she were worried solely on his behalf; he could not return home at night without facing interrogation. Most of the scant conversation she directed his way had to do with his schedule. Where was he going, who was he going there with, what time would he get home? Because the truth would have sounded so bizarre, Mark found himself inventing tasks and errands that the Nancy of old would have seen through in an eye blink. Checking out the new puppies at the dog-breeding business run by a classmate's parents, going to the county museum to wander through the exhibits, taking the nature trail alongside the Kinninnick River were things he'd enjoyed doing in grade school. At fifteen, he was no longer friends with the boy whose parents bred border collies, and the dioramas of alert-looking Indians and Mr and Mrs Neanderthal in the Millhaven County Museum retained nothing of their old ramshackle appeal. And his almost magically clueless parents would never find out in a million years, but the nature trail had disappeared when a budget cut had let the banks of the Kinninnick revert to a secretive brushy wasteland lately popular, according to the teenage bush telegraph, as a pickup bazaar for gay men.

Mark did not enjoy lying to his mother, but he was sure that telling her the truth would give rise to a hundred new questions, none of which he could answer. He could not explain why he should have become so fascinated by the house on Michigan Street, but fascinated he was. He would no longer have argued with the word 'obsessed.' In fact, Mark liked being obsessed. Being obsessed absorbed into itself a good deal of his concern about his mother. When his attention was focused on the house, his mother might as well have been on the other side of the world.

Or on the moon. The house seemed to vacuum his ordinary concerns out of his mind and replace them with itself. Although Mark knew that his idea was absurd, 3323 North Michigan Street felt as much an active partner in his obsession as himself. Present from the first moment the place revealed itself to him, the sense that it possessed a will, even the capacity for desire, had taken hold in him while he and Jimbo had stood before it with their skateboards in their hands. When they returned to Michigan Street, Mark could feel in himself very little of the afternoon's hesitancy. Half of him wanted to go up the flagged walk and prowl around the house; the other half was content to do no more than stand on the sidewalk and let his eyes roam over the roofline, the porch, the front windows. Dark to the point of opacity that afternoon, the windows were now, a couple of days later, a dead, flat black. To see anything through them, he would have to hold a flashlight up to the glass.

What would the flashlight reveal? An empty room. There was no point in even thinking about going in there. Mark had no interest in seeing a handful of dusty, long-neglected rooms.

Yet something kept him rooted to the sidewalk, resisting Jimbo's irritated suggestions that they go back to his house and watch some TV.

After twenty minutes, Jimbo persuaded him to leave. The two of them went to his house and spent hours switching back and forth between music videos and foul-mouthed cartoons on the elderly fifteen-inch Motorola in Jimbo's room. At ten-fifteen, he went downstairs; did his utmost not to ogle Margo Monaghan while bidding good night to her and a red-faced Jackie, tilting a nice slug of Powers Whiskey into his glass; proceeded homeward past vacant porches and lighted windows, in his mind seeing only the dull, remembered face of Shane Auslander and hoping that he had run away to Chicago, or New Orleans, or somewhere else where weed was plentiful; turned up his own path to his own porch and let himself in through his own unlocked front door; and for some reason experienced a burst of apprehension instantly rationalized by his father's growl of unwelcome.

Philip looked at his watch. 'Break out the champagne, he's a whole five minutes ahead of his curfew.'

'I was watching TV at Jimbo's,' he said.

Supine on the davenport, his mother pulled herself from the depths to ask, 'You were there all night?'

'Pretty much,' he said. 'We went over to the fountain for a little bit.'

'I don't like that crowd at the fountain,' Philip said. 'Trouble just waiting to happen.'

Upstairs, Mark switched on the radio. An old Prince tune filled the air with a toxic perfume. He unlaced his sneakers and tossed them toward the closet. Mark peeled off his shirts and let them drop to the floor. Ditto his socks. Soon afterward, his teeth brushed and various previously unwashed parts of his body more or less washed, he was back in his room picking up his jeans and putting clothes into the wicker hamper. While engaged in these humble duties, Mark remembered that his window looked directly down at the alley, and also, therefore, onto the rear of the house across the alley. He dropped his clothes, scrambled across the room to the window, and thrust his head and shoulders into the humid night.

Light from his window and from the kitchen beneath made pale, oblong rectangles on the patchy yard. Beyond the rectangles of light could be seen only shapes and the vague suggestions of shapes. A faint gleam on the boards of the ruined fence led toward the hazy darkness of the alley, its dimensions sketched by faint moonlight. Beyond the outline of the eight-foot wall loomed the bushy crowns of trees. Mark had the faint memory, more like that of something glimpsed in passing than actually seen, of the great trees rising behind the cement wall. For a moment, disappointment like a red-hot awareness of loss burned at the center of his body. He would never be able to see the back of that house from his window, at least not until October, when the leaves fell.

How many Octobers had he –

– without *once* bothering to look –

Mark switched on his bedside lamp, punched

off the main bedroom light, and padded back to bed to continue reading the book he had taken a few days earlier from a shelf in the kitchen, a previously unopened copy of one of his uncle's novels that had been inscribed to his parents. *For Philip and Nancy/Something for the wee hours/With Love,/Tim*. A sporadic reader at best, Mark had been reluctant to sample his uncle's work, but he had soon found himself enjoying *The Divided Man*. It had a built-in dread that made him want to keep reading, and to judge by the street names, a big part of the book seemed to be set in Millhaven. Twenty minutes later, the lines of print began to melt into dream-sentences. He turned off his light, rolled over, and fell effortlessly into unconsciousness.

As a cabbie dreams of driving, a baker of his loaves, Mark dreamed of standing on the pavement in front of the abandoned house, now abandoned no longer. Men and women, some of them with children, congregated on the narrow porch and passed in and out of the front door. Whenever Mark looked at the front windows, he saw the partygoers, the visitors, the celebrants moving around in the crowded living room. Among those arriving were policemen, ax-carrying firefighters in yellow-striped coats, and sailors in dress whites, a UPS driver, his father's boss, a man in a diving suit and scuba gear . . . and some small children, four-year-olds he had known in nursery school but had not seen since. Whenever the front door opened, cheerful music came to him. Mark felt an overwhelming desire to go up onto the porch and join the party, but some mysterious reluctance held him back. He felt shy, awkward, out of place: apart from Mr Battley, who didn't count, the only people he knew were the nursery school children.

From the porch, a famous blue eye winked at him, and a famous smile stopped his heart: Gwyneth Paltrow! And who stood beside her but Matt Damon, grinning like crazy and winding his hand in the air, saying *Come on, Mark, get up here!* And there, beside Matt Damon, was Vince Vaughn, surely; and peeking out from behind Vince, wasn't that Steven Spielberg, with his arm around Jennifer Lopez? *You know you belong here with us*, Gwyneth's smile said. *I can't believe how stupid you're being!*

Resist Gwyneth Paltrow? Hold out against Gwynnie? He stepped off the sidewalk onto the walkway and began to move toward the party. As he approached, the people on the porch began to slip into the house, first Steven Spielberg and J.Lo, then Ben Affleck – whom he hadn't even seen before! – and Matt Damon, then even Gwynnie, and by the time he reached the steps only two skeletally thin policemen remained on the porch, gazing down at him with their hats pushed back on their heads and their collar buttons undone. Their teeth jutted from their shrunken gums like the teeth of the dead. No more than skin adhering to bone, the policemen leaned toward him. From the house came an odor of rot, floating atop a sour wave of hurdy-gurdy music. One of the cops reached out to take his hand, and Mark understood that this jackal-like figure, no more alive than an image on an Egyptian tomb, wanted him to meet Shane Auslander. He jolted back, his heart accelerating in shock and fear, and saw that he had not been quick enough. The jackal's dirt-encrusted hand had already closed on the fabric of his sleeve. Mark screamed in panic and without transition found himself sitting up in bed, panting as though he had run a marathon.

Gradually his panic left him, and he got out of bed and went to his window. Out in the night, something *happened:* a bloated, dark shape melted through the barbed wire at the top of the wall and – he thought – dropped into the alley. It might have been a cat; it might have fallen inside the wall, not into the alley. Mark's reawakened terror, cold as dry ice, brushed his stomach and his lungs. That had not been a cat, unless cats grew to the size of pigs. And he was almost certain that it had jumped down into the alley.

Fear made him imagine the thick, somehow misshapen thing sliding across the alley and crawling over his father's useless fence. Unable to move or look away, Mark peered down. It was there; it wasn't; it was. Too frightened to close his window against whatever might be invading his backyard, he put his hands on the sill and leaned out. A vague movement in the darkness below showed him the creature sliding down the pitch of the fence and moving closer to the house. Soon it will have come halfway across the yard, and then . . . Two shiny orbs, cold and reflective as steel bearings, looked up at him. Chill with terror, Mark yanked himself back through the window, in the process banging his head painfully against the bottom of the frame.

For a second he had the oddest feeling, that of having awakened a second time. The house, Matt Damon and Gwyneth Paltrow, the ghoul policemen with jutting teeth and grimy hands, they had been a dream inside a dream.

But instead of being in bed, he was still standing at the window, and the back of his head hurt like crazy. The bright insistent flare of pain from the tender place at the back of his skull seemed to anchor his feet to the floor, to locate him more firmly in the rational world. On the whole, it was as if he *had* been yanked out of a dream. Hesitantly, Mark leaned down and looked out the window again. The cold eyes had vanished; had never actually been there. No bloated monstrosity had come creeping toward his house, of course not. Mark half-closed the window and got back into bed. His heart was beating in his chest like a trapped animal.

Too disturbed to close his eyes, Mark lay awake for what seemed to him most of the night. By every measure less subjective and impatient than his, he fell asleep half an hour later. If he had any further dreams, they vanished from his mind the moment his mother, on the way to the bus stop on Sherman Boulevard, slammed shut the front door and woke him up. His father would already be downstairs, reading the newspaper in the morning's hunt for fresh outrage and eating a characteristically suicidal breakfast of four cups of coffee and a sugar-plated Danish pastry, to every bite of which he conscientiously applied a generous smear of butter. Philip had no real work to do during the summer, Mark supposed, but every morning he got up in time to arrive at Quincy a minute or two before 8:00 A.M. Once there, his father shuffled papers or talked on the telephone until 5:00 P.M., when he could no longer justify staying away from home. To avoid all contact with his father until late in the afternoon, therefore, Mark had only to delay his own arrival in the kitchen for another fifteen minutes.

Before he slipped out of bed and tiptoed down the hall to the bathroom, he went to the window and looked down at the scene of what he now had no doubt had been a secondary and half-wakeful nightmare. The backyard looked as peaceful as he had expected it to be. The fence had not been flattened closer to the ground; no rags or bits of skin clung to the barbed wire. As far as he could see, no footprints, or animal tracks, or anything of the sort had been added to the marks left by Jimbo and himself over the past few weeks.

As soon as he got downstairs, Mark went out through the kitchen door. He saw no more evidence of intrusion than he had from the bedroom window. The packed earth between strips of grass yielded a few sole prints from a pair of DC Mantecas and nothing more – certainly no hoof marks or paw prints or whatever kind of trail would have been left by the creature he had imagined crawling over the fence.

In the alley, the cobbles showed no fresh marks or stains, at least as far as he could see. But of course nothing had dropped from the top of the wall. Nothing, especially not some large animal, could have passed through the barbed wire up there without leaving some traces behind.

With some portion of the relief experienced by a man recovering from an addiction to a bad love or a seductive drug, Mark went back inside to have a glass of milk and a bowl of Chex. As if in imitation of the abandoned house, the morning's *Ledger*, rumpled from his father's hunt for outrage, abruptly lurched into visibility at the center of the breakfast table. This time, however, Mark knew exactly what had caught his notice. A headline on the first page read FEAR FOR FATE OF LOCAL TEENAGER. From immediately below the headline, Shane Auslander looked out at him, not quite meeting his eyes. It was the photograph he and Jimbo had seen in Sherman Park.

The article told him that Shane Auslander, a sophomore at Holy Name Academy and a resident of the city's North Side, had been missing for five days. He had last been seen leaving his house to join the evening gathering in Sherman Park that had lately been the source of neighbors' complaints about excessive noise and disorderly behavior. Drug trafficking was suspected at these gatherings, but the police had no evidence that the Auslander boy had been the victim of drug-related violence. They feared, however, that his disappearance could be related to that of fifteen-year-old Trey Wilk, who had ten days earlier left a classmate's house to walk home late in the evening and failed to arrive. The officer in charge of the two cases, Sergeant Franz Pohlhaus, stated that any connection between the two disappearances would be rigorously investigated and that police were pursuing all available leads. In response to a reporter's question, Sergeant Pohlhaus said that while he could not comment on the safety of the two missing boys, the chances of a happy ending to such cases tended to diminish over time. Questioned as to the period of time most conducive to a safe return, he said, 'We don't have too much experience of this kind of situation here in Millhaven.'

Another glance at Shane Auslander's photograph brought with it an unpleasant jab of remembrance. An unwelcome fragment of nightmare flickered in view, and he glimpsed something feral extending a bony hand to yank him out of his life. Goose bumps raised on his arms, and little dark hairs stuck up like quills. Hastily, Mark turned to the arts pages and grazed over the movie advertisements. He had nothing to do until Jimbo Monaghan finally got out of bed, an event that in summertime rarely took place until eleven o'clock had come and gone.

Mark put his dishes in the sink. Hoping to both save his mother some unnecessary worry and preserve his mobility, he folded the newspaper and thrust it into the wastebasket.

Without having made any conscious decisions, he wandered out the back door into the yard. His feet took him to the place on the defeated grass and exposed earth where the monstrous creature had seemed to lift its snout and look up at him. He smiled, thinking that he should send his uncle Tim an e-mail telling him that *The Divided Man* had given his nephew a grade-A nightmare. Maybe people wrote stuff like that to him all the time. *Your book scared the hell out of me. Thanks!* Mark did not feel so grateful.

Mark discovered that while conducting a kind of mental dialogue with his uncle, he had stepped over his father's broken fence and moved into the middle of the alley. This morning, the eight-foot wall still looked ugly and said *Keep out*, but it did not seem quite so sinister. Lots of people took what other people considered excessive measures to make sure they got the privacy they thought they needed.

And where was he walking now but down to the lower end of the alley to Townsend Street? And at the bottom of the alley which way was Mark turning, east toward Sherman Boulevard, where he could kill a little time mooching around in the shops, or west toward Michigan Street?

It occurred to Mark that he was retracing his path of yesterday afternoon, when he had rounded the corner of Townsend and Michigan on his skateboard. This time, he wanted the reassurance of finding that the front of the house held no more fascination for him than the wall behind it now did. He wanted his normal world back again.

Mark came around the corner, looked for an introductory moment up at the whole of Michigan Street, and felt the breath in his lungs turn to vapor. Even before he had taken in any details, his nerve endings had registered a sense of essential *wrongness*. For perhaps as long as five or six seconds, familiar Michigan Street struck him as enemy territory. Only then did he notice the profound stillness. Drained of life and dimension, Michigan Street was as flat and dead as a landscape on a billboard. Skip lay curled on his porch as if dead. Mark's knees weakened and trembled, and his heart stuttered in his chest.

With an enigmatic, self-conscious authority that suggested he had been there all along, a thick-bodied man facing the other direction stood silhouetted against the dead sky at the top of Michigan Street. He was there now, in any case, and perhaps he had been posed up there from the start, and in his shock, Mark had failed to see him. The sense of wrongness flowed from this man, Mark understood – this figure with his back turned. Mark took in the unkempt black hair curling past his collar, his wide back covered by a black coat that fell like a sheet of iron to the backs of his knees. Willful, powerful wrongness came off of him like steam.

No, Mark thought, this creature had not been standing at the top of the street all along. He had set the scene, then placed himself in it. He had created an effect, and the purpose of the effect was to get Mark's attention. With the clarity that sometimes follows in the wake of terror, the boy saw that he had been given a warning. A warning against what, the being at the top of the street would let him figure out later. For now, it was enough that he knew he'd been warned.

A recognition bloomed at the center of his terror. *Oh*, Mark understood, *he's what I saw last night. He climbed over the fence and came into our backyard*. He saw the vague snout lift and the empty steel-colored eyes find him at his window.

Then one of those new, funny-looking Chryslers turned left at the top of the street and rolled directly past the place on the sidewalk where that *thing* had been standing with his back to Mark. On his porch, Skip dragged himself upright and, without much urgency, barked twice. Like Mr Hillyard's mutt, Mark forced himself upright. The ground beneath him swayed right – left, then right – before settling down.

Everything inside Mark's body and most of his appendages seemed to be trembling, hands knees stomach heart viscera. It was almost funny, watching his hands jitter. The way his knees were jumping around, he was amazed that the legs of his jeans were not shaking. All of a sudden he was sweating like crazy.

Let's pretend we have a clean slate, he thought. *Let's go up and look at that place as though nothing had happened before this moment.*

He was going to waste a couple of minutes standing in front of a house that was rotting away from within. After he got tired of standing there, he would walk away.

A sentence from his uncle's book popped into his mind: 'What was at stake here, he thought, was the solidity of the world.' All right, how solid *is* the world? This time, he told himself, he would look at that house as never before. What could be seen, he *would* see; if it was nothing but an empty shell, he would go away knowing that his imagination really needed to be held in check.

Set thirty feet before him on its slightly tilting lawn, the house appeared subtly to shift its ground without actually moving in any way. Mark stood stock-still, as immobile as Skip had been a few minutes earlier. The house looked exactly the same, but it had altered itself nonetheless. In some internal fashion he had no hope of identifying, the house had adjusted to his presence. Mark waited. Chill drops of sweat glided down the sides of his chest. Unconsciously, he had balled his hands into fists, and the muscles in his calves and upper arms became unbearably taut. His eyes seemed to grow hot with the concentration of his staring. Mark's entire body felt as if he were straining against an immovable force.

He dared not blink.

Then he wondered if he had missed it anyhow – a faint change in the texture of an area of darkness beyond the right front window. Too vague to be defined, the difference nearly escaped his notice. Mark could not be certain that he had not invented what he thought he had seen. Now the darkness behind the window presented a uniform charcoal gray. A second later, he thought he saw the slight alteration occur again, bringing with it this time a suggestion of solidity and movement.

The thought of that bulky figure from the top of Michigan Street hanging back in the darkness while looking out at him caused a sudden pressure in his bladder. Behind the window, an indistinct portion of the general shadow drifted forward and acquired an unmistakable solidity. Another step brought into greater visibility what could almost be identified as a human head atop a human body perhaps smaller and slimmer than that of the creature who had so alarmed him. With another gliding step, the dark figure emerged into sharper, though still uncertain, focus.

To Mark, the figure seemed too small and slight to be anything but a girl. The person inside the house had come forward to see him, as well as to be seen by him. She hung unmoving in the obscurity beyond the window, declaring her presence, exactly as the house had declared itself. Look at me, take me in, I am here. The house and its inhabitant had chosen him. That he had been chosen implied an invitation, a summons, a pact of some kind. Something had been decided, he knew not what, except that it had been decided in his favor.

Mark stepped forward, and the being inside the house filtered backward into darkness and invisibility. If he wished to hold on to its approval, he could go no farther.

Behind him, a voice said, 'Yo, don't you ever do anything else?'

Startled, Mark jumped. Jimbo stepped up beside him and laughed. He jabbed the nose of his skateboard into Mark's back. 'You jumped a mile!'

'You surprised me,' Mark said. 'What are you doing up so early anyway?'

'My mom freaked when she saw the paper this morning. Remember the cop showing us that picture of the missing kid?'

'Shane Auslander,' Mark said. 'Yeah, I saw that story, too. I bet she wants you never to go back to the fountain.'

'I had to promise her,' Jimbo said. 'You look like shit. Honest to God. Didn't you get any sleep last night?'

Mark could not tell Jimbo about anything that had happened to him since they had last seen each other. It felt completely private, like a secret only he could know. 'I slept fine. Like a baby. Like a log. Like the *dead*. Now tell me something, bro. Do you think that house is really empty? Completely empty?'

'Here we go again,' Jimbo said. 'Wanna go to the dump and shoot rats?'

'No, *do* you? I mean it.'

Jimbo cast an irritated glance at the house, then looked back at Mark. 'Isn't that what got you started in the first place? That it was empty?'

'That was part of it, yeah. That the place was empty. In a neighborhood like this, you'd think an empty house would stick out.'

'More like it fades out,' Jimbo said. 'Honest, I don't get what the big deal is here.'

‘Maybe I ought to get inside there one of these days. Find out for sure.’

Jimbo raised his hands and stepped back. ‘Are you nuts? You want to see inside? Take a look in the window.’

Mark knew he could not do that. The force field kept him at the distance of the sidewalk. It would be easier for him to break in than to walk up the path, mount the steps, and stare into the window through which he had seen that shadowy figure.

‘Let’s go to my house, so I can get my board,’ he said.

For the rest of the day, they rolled down the handicapped ramps and wide concrete steps of an abandoned construction site located on Burleigh, a short bus ride away. Mark forced himself not to speak about 3323 North Michigan Street, and Jimbo was so grateful that he took pains to veer around the subject whenever it threatened to draw near. They had the place to themselves. No older kids showed up to make fun of their technique or to try to bully them out of their equipment. No aloof, silent loner appeared, as sometimes happened, to shame them with the chasm between their skills and his. Both Mark and Jimbo made three failed attempts to jump across a three-foot gap in a concrete railing; they scraped their wrists and acquired bruises on their shins, but did no serious damage to themselves. Around noon, they rolled down the block to a BK for bacon double cheeseburgers, fries, and chocolate shakes, and while they feasted they agreed that Eminem had changed hip-hop forever, yo, and that Stephin Merritt was the best singer of Stephin Merritt songs. After their lunch, they trundled back on their handsome boards to the construction site and rubbed their sore spots and decided to take another shot at that gap in the concrete railing. Both of them made it across on their first after-lunch attempt, and in the words of Eminem, they asked the world if they could have its attention, please? For the rest of the afternoon, leaving aside a few minor falls, it was as if they could not make a mistake, either of them, and they rode the bus back to Sherman Boulevard in happy and proud exhaustion, fondling their scrapes and bruises like medals. They would never again share a day of such uncomplicated pleasures; it was the last time they were ever able to enjoy themselves in this way, together, like the boys they were.

9

BY SPEAKING WHEN he knew he should remain silent, Mark brought some of the coming difficulties down upon himself. After dinner, his father escaped into his 'den,' he claimed to read an article in the latest *Journal of Secondary Education*, but just as likely in order to leaf through the old issues of *People* and *Entertainment Weekly* piled in his magazine rack. Coasting along on autopilot, Nancy had put together a mushroom soup–tuna casserole with a crust of crumbled potato chips identical to those that would feed her husband's guests on the afternoon of her funeral. When Philip scuttled off, she stacked their three plates and carried them into the kitchen. She seemed so distracted that Mark wondered if she would remember how to work the dishwasher.

He followed her into the kitchen, where she was dreamily running water over the plates. Her face, which had been concentrated into a brooding network of lines, twitched into an unconvincing smile at the sight of him.

'Are you all right, Mom?' he asked.

She responded with a phrase she would repeat two nights later, when Mark would find her seated on the edge of the downstairs bathtub. 'I'm fine.'

'Are you really? I don't know, you just look kind of . . .'

Visibly making an effort to imitate her normal self, she straightened her shoulders and gave him a look of mock rebuke. 'Kind of what?'

The only answer he thought he could give was a weak 'Tired?'

'Maybe I am tired. You know what?' Now her smile communicated some actual warmth. She reached out and rubbed the top of his head. 'I wouldn't exactly mind a little help in the kitchen. Your father would only get annoyed if I asked him, but maybe there's some hope for you.'

'Sure,' he said, and held out his hands for the rinsed plates. 'I was thinking you maybe looked sort of worried, too.'

'Maybe looked sort of worried.' Nancy spoke the words as if testing her understanding of a foreign language.

'Yeah,' Mark said. She still had not handed him the plates.

'Why shouldn't I be worried? At work today, Mack and Shirley told me that someone's been abducting teenage boys right in this part of town. From Sherman Park! Mack said, "Nance, I hope you're keeping your boy away from that fountain at night."'

With that, she handed him the dripping plates. Mark bent over and began inserting them into the bottom rack of the dishwasher.

'But you do go there, don't you? You and Jimbo hang around that fountain almost every night.'

'Probably not so much anymore.' He straightened up and held out his hands for whatever she would give him next. 'Now they have cops all over the place. They ask you all these questions. It's so stupid.'

'I don't think that's stupid. It's what the police should be doing.' She handed him two water glasses with a touch of belligerence.

'Not if they want to catch the guy,' he said. 'This way, all they're doing is guaranteeing that fewer and fewer kids will go there every night, until nobody's there at all. I don't think the bad guy, if there is a bad guy, is going to stop what he's doing, I just think they won't know where to look for him anymore.' He put the glasses into the machine and held out his hands for two more.

'So what do you think they should do, Mark?'

'Go to the park, but stay out of sight. Conceal themselves. Go in disguise. That way, they might have a chance.'

'And use you kids as decoys? No thanks, Buster Brown.' She shoved another glass into his hand and took his cereal bowl from the sink. 'I don't think I want you going to that park at night anymore. At least not until they catch the man who's been taking these boys. I don't care if the Monaghans let Jimbo sashay over there every night. Jimbo isn't my son. He can go alone, or you and he can either stay home or go somewhere else. You know, you could join a church youth group. Shirley's daughter, Brittany, has a lot of fun at her youth group. She uses it like a club. They even have dances.'

'I don't want to join a church youth group with Shirley's daughter. Please.'

'I want you to think about it. Please. You and Brittany could, I don't know –'

'Mom, sorry. There's something I've been meaning to ask you about.'

She closed her mouth on her unfinished sentence and nodded at him, frowning. Uncertain if this was actually a good idea, Mark said, 'Is there some kind of story about that empty house right in back of ours?'

For a second, his mother's mouth hung open and her eyes lost focus. The cereal bowl dropped from her hands and smashed against the floor, separating into three sections and a scattering of white powder. Nancy stared down at the remains of the bowl without moving her hands.

'What?' Mark said. 'What's wrong?' he added, this time meaning something different.

Slowly, Nancy lowered herself. She did not change the position of her hands until she could touch the floor, after which she piled up the three large sections of the bowl and nested them together. 'Nothing's wrong, Mark,' she said. 'Get the whisk broom and the dustpan, will you?'

Feeling blocked and almost rejected, he spun away to fetch the pan and brush from the broom closet. When he knelt beside his mother, she snatched the things away from him. 'Go on, I'll do it. I mean it. I dropped the darned thing, didn't I?'

Mark stepped back and watched her brush the fragments into the dustpan, go after the powder, then continue sweeping the whisk broom over the same patch of kitchen tile until she appeared to be attacking invisible fragments. He was determined not to leave her side until she at least looked at him.

Evidently, she had been gathering herself to speak while she rid the tiles of nonexistent particles, and she spoke without looking up. 'You were asking me about that empty house on Michigan Street, weren't you?' Her voice was deliberately uninflected.

'Come on, Mom. Stop pretending.'

She glanced up at him. 'You think I'm pretending? What do you think I'm pretending about?'

'I'm pretty sure you know something about that house across the alley from us.'

'You can think what you like.' She stopped moving the whisk broom over the tiles.

'Mom, that's why you dropped that bowl. It's obvious.'

Nancy got to her feet without taking her eyes from him. 'Let me tell you something, Mark.' She waved him aside so she could dump the fragments of china in the wastebasket. 'You have no idea on earth what is obvious. None.'

'Then tell me,' he said, more alarmed by her present manner than he had been earlier.

'You're interested in that house for some reason, that's clear. Have you done anything about it, Mark?'

'What do you mean?'

'Have you been sneaking around that place?'

'No.'

'Have you ever tried to break in?'

'Of course not,' he said, stung.

'All right. *Don't.* Stay away from that place. Everybody else does. Did you ever think about that?'

'I only noticed the place about a day ago.'

'I'm sorry you did.' Her gaze grew more intense. 'Answer me this. Let's say the reason you never noticed that house before now is because everyone else around here ignores it. Does that make sense to you?'

He thought about it, then nodded.

'Now I'm just guessing, okay? I think something terrible happened in there – something really, really bad, and that's why everybody leaves the place alone.'

'But what about the people who came here too late to know about it?' *Like us*, he could have added, but did not.

'It's *obvious*, Mark. Something's wrong, and they smell it. One of these days, the city will knock the place down. Until then, it's better to forget about it.'

'Okay,' Mark said.

'So that's what I want you to do.'

'Well, I can't really *forget* about it, Mom.'

'Yes, you can. At least you can try.' She came a step closer and gripped his arm.

'Fine,' he said. The wild expression in her eyes frightened him.

'No, not *fine*. Promise me you'll stay away from that house.'

'Okay.'

'Say it.'

'I promise.'

'Now promise me you'll never go inside that place.' She opened her mouth, closed it, opened it again. 'For as long as I live.'

'Yo, Mom, you're scaring me.'

'Good. Being scared isn't going to hurt you. And don't say *yo* to me. Now, say it.'

'I'll never go inside that house.' Eyes blazing, she nodded at him. 'For as long as you live.'

'Promise.'

'I promise. Mom, let go, okay?'

She released him, but her fingers seemed still to clamp into his skin. He rubbed his arm.

'So what are you going to do tonight?'

'Probably we'll just walk around, maybe go to a movie.'

'Be careful,' she said, unerringly placing her fingers on the developing bruises they had just given him.

Skateboard in hand, he fled through the back door. To his surprise, Jimbo was waiting for him, leaning against the concrete wall on the other side of the alley.

They began drifting back up the alley toward the Monaghan house and West Auer Avenue. 'The park is fucked,' Jimbo said. 'All those cops around the fountain, nobody'll be there.'

'Except for the pedophile child murderers. No more fun for those guys. "Dude, where'd they all go? I got two spaces left under my back porch."'

'Playgrounds and shopping malls, man. All you need is some Milk Duds and a van.'

Mark snorted with laughter. *Some Milk Duds and a van.*

An earlier subject returned to him, so swiftly its velocity might have pushed him backward. 'I asked my mom about that house, and she went completely nuts.'

'Oh, yeah?' Jimbo appeared to be more interested than Mark had expected him to be.

'She made me promise never to go inside there. At least not while she's alive.'

'That gives you about a fifty-year wait.'

'Why would she think I wanted to go in there in the first place?'

'Does she know how screwy you are about it?'

'No! And I don't think I'm so screwy, either. There's something I wasn't going to tell you, but I think I will. Then you can decide how screwy I am.'

'Where are we going anyhow? We could take

a bus downtown to the mall, see if there are any good new CDs.'

'Will you shut up and listen to me?'

Mark stopped moving; after a few paces, Jimbo stopped too. 'What?'

'Are you interested? Are you going to listen?'

'Well, yeah, but I could listen to this thing you didn't want to tell me on the bus, too.'

'I think I saw someone in there today.'

Jimbo came nearer, his head tilted to one side. So he was interested at last. 'What do you mean? Through the window?'

'Of course through the window, dumbbell. How else could I see someone?'

'Who was it?'

'I couldn't see that clearly. It was like this person was sort of hanging back far enough to hide in the darkness, you know, but close enough to show me she was there.'

'You think it was a woman?'

'Maybe. It could have been.'

Mark tried to remember what he had seen: a shape moving toward him through layers of darkness, then moving back into invisibility. The shape had been without any specific age or gender, yet . . .

'We should go look,' Jimbo said, firmly.

'I thought you wanted to go downtown.'

'I can't afford to buy any CDs until the weekend, and neither can you.'

Jimbo set off down the alley in the direction they had come. 'I asked my parents if they knew anything about that house, too. They said it was already vacant when we moved here.'

'My mom loses her mind just thinking about the place. She made me promise – oh, I told you.'

The high concrete wall rose up along their left side, and Jimbo patted it as they went by. 'This thing does look pretty sinister, now that you mention it. I mean, it's not exactly normal, is it?'

At the bottom of the alley, the cobblestones gave way to ordinary pavement. They got on their boards and propelled themselves around the corner onto Michigan Street.

'Next time, I'll bring my old man's field glasses,' Jimbo said. 'They're good, yo. With them, you can practically see the footprints on the moon.'

The house sat on its narrow lot exactly as before. Its windows reflected nothing. The burn marks appeared to ripple across the bricks. The boys' wheels sent out rolling, unbroken rumbles that boomed in Mark's ears like shock waves. It sounded as though they were making three times more noise than usual, creating a din that would rattle the dishes on the shelves and shake the windows in their frames.

Mr Hillyard's dog raised its long, big-nosed head and uttered a dispirited woof. Mark thought he saw a curtain on the porch window twitch back into place. They had awakened the dog; what else had they roused into life?

'We could go back to that place on Burleigh,' Mark said. 'It won't get dark for at least an hour.'

'Let's stay here,' Jimbo said. The idea of the unknown girl had provoked a new, heightened interest in him. 'If she's there, she'll hear us. Maybe she'll look out the window again.'

'Why would she?' He sounded doubtful, but his heart stirred.

'To see you,' Jimbo said. 'That's what she was doing the first time, wasn't it?'

'If it was a she. If it was anyone at all.'

Jimbo shrugged and spun his board around, for once reasonably smoothly. 'Maybe she ran away from home.'

'Maybe,' Mark said. 'One thing's for sure. Nobody's going to bother her in there.' Then he wondered: was that true? He felt queasier than he wanted Jimbo to notice.

For another hour, they pushed their skateboards uphill and rode them down, jumping off curbs and doing ollies. A few neighbors stared at them from porches or windows, but no one complained. At least once every couple of minutes, one boy or the other glanced at the front windows of 3323, without seeing any more than an opaque surface, like a film over the glass.

Just as it began to get dark, Jimbo looked at the house for the thousandth time and said, 'We're such a couple of dopes. We're acting like we're afraid of the place. We should just go up and look in the window.'

'I can't do that,' Mark said quickly. 'I promised my mom.'

'You promised not to break in, not that you wouldn't look in the window!'

'It was more like I promised to stay away from the place,' Mark said, not quite telling the truth. 'I just *can't*.' He waited a second. 'But you didn't make any promises, did you?'

'The only place I said I'd stay away from is the fountain.'

'Then I guess you could take a look,' Mark said.

Jimbo handed him his skateboard and ran across the street, bent over like a parody of Groucho Marx. He vaulted across the sidewalk, sped over the ground, and took the stairs in two jumps. On the porch, he crab-walked along the fire-scorched wall to the window. Only his head was visible. Mark watched him cup his hands over his eyes and peer inside. Jimbo moved half a foot to his right without taking his hands from his eyes. Half a minute later, he dropped his hands, half-stood, and, shrugging, looked across the street at Mark. He shook his head and made a palms-up sign for confusion before jumping down from the porch and running back across the street.

'Did you see something or didn't you?' Mark asked.

'There might be something in there – some person, I mean.' Jimbo drew his entire face into a squint. 'I don't really know what I saw. It was like something was hiding from me.'

'A guy? Because I really do think I saw a girl in that room.'

'Yeah?'

Mark nodded. Over the past half hour, the impression had been growing in him: a girl, a young woman, had permitted herself to be glimpsed. It was like an announcement, or an invitation.

'I have an idea,' Jimbo said. 'It's getting dark in about half an hour. Let's go back to my house and pick up some stuff.'

'What?'

'Stuff.'

Jimbo flipped his board into position, grabbed it with his feet, and sailed down the street, pumping his body for speed. Mark rolled downhill after him. Six feet ahead, Jimbo swung through the corner, popped himself onto the sidewalk, and kept sailing until he reached the alley, where he jumped off his board, scooped it up, and ran toward his house. Mark trotted along in his wake, thinking that whatever Jimbo wanted to take from his house, he was pretty dedicated about it.

Then he remembered: the fancy binoculars.

'Wait here,' Jimbo called over his shoulder, sprinting across his backyard to the kitchen door. The light over the sink burned yellow in the window; behind it, light from the living room washed a long rectangle across the floor. Mark heard Jimbo's voice raised in argument, then his father's voice, louder and more aggrieved. He settled down to wait.

By slow degrees, the air thickened and gathered itself. At his feet, the separations between the cobblestones filled with shadows. A familiar alto voice drifted from the kitchen window, calm and soft as a summer cloud. His mother at his shoulder, Jimbo reappeared in the door. For an instant, Mark wished he could let Jimbo go his way while he slipped into the kitchen to spend an hour with Margo Monaghan. The door closed, and his ideal woman disappeared. Jimbo came bouncing toward him, carrying a leather case in one hand and in the other, something black that looked like a club. He held his skateboard clamped against his side. When Jimbo reached the end of his backyard, Mark saw that the club was a Maglite.

'That isn't going to work, you idiot,' he said. 'When you shine a flashlight on a window at night, you just see the reflection.'

'If you're holding the flashlight, yeah. But what if I hold the field glasses, and you hold the flashlight?'

'It won't work,' Mark said.

'You don't want it to work. You don't want me to see your girlfriend.'

'My girlfriend, sure.' At the center of his being, Mark knew that his friend was right; he wanted this experiment to fail.

Up on Michigan Street, streetlamps cast shining pools of light. Unnoticed, night had come upon them. The sky seemed one shade lighter than the inky blue of the earth. A single star pierced the great bowl above.

'I still don't see how this can work,' Mark said.

Jimbo switched on the big flashlight and shone it directly into Mark's face, dazzling him. 'You look scared.'

'I'm not scared, you blinded me!' Mark raised his hands in front of his eyes.

'Move over there and stand still.' Jimbo lowered

the flashlight and swept the beam in a long, erratic arc onto the pavement in front of the Rochenko house. 'Get over there. I'll keep marking the spot.'

'Where will you be?'

'Never mind, just get to your spot.' Even more irritated than he had been earlier, Mark moved into the street and walked toward the yellow ellipse cast on the sidewalk by the Maglite. Bright windows showed television screens. A middle-aged black man in a Cubs T-shirt sat in his living room reading a hardback book the size of a dictionary. In the next living room uphill, an obese white man of no determinate age in a mesh T-shirt propped a can of beer on his gut. The streetlamps hung silhouetted against the oddly light sky, soon to darken. Except for the warmth of the evening, the look of the street reminded him of wandering in costume down this street on Halloween night and imagining, half in pleasure, half in terror, that occult presences shared the evening.

When he reached the spot, the ellipse disappeared at a click from the Maglite. He set down his board.

'Okay,' Jimbo said. 'One sec.'

Indistinct in the wide lane of darkness between lampposts, he jogged toward Mark. The binocular case swung on its strap like a fat handbag. When he reached Mark, he passed the heavy flashlight into his hands. Mark switched it on, and a streak of yellow light cut through the air and pooled on an empty lawn. Jimbo hissed, 'Turn it off!'

'Don't pee in your pants, Jim Boy,' Mark said, obeying. 'All right, now what?'

'Now I go over there and get ready to give you the word.' He was pointing back across the street to a position ten or fifteen feet down the mild hill. 'Don't do anything until I tell you to.'

'You are so annoying,' Mark said.

'Yo, who started this? Me? Wait for the signal.' The skateboard still clamped beneath his elbow, the leather case dangling from one hand, Jimbo swung away and sauntered diagonally down the street. He seemed to be moving with deliberate lack of speed, as if to maintain his own composure while shredding his friend's.

Jimbo mounted the opposite curb and took a few additional paces downhill to the western edge of 3323's plot line. He lowered his skateboard to the narrow strip of grass between sidewalk and curb and fiddled with the strap of the case. Mark could barely see what he was doing. A small, bulky object that must have been the binoculars separated from its container, and Jimbo bent over to lower the case to the ground. He straightened up and toyed with the binoculars before raising them to his eyes. Mark thrust the Maglite out before him like a baton. He placed his thumb on the switch.

Jimbo lowered the glasses again, shook his head, fiddled with the lenses, and once more raised them to his eyes. Getting the house into focus seemed to take him an eternity. Mark thought, *I guess he isn't so eager to look through that window after all*. Then he realized that Jimbo would scarcely be able to see the porch, much less the window, until the Maglite played on them. Two, three slow seconds ticked by, then a fourth, a fifth.

I was right, Mark said to himself. *Now that he's so close, Jimbo doesn't want to do it.*

Neither did he, it came to him: not this way. They were doing it all wrong, coming at it from the wrong angle, invasive and clumsy. If he had truly seen the slow dance of advance and withdrawal he thought he had seen, that person, that young woman, that girl was going to hate what they were about to do.

A millionth of a second earlier, the absolute certainty of having seen a young woman in the house had taken root in his mind.

Jimbo steadied the field glasses. He commanded, 'Now!'

Unhesitatingly, Mark pushed the switch, and a fat ray of light from the eye of the Maglite cast a wide, dull yellow circle on the front of the porch. Even before Jimbo ordered him to do it, he raised the circle to the window. The flat circle of light spread across the glass like an oil stain.

Jimbo stiffened and jumped backward. With uncoordinated, almost spastic movements, he lowered the binoculars and staggered to the edge of the sidewalk, dragging the binoculars along the ground. His feet wandered from beneath him. He folded over, went down, and struck the lawn bottom first. His trunk toppled backward, and his legs twitched.

Mark hit the button on the Maglite's shaft, and the light snapped off. In the sudden darkness, he could make out Jimbo lying like a corpse on the lawn in front of 3325. Fear probed Mark's stomach. He was not sure he could move. A second later, he found that he had already begun to walk across the street.

His mind felt curiously empty; he felt strangely empty all over, as if he were a blank sheet of paper waiting for a pencil's rough, awakening bite.

Jimbo's hands lay limp at his sides, his head back against the grass. Mark knelt beside him and watched his eyelids fluttering. A combination of anxiety and fear made him want to kick his friend in his ribs.

Jimbo blinked up at the sky. He licked his lips.

‘What did you see, man?’

‘Whoo.’ Jimbo was staring straight up.

‘When I put that light on the window, you jumped backward about a foot. Then you *fainted*.’

‘Well, that’s your story.’ Jimbo’s face seemed drawn and sunken, as if suddenly aged. ‘Here’s *my* story. I didn’t see shit and I want to get out of here.’ He folded his hands on his stomach, took a deep breath, and sat up. ‘Could you get my dad’s field glasses?’

Mark got the glasses from the sidewalk and handed them to him.

‘Where’s my board?’

Mark found it with the flashlight, and Jimbo got up and gathered it in so slowly it seemed that his joints ached. He turned around and held out a hand for the Maglite, which he shoved into his waist-band. Mark walked around the corner and into the alley with him, but Jimbo remained silent until they reached the ruined fence and the concrete wall. ‘See you tomorrow,’ he said, telling Mark to go no farther.

Part Three

A RIP IN THE FABRIC

10

AFTER RETURNING TO Millhaven in response to Philip's alarming call, Tim Underhill questioned nearly as many people as would a conscientious reporter doing man-on-the-street interviews in the week before an election. He would have flown to Alaska if he thought an Alaskan had seen Mark on the day of his disappearance, or could give him any information about that disappearance.

As the days went by, Tim felt an ever-increasing desperation. He loved Mark more than he'd known, he discovered: for his promise, his striking good looks, the underlying sweetness of his character – and for his angers and frustrations and moments of reckless bravado. He was a kid, after all, and if you were to love him sensibly and well you had to take him as he came. Tim had wanted his nephew to visit him in New York. He thought a boy like Mark should see the great city and sense its million opportunities, begin to appreciate its gritty essential goodness, and come to understand that New York City was really the opposite of what people living in other parts of the country tended to imagine it to be, was more honest, more generous, and more considerate than other towns and cities. Such was his New York, anyhow, and that of most of the people he knew.

In the days after he returned to Millhaven, during his encounters with men and women who might have seen more than they knew but probably had not, Tim Underhill was forced to acknowledge the extent to which he had thought of Mark, consciously or otherwise, as a kind of son. Of course he could not speak of this to Philip; two successive losses had shattered his brother and turned him into a hollow creature dependent on Tim for whatever hope he could permit himself to feel. In the absence of anything else to do, Philip continued to go to work, but since 'work' had not involved anything serious for something like two weeks, the vice principal's office represented chiefly a bolt-hole free of the emotional associations inevitable at home.

Tim wished that Mark *had* fled 3324 North Superior Street for 55 Grand. He wished he had earned his brother's rage. Rage, he thought, was better than hopelessness. Philip never confessed it, but he had settled for the bleak comfort of hopelessness the moment the voice of a WMTG newsreader coming from the portable radio on his desk had distracted his attention from an elaborate doodle with the announcement that a third name had been definitively added to that of Shane Auslander and Trey Wilk. This announcement had come at the top of the three P.M. local news. Within the hour, Sergeant Franz Pohlhaus of the Millhaven Police Department was reporting the discovery of the corpse of sixteen-year-old Dewey Dell in the underbrush along the eastern bank of the Kinninnick River. It was thought that the perpetrator had been forced to dump Dell's body in haste before he could dispose of it as he had those of Auslander and Wilk. *And Mark*, Philip told himself, only half-consciously aware that he had just abandoned all hope of hope.

Dewey Dell's body was found along the neglected riverbank the day after Tim returned to Millhaven. On the day he arrived, Tim found Philip taut as a drumhead. If Philip were a smoker, he would have been burning through four or five packs a day. Tim demanded that his brother join him for dinner at Violet's, the show-offy restaurant carved out of the Pforzheimer's lower depths, and for the sake of propriety Philip calmed down enough to eat a meal without jumping up to check in with the police. That night, he still thought his son probably had taken the Greyhound to Chicago, or some such place, fleeing from reminders of what he had seen. And Philip insisted on meeting Tom Pasmore; he wanted the detective's voodoo to locate his son. For the first half hour in Violet's, Tim labored to convince Philip that if they were to stand on Tom's doorstep and ring his bell, Pasmore, friend though he was, would refuse both to meet them and to have anything to do with Mark's case. Philip refused to be convinced, so Tim pulled out his cell phone and proved his point. Tom Pasmore did, however, agree to meet with Tim later that evening.

After Philip's reluctant departure, Tim piloted the swan boat of his rented Town Car to Tom Pasmore's house on Eastern Shore Drive, and Tom, who was exceptionally pleased to see him, did some mild voodoo with his computers and reported that, as far as he could see, Mark had not taken a bus to Chicago or anywhere else in the past month. He promised to be as helpful as he could, but, as predicted, he declined to meet Tim's brother unless the meeting became absolutely necessary.

The next day, Tim joined Philip for breakfast,

watched him go off to work, and started the laborious process of ringing the neighbors' doorbells. When that grew tiring, he went to Sherman Park and joined two police officers, Nelson Rote and Tyrone Selwidge, engaged in the task of questioning people about the missing boys. Rote and Selwidge had three photographs, and he had two, both of Mark. When they showed their photographs, he showed his. No one could remember seeing any of the boys leaving Sherman Park with anyone, although two women pushing baby strollers said that Mark's face was familiar. They did not know his name, but they had seen him in the neighborhood.

'He's such a good-looking boy,' said one of the young mothers. 'I mean, really. I have this friend, she'd – oh, sorry.'

Shortly after three P.M., Tim's cell phone burst into tinny song, and he ripped it from his pocket, startling Jimbo Monaghan, whose house he had reached after his return to Superior Street. No, the caller was not Mark, as had seemed possible for the space of approximately two seconds. Philip had just heard about the fate of Dewey Dell on WMTG.

'Mark used to go for walks down there,' Philip told him. 'Right where they found the body, on that riverbank. We thought it was so safe! They had a walking trail and a bicycle path. Doesn't that sound safe to you?'

Tim guessed it did.

'Nothing's safe,' Philip said. 'Not these days.'

Tim could hear in Philip's voice that he no longer believed that Mark was still alive. The pain of his death was more bearable than the pain of uncertainty.

'They have a name for the guy,' Philip said. 'The Sherman Park Killer.'

Having heard that a boy's body had been discovered, Jimbo Monaghan was staring pop-eyed at Tim.

Tim lowered one hand through the air, palm down and fingers splayed, telling the boy to wait another few seconds. 'The press always gives sexy names to psychos who haven't been caught,' he said to Philip. 'Listen to me. I haven't given up on Mark yet. This new kid wasn't found anywhere near Sherman Park, right? And so far; nobody really knows what happened to Auslander and what's-his-name, Wilk.'

'You have to talk to Tom Pasmore again.'

'He's doing what he can.'

Tim broke contact and slipped the little phone back into his jacket pocket.

'Sorry, Jimbo. We were just getting to the good part. You're standing there with the binoculars,

Mark switches on the Maglite and . . . what, everything goes black?'

'The next thing I know, I'm lying on the grass, and Mark is looking down, talking at me.'

'Saying what?'

'"You jumped about a foot and you passed out, man." Like that.'

'Is that what you did?'

Jimbo stirred on his chair, for a moment resembling a mouse under the gaze of an attentive cat. There was a cold can of Coca-Cola before him, a glass of ice water before Tim. From the basement stairs came the sound of Margo Monaghan opening the door of the dryer.

'I guess,' Jimbo said.

'And that was because of something you saw?'

Jimbo looked away and shrugged.

Tim leaned forward and put his elbows on the table. 'Mark told you he thought he'd seen a girl in that room?'

'Yeah.' Jimbo swallowed and looked away. 'That's why I wanted to use the, you know, field glasses and stuff. I thought we could maybe catch her when she wasn't expecting it.'

'Who did you think this girl might be?'

Jimbo gave him a quick sideways glance. 'Maybe a runaway?'

'And what if you were right about that?'

'We could help her. Bring food. We wouldn't turn her in, or anything.'

The earnest expression on Jimbo's face told him that he was trying to put himself and Mark in as noble a light as possible. He was hiding something, and Tim thought that he was doing it for Mark.

'So did you see this girl?'

Jimbo crossed his arms over his chest.

'Sure doesn't sound like it,' Tim said.

'I didn't see any girl.' The boy screwed up his expressive face and stared at the gaudy little Coca-Cola can.

'Jimbo, do you think the house on Michigan Street was involved in some way with Mark's disappearance?'

The boy's head swung up, and his eyes briefly met Tim's. His Adam's apple jerked in his throat.

'I would really hate being forced to think that abduction by some homicidal creep was the only way to explain Mark's disappearance. The only thing worse than that would be no explanation at all.' Tim smiled at the boy. He forced himself to proceed slowly.

'Look, Mr Underhill, I don't really know much. I don't even know if Mark was making everything up . . .'

'If he was, he probably had a reason.'

In Jimbo's frank stare, Tim could see that he was deciding to part with a share of his secret.

'You can't tell anybody about this, okay?'

Tim leaned back and put his hands together.

'When the light hit the window, I thought I saw a guy in there. He was hiding way back in the room.'

Jimbo's hands were trembling. He licked his lips and glanced at the door to the basement. 'He was looking right at me.' A tremor like an electrical current moved through the boy's entire body. 'I was so scared.'

'No wonder,' Tim said.

'He was pretty big. Big head. Big shoulders. Like a football player.'

'He was just standing there?'

'It was like he *stepped forward* – like he deliberately moved into the light – and I saw his eyes. Looking at me. They were like ball bearings or something – silvery. Then I turned away, but he was already gone. I don't remember anything more until Mark was bending down over me.'

'Did you tell Mark any of this?'

'I wanted to get home. He came over the next day, and that's when I told him.'

'He must have been very interested in what you had to say.'

Jimbo enacted an entire series of you-have-no-idea gestures, looking skyward, raising his hands, shaking his head. When he looked at Tim, his eyes were the size of eggs. He really was a natural comedian, and under other circumstances, this little performance would have made Tim laugh out loud. However, what he said in response took Tim completely by surprise.

'*Interested*? He told me he looked out his window in the middle of the night and saw the same guy, looking up from his backyard! And after he got up that morning, he saw him again, standing at the top of Michigan Street with his back turned.'

'How could he tell it was the same man?'

Jimbo leaned forward and whispered, 'This isn't any normal guy. Believe me, you'd know him.' The boy's face squeezed around a sudden access of fear, and his voice dropped. 'Remember the party thing after Mrs Underhill's funeral?'

Tim nodded.

'Mark saw him there.'

'In his *house*?'

'Standing in the kitchen, with his back to Mark. Facing the door. Nobody else saw him.'

After struggling to find a question, Tim at last asked, 'What did Mark think he was doing there?'

Margo Monaghan's footsteps sounded on the

basement floor. Jimbo leaned even farther forward. 'He thought it was a warning.'

The cell phone trilled in Tim's pocket. Both he and the boy jolted upright in their chairs. This time, Tim had no sense of suspended, heart-breaking possibility; he knew who had called him before he heard his brother's voice. Unable to last out the rest of the day in his office, Philip was begging him to come home.

Embracing a woven yellow basket piled high with newly laundered clothes, Jimbo's mother emerged into the kitchen. The odor of fresh laundry still warm from the dryer contrasted with the drawn, unhappy expression on Margo's face. She moved alongside her son and said, 'I hope you're telling Mr Underhill everything, Jimbo. I know there are things you think you can't tell me, but this is your chance to get it all off your chest. Are you listening to me?'

Jimbo muttered that he heard her.

'This is serious stuff, kiddo. Your best friend is *missing*. Another boy was found *dead*. Am I getting through to you?'

'Uh-huh.' He could not meet her eyes.

Margo rapped the palm of her hand on the top of her son's head and turned away. Soon her footsteps were moving up the stairs. Tim looked at the cringing boy on the other side of the table.

'Jimbo, even your mother knows you're still holding out on me.'

The boy slumped deeper into his chair.

'But she doesn't know anything about that house, does she?'

Jimbo sighed. He could not trust himself to look up at Tim. 'We should have stayed away from that place.'

Tim remembered seeing the two boys walking through Cathedral Square and turning onto Jefferson Street. 'You didn't want to have anything to do with it, did you?'

'He wouldn't listen to me,' Jimbo said. 'Mark went crazy, sort of. Of course, he had a really good reason to go crazy.'

'Tell me,' Tim said.

And Jimbo told him – told him more than he had intended to, certainly.

Mark, he said, had been kind of weird after the Maglite incident, seeming to be both angry and confused. He thought he had been warned away from the house on Michigan Street, and he had developed certain fixed ideas about it. At the same time, his mother had become a source of tremendous worry.

Two nights after Jimbo's scare and subsequent fainting, Mark had come home half an hour after his curfew, and instead of getting the interrogation he expected, he had come across his mother sitting on the edge of the downstairs bathtub, dazed and blank with what he thought was fear. After that night, she seemed to deteriorate a little more every day.

'And, see, we thought there were two people hiding out in that house,' Jimbo told Tim. 'That big guy in the black coat and a girl. We spent hours hanging out on the other side of the street, hoping to see the man leave the building. He had to buy food, didn't he? Especially if he was keeping the girl prisoner, like we thought he was. Or maybe what Mark thought was a girl was really Shane Auslander, you know? He was a pretty skinny kid, after all. One afternoon, we called the police and told them the Sherman Park guy was hiding out in the house, but nothing happened. I don't even know if they looked at the place.'

'They never checked it out?'

'We never saw 'em do it.' He lifted his shoulders and let them drop. 'They never called us back, either. That's the last time I ever try to do anything for the cops, yo.

'So there's that house, and there's his mother. And his mother *knows* something about the place, he's really sure of that. Every day, she gets a little worse. He told me, 'It's like she thinks the Black Death is in that place. She's turning into one of those old peasant ladies back in Eastern Europe, where her ancestors came from. Like the old women in *Dracula*, all wrapped up in black?' That's what he said. And what's eating at her? Whatever she knows about that house! Which made him get even more cranked about the place.'

Jimbo glanced at Tim, bit the inside of his cheek. 'He thought maybe there was something inside there that could explain why his mom was dragging around like she was. Something like pictures, or old papers, or what, bloodstains, even.' The boy looked profoundly uneasy, and a trace of anger flashed in his eyes. 'He wanted to get a look at it. That's how it went down. Since that one day, we never saw anything or anybody in there, and nobody went in or out, either. If the Sherman Park Killer ever used to hide out there, it sure looked like he took off. And you know what?'

The anger flared again in the boy's face.

Tim said, 'I have no idea.'

'He didn't trust me. That jerk. He was going to go against his precious promise, and he didn't want me along.'

'Jimbo, for God's sake, what did he do?' Tim asked, knowing that he was getting somewhere at last.

'He broke in – he smashed a hole in the rear window, and he got inside. He told me about it afterward, but right then he wanted me out of the way. So naturally, the asshole lied to me.'

In a cell-phone conversation after dinner that night, Mark had surprised Jimbo by suggesting that they see what was happening at the fountain. If they went together, they would surely be safe from whatever had befallen the missing boys. The greatest danger they faced was that Sherman Park would wind up being even more boring than hanging out on Michigan Street.

Mark's proposal delighted Jimbo, who wished to stay as far as possible from the man whose eyes had found him through his father's binoculars. And although by going to Sherman Park they would undoubtedly be breaking the letter of their vows – they might as well be honest about it – the meaning, the soul, of the vows remained intact, since the presence of half a dozen cops like Officers Rote and Selwidge guaranteed the continued well-being of any adolescent within a hundred-foot radius of the fountain. Actually, their parents should have been begging them to spend their evenings in Sherman Park.

Up the alley they went, Jimbo feeling a happy relief at the return of their customary occupations. So much of the past few days had the flavor of dreamlike confinement in someone else's irrational designs. Now he felt an unexpected lightness of spirit, as if he had been set free in a restored world.

On West Auer Avenue, a man in a gray University of Michigan football T-shirt, gray cotton shorts, and flip-flops was washing a dark blue Toyota Camry in his short double-wheel-track driveway. Heavy-looking muscles stood out on his arms and legs while he scrubbed the Camry's hood. As the boys approached, he looked toward them and smiled. Helplessly, they fell into their homeboy stroll.

'Ah, youngbloods,' the man said. 'How y'all doin' tonight?'

'Hangin' in there,' Jimbo said.

The man leaned against his car and smiled at them. 'That seems to be working out just fine. Be sure to take care of yourselves, all right?'

The day was still hot, and the shops still stood open. Bored clerks lounged against counters, sneaking looks at their watches. Widely separated cars trolled along the boulevard. The only other people on their side of the street were an old woman bent nearly parallel to the sidewalk and a man who recently had been thrown out of a liquor store. He was aiming punches at a parking meter. The old woman carried a string bag containing a single head of iceberg lettuce.

'I'd really like to get out of this nowhere town,' Mark said. 'I should e-mail my uncle Tim and ask if I could come to New York and stay in his place.'

'Would he let you?'

'Sure he would, I think. Why wouldn't he?'

Jimbo shrugged. A second later, he said, 'Maybe I could come with you.'

'Maybe,' Mark agreed. 'Or I could just go and send you a postcard.'

'You fathead skell.'

'No, you're a fathead skell,' Mark said, and for a time the two of them sniggered like children.

'A lot of great-looking women live in New York. They're all over the place, bro. They're lining up at every Starbucks in the city.'

'Yo, and what would you do with them?'

'I know what to do,' Jimbo said.

'You know what to do with your right hand.'

'I didn't hear any complaints from Ginny Capezio,' Jimbo said.

'Ginny Capezio? Give me a break. She's so hopeless, she'd go down on that guy.' He waved toward the rummy, who had finished punishing the parking meter and seemed now to be looking for a soft place to lie down.

Virginia 'Ginny' Capezio had administered brisk oral sex to a number of the boys in Quincy's ninth grade, among them Jimbo but not Mark. According to Ginny, oral sex did not count as actual sex.

'You're jealous, that's all,' said Jimbo.

He was jealous, Mark silently admitted, but of Jackie Monaghan, not his son. Also of everybody who had ever had sex with an attractive, or even a semi-attractive, woman. Ginny Capezio had fat legs and the disconcerting beginnings of a mustache, which her father forbade her to remove. Mark did not suppose that his inventions concerning a gorgeous and brilliant girl named Molly Witt, who after having been universally desired at Quincy had left the previous year, had ever convinced Jimbo. Mark wasn't even sure why he had lied about Molly Witt. It had happened in a weak moment, and after that he was stuck with it. Fortunately, they now reached the street corner diagonally across from the park's entrance, and checking the traffic to make sure they could run across the street without waiting for the light to change gave him an excuse to ignore Jimbo's remark.

They trotted across the street, and the same thought floated into two heads, that they should have brought their skateboards. The paths and benches, in themselves no less suitable for skateboards than the building site's ramps, converged at the wide, curved bowl of the fountain, which was large enough for some halfway serious fun.

Knowing nothing of the shadows gathering about them, the boys began walking toward the fountain on the broad, long path, imagining their skateboards bumping and rumbling over the grooved stone flags. Imagined pleasure would be all the pleasure to be enjoyed at Sherman Park that evening: a small group of boys in baggy jeans perched on the lip of the fountain, ignored by two police officers who appeared to be talking to their girlfriends on their cell phones but were probably engaged in official business.

To look upon this scene was depressing; to join it would have been unthinkable. In a single shared gesture, the boys wheeled around and drifted toward the nearest bench. One of the policemen gave the boys a quantifying once-over.

Jimbo jumped to his feet and said, 'What are we going to do?'

'I think I'll go home,' Mark said. 'I don't feel very good.'

They returned the way they had come, past the nearly empty stores and the rows of houses beside driveways leading nowhere. The athletic-looking man washing his Camry waved as they passed him, and they waved back. They turned into the alley and walked the fifty feet to the Monaghans' backyard.

‘Want to come in?’ Jimbo asked.

‘Not now,’ Mark said. ‘Tomorrow, we’ll hack around on our boards, okay?’

‘Okay.’ Jimbo pretended to punch Mark’s stomach, grinned, and jogged across the backyard to his kitchen door.

Mark waited until Jimbo had gone inside before continuing down the alley. At its southern end, he turned right onto Townsend, then right again onto Michigan Street, where he walked slowly up the block on the west side of the street, checking the porches for people who might see what he was about to do.

If someone had asked Mark what he intended to do, he would have said, *I want to test the air*.

Satisfied that no one was watching him, he moved at twice his normal pace up to the property line at 3323, glanced quickly at the other side of the street, spun around and raced over the tilting lawn. When he had run past the side of the house and veered toward the backyard, he stopped short, startled by what he was looking at.

For the first time, Mark realized that the other residents of Michigan Street had been mowing the areas of the lawn visible from the street. Behind the house, the lawn had disappeared beneath a riot of tall weeds and field grass. Queen Anne's lace and tiger lilies shone within the waist-high growth. Circles of dead leaves and gray mulch surrounded the bases of the giant oak trees. Mark felt as if suddenly he had been transported to another country. Insects buzzed. As soon as he waded into the tangle, a small animal exploded into motion near his right foot and scurried deeper into the tall grass. Startled by what had been done to the rear of the house, he scarcely noticed the ruckus. It had been modified out of all recognition. He realized that he was looking at what the eight-foot concrete wall had been built to conceal.

Alongside the kitchen on the uphill side of the house, someone had added a strikingly eccentric structure. To Mark, the addition only barely suggested the existence of anything that could be considered a room, but a room he supposed it had to be: a room like a space in a steeply pitched attic. The roofline dropped to within three feet of the ground and met a short exterior wall. It looked like the side of a big, big pup tent made of roofing tiles. He could not imagine why anyone would build such a thing – a long, windowless room pinched down into itself by a steeply slanting roof.

In the few moments since he had come around the side of the house, the air had truly darkened. Hasten hasten, night comes on. Mark pushed through the tall field grass, and the tiger lilies bobbed their heads. Another little life shot panicked away from his foot. A dry, jungly odor of rot arose from a clump of bindweed.

Close up, the added room proved to be ill-constructed and in need of repair. Nothing quite lined up or lay flat. Long chips of paint had flaked off the boards alongside the kitchen door. Mark went up three broken steps and peered through a narrow glass panel. A layer of gray dust kept him from seeing any more than the vague shapes of the counters and the arched entrance, identical to that in his house, to the dining room. The arch carved in the wall looked like a trick of perspective. He rattled the doorknob.

The air around him had advanced another stage toward nightfall, though the sky was still almost bright. Mark peeled the topmost shirt off his body and wrapped it around his right fist. He had been seeing himself do this since leaving Jimbo; now it felt as though he were acting mechanically, without volition. Hurry hurry, little boy, do your worst, dark dark night approacheth. He punched the narrow window with his padded hand. Shards of dusty glass flew inward, clattered tinkling to the floor, and burst into fragments. So softly he barely noticed, something odd and as physical as a smell streamed through the broken window and fastened on him. Jagged sections of broken glass clung to the sides of the frame, and these he snapped off with sharp, efficient raps of his hand. He unrolled the T-shirt from his hand, brushed off shards of glass, draped it around his neck, and reached in. His fingers found the doorknob, which felt simultaneously gritty and sticky, almost greasy. He revolved the knob, unlocking the door, and withdrew his arm. Then he opened the door the width of a boy's slender body and, in accord with the plans he had decided upon hours earlier, slipped into the dark kitchen.

For a second or two, he was able to register a sense of emptiness and neglect that suggested absolute abandonment. On the wall to his left, he took in a closed door that must have opened into the pup-tent room. Then whatever had settled on him after he broke the window clamped down like a vise. His eyes failed, and he found that he could not draw breath. Hopelessness and misery thickened around him like a reeking cloud. His stomach and his bowels churned. What had invaded him? Frantic with disgust, Mark cried out. He could barely hear his own voice. When one of his hands struck the back door, he whirled toward it. As if the door had come violently to life, it rapped his chest and his elbow. Layer upon layer of stinking gauze seemed to drift like spider webs down upon him. His right hand blessedly found the doorknob. He thrust himself through the frame and slammed the door behind him. Invisible webs and filaments seemed to float out in pursuit. When he wiped his eyes, the sight of his hands – trembling, so pale! – informed him that his vision had returned.

11

'OH, YOU HEARD me talking to Jackie Monaghan about that "heroism" business?' Philip asked. 'Believe me, there's no point in talking about that subject.'

'Humor me,' Tim said. 'Tom Pasmore mentioned it the other day, but he didn't know the whole story.'

The brothers were driving east on Burleigh in Tim's swan boat, to which Philip had agreed both for the sake of comfort and on the grounds that riding in the passenger seat allowed him to scan the sidewalks more effectively. Three hours earlier, the radio announcement about Dewey Dell had given him leave to swap the agony of hope suspended for the comfort of despair, but believing that his son was dead did not release him from the obligation to act as though Mark might still be at large. After Tim had driven twice around Sherman Park, expanding his circle outward, Philip overruled his plan of making a third, wider circuit by telling him to drive toward the lake.

He pretended to scrutinize a group of teenagers hanging out in front of a drugstore. At last he looked back at Tim. 'Heroism! That's a laugh. Really. Nancy's family was a lot of things, but heroic was never part of the deal.' He took his eyes from Tim and seemed to look at the windshield instead of through it. 'You ought to do background checks on everybody related to the person you think you want to marry, that's all I can say.'

'You have to admit,' Tim said, 'it's an odd twist in the Joseph Kalendar story.'

'Everything about Joseph Kalendar's story is twisted. I can't believe you didn't know about this. I guess it all came up while you were still frisking around in the Far East. The guy was a good carpenter, but everything else about him was crazy. Kalendar raped and murdered a bunch of women, and he killed his own son. He probably killed his wife, too, so he could have a nice, empty house to play in.'

'What year are we talking about?'

'Kalendar was arrested in 1979, 1980, I can't

remember which. Turn south on Humboldt and get on Locust. We'll drive past that little park over there.'

'You want me to drive to the East Side?'

'You never know,' Philip said, meaning that it was impossible to predict where a teenage boy might go when he ran away from home.

'Did you and Nancy ever get together with the Kalendars? He was her first cousin, after all.'

Philip shook his head. 'I hardly knew the guy existed until one day Nancy told me that his wife had come over to see her. This was when we were living in Carrollton Gardens. Way west. What a mistake. I hated it out there. Bunch of snobs talking about golf and money.'

'Kalendar's wife went to see Nancy? When was that?'

'Around '72, something like that. It was winter – a miserable winter. We'd only been married about two years. When I got home from work, Nancy was very upset. She refused to talk about it. Then she finally 'fessed up, said her cousin's wife had been out to see her. I don't remember the woman's name, something like Dora, Flora, who knows? She probably wanted money. Of course Nancy knew better than to give her any. We were thinking about starting a family, and I would have hit the ceiling if Nancy had given my hard-earned money away to her fruitcake cousin.'

'And Nancy was upset.'

'Very. Very disturbed about the whole thing.'

'Did she seem guilty to you?'

'That's one way to put it. Guilty and upset. Stay away from those people, I said. Don't ever let them come out here again.'

'Did you ever meet Kalendar?'

Philip shuddered.

'Nancy must have known him, though, at least during her childhood.'

'Yeah, sure, she knew him. I guess he was sort of okay as a kid, but he started to get weird pretty soon. The trouble was, nobody knew how weird. Nancy said this thing about him once – after he got arrested. She said it was scary just being with him.'

'How?'

'Nancy said he made you feel like all the air was sucked out of the room. Nobody ever knew what happened to his wife. I bet he killed her, too, and got rid of the body. For sure, she disappeared.'

'How long was that after she came out to see Nancy?'

Philip looked at him in surprised speculation. 'Four, five weeks. Nancy called them in the middle of the day, hoping he was out in this little workshop he rented on Sherman Boulevard. But Kalendar answered, said he had no idea where she was. Myra, that was her name! Dumb bitch, you have to feel sorry for her, hitching up with a guy like that.'

'Still, there was the heroism thing.'

Philip laughed. 'The first time Joe Kalendar got famous. We're getting close to Shady Mount Hospital. Turn left. Let's drive north for a while.'

Tim thought that Philip wanted to wind up on Eastern Shore Drive, where the spectacle of mansions inhabited by people whose children were legacies at Brown and Wesleyan would further divert him from the reality of his situation. He was looking for distraction, not Mark. Philip had given up; now he was merely waiting for the police to find the body.

'Happened back when I was first getting to know Nancy. The summer I was nineteen, 1968. Of course, you wouldn't know anything at all about this stuff, you were away killing Commies for Christ, weren't you?'

Tim smiled. 'Most of the guys in my platoon liked to call 'em gooks.'

'Slants,' Philip said. 'Slopes.'

'You know, you could always tell people you were there.'

'Sometimes I do,' Philip said.

'I'm sure,' Tim said. 'Anyhow, Kalendar saved the lives of two children?'

'The story was all over the local paper. The house next to his, a plug shorted out and bang, electrical fire. It was like six in the morning. It takes about ten minutes for the whole house to fill up with smoke. Joe Kalendar happened to be messing around in his backyard, and I guess he smelled the smoke or something.'

'He's messing around in his backyard at six o'clock in the morning?'

'Maybe he was having a fresh-air pee. Who knows?'

'Who lived in the other house?'

'A black family – two little girls. Guy was a bus driver, something like that. Later on, he said Kalendar basically hadn't given him the time of day since he moved onto the block, but what he did proved that blacks and whites could get along fine, at least in the city of Millhaven. That bilge was exactly what people wanted to hear. Especially then, one year after the big riots – Detroit, Chicago, Milwaukee. People lapped it up, turned Kalendar into a symbol.' He smiled. 'Of course, Kalendar had no time at all for black people.'

'What did he do, rescue the children?'

'Both of them. The parents weren't even out of bed when he hit the door. Wasn't for Kalendar, everybody would have died of smoke inhalation. According to the bus driver, he smashed down the door and bulled straight in. He's shouting, "Where are you? Where are you?" The kids more or less run into him, or he runs into them. He grabs them and hightails it out the door.'

'Were the parents still in bed?'

'Standing right in front of the door, trying to figure out what to do next. Dazed and groggy and all that, but I hardly think the bus driver was Mensa material anyhow. Kalendar ran back in and slammed into him and his wife and shoved everyone outside.'

'So he saved them all.'

'You could see it that way. Kalendar didn't want to stop there, either.'

'He thought more people were still inside?'

'The bus driver told the reporter that Kalendar was fighting to go back in when the police and the firemen showed up and restrained him. All this came out all over again when he got arrested, that's the reason I remember it.'

Tim turned left onto the pretty street called An Die Blumen, making his way toward the lake. Barely pretending to look for Mark, Philip let his eyes drift over a little knot of teenage boys and girls walking east, carrying tennis rackets and soft Adidas and Puma bags. They had the bland confident good looks produced by wealthy parents, private schools, and a sense of entitlement.

'I wish I could afford to live around here,' Philip said. 'Instead of that dopey Jimbo Monaghan, Mark could have friends like those kids. Look at them – they're completely safe. They're going to go through life laughing and carrying tennis rackets. And do you know why? Because this is a long way from Pigtown.'

Tom Pasmore had grown up around the corner from where they were, and his childhood, Tim knew, had been neither safe nor stable. He turned onto Eastern Shore Drive, and Philip swiveled his head to look at the great mansions. In one of them, a man had murdered his wife's lover; in another, a millionaire given to black suits and Cuban cigars had raped his two-year-old daughter; in another, two off-duty policemen acting as paid executioners had murdered a kind and brilliant man.

'Jimbo wasn't good for Mark,' Philip continued.

'You're kidding me.'

'Believe me, I know kids, and those two were not in the mainstream. To be honest, they were a couple of losers. And if you ask me, they were getting way too close. You could see it in the music they liked. They didn't listen to normal people. All that airy-fairy stuff gave me the creeps.'

12

ON THE NIGHT Mark first broke into the abandoned house, the lost girl, who was the girl she had declined to rescue, came again to Nancy Underhill. Her son had left for the evening, and Philip had vanished into his 'den,' where he would remain until 10:00 P.M., at which time he would emerge, announce that he was going to bed, and look at her as if any deviation from his schedule was an indication of questionable thought processes. At 10:30 on the dot, he would sit bolt upright in bed and listen for the sound of Mark either opening the front door or walking from the backyard into the kitchen. If he failed to hear Mark return before his curfew, he would instruct her to 'work out' a suitable punishment for 'your son,' then lie back, roll over, and, having fulfilled his duties as CEO of the Superior Street Underhills, return untroubled to sleep.

She had been seated on the davenport with her legs beneath her and a cold cup of coffee before her on the table, staring at, but not seeing, a rerun of *Everybody Loves Raymond. Everybody Loves Raymond* was camouflage. Philip detested the program and was unlikely to investigate her state of mind if he found her watching it.

Instead of a scene in which an actor named Ray Romano was pretending to argue with his father, Nancy was looking at something else entirely, a scene that replayed itself across the screen of her inner eye. Nancy's scene took place not in a fictional Long Island living room, but in the kitchen of a quick-and-dirty tract house constructed by a shady contractor named James Carrollton, then in the second year of a three-year stretch for tax evasion. Standing in for Ray Barone, sportswriter and father of three, was Nancy Underhill, a suburban housewife, still childless after two years of marriage; and before Nancy was Myra Kalendar, the wife of her terrible cousin Joseph, who in adolescence had spirited the neighbors' dogs and cats away to distant lots, doused them with lighter fuel, and set them on fire. Joseph had referred to this activity as 'making torches.'

Myra sat across the table in the tacky suburban

kitchen and begged for help. Myra had no friends. She could talk to no one but Nancy. Joseph would kill her if she went to the police. She begged not for herself, but for the daughter who since birth had been Joseph Kalendar's private project and plaything. In the year of the appeal, Lily Kalendar was six years old and a secret from both the state and the school board. Until this moment, she had been a secret from Nancy, too. Joseph took his daughter out of the house only at night, to conceal her from the neighbors. The one time Lily had managed to go outside during the day – to escape! – she had hidden in the alley, and her father had gone crazy with rage and worry. When he smelled smoke, he saw that it came from the house of a black neighbor with two daughters Lily had often seen playing in their yard; he assumed that his daughter had fled there. On his return, coughing and red-eyed and reeking of smoke, Lily had crawled weeping out of hiding, begging for mercy.

Instead, Myra said, she got the beating of her life. Her father loved her, she was the love of his life, and her disobedience would cost her dearly. And after that, Joseph had built a special room to hold his beloved daughter and a special wall to hide the room. But that was only two of many modifications Joseph had made to their house.

The worst was . . . she did not want to say it.

The scene played and replayed in Nancy's mind and memory as she stared blindly at the television set. Myra sobbing, she herself trembling and lowering her head, thinking, *Philip is right, she's unbalanced. None of this is true, she's making it up*. Nancy knew what she had done; she had backed away. She had said to herself, *Myra had a miscarriage, we all knew that. There isn't any daughter, thank goodness. They're both crazy*. Fear of her dreadful cousin had led her to betray her niece. Eight years later, the headlines had shown the world what her cousin was capable of, but Nancy could not lie to herself: she had already known.

Mark surprised her by coming home early. After giving her one of those looks that had become familiar to her, Mark muttered something about being tired and disappeared into his room. At 10:00 P.M., as if summoned by one of Quincy's timetable bells, Philip popped into the living room and announced that bedtime had come. Alone, then, she sat in the living room until the next program had chattered to a conclusion. Nancy turned off the television and in the abrupt silence understood that her worst fear had been realized. The world would no longer run along its old, safe tracks. There had been a rip in the fabric, and bleak, terrible miracles would result. That was how it came to her, a tear in the fabric of daily life, through which monstrosities could pour. And enter they had, drawn by Nancy's old, old crime.

For she knew her son had not obeyed her. In one way or another, Mark had awakened the Kalendars. Now they all had to live with the consequences, which would be unbearable but otherwise impossible to predict. A giant worm was loose, devouring reality in great mouthfuls. Now the worm's sensors had located Nancy, and its great, humid body oozed ever closer, so close she could feel the earth yield beneath it.

Nancy's own sensors prickled with dread. Moments before she was able to raise her eyes and look at the arch into the little dining room, she knew her visitor had returned. There she stood, the child, a six-year-old girl in dirty overalls, her bare, filthy feet on the outermost edge of the faded rag rug, her small, slim, baleful back turned to Nancy. Her hair was matted with grease, possibly with blood. Anger boiled from her and hung in the dead air between them. There was a good measure of contempt in all that rage. Lily had come through the rip in the fabric to cast judgment on her weak traitorous aunt, that fearful and despairing wretch. Oh the fury oh the rage in a tortured child, oh the power in that fury. She had come also for Mark, his mother saw. Mark was half hers already, and had been from the moment Joseph Kalendar's hellhouse had surged out of the mist and knocked him off his stupid skateboard.

13

IT AMAZED Jimbo Monaghan how dumb smart people could be. If *he* understood the reason for most of what Mark had said and done over the past five days, it could not be all that difficult for anyone to grasp. Especially when the reason was so obvious. Mark had come home in the afternoon, strolled into the little downstairs bathroom to take a leak, and in a tub full of tepid, bloody water, discovered the naked corpse of his mother with a plastic bag over her head. The film of condensation on the inside of the bag kept him from making out her face. Mainly, he could see her nose and the black, open hole of her mouth. A second later, he noticed the paring knife dripping blood onto the tiles beside the tub. *At first I thought it was some kind of horrible mistake,* he told Jimbo. *Then I thought if I went out into the kitchen and came back in, she wouldn't be there anymore.*

All that time, his heart seemed not to beat. He thought he had hung in the doorway for an incredibly long time, looking at his mother and trying to make sense of what he saw. Blood pounded in his ears. He moved a step forward, and the tops of her knees came into view, floating like little pale islands in the red water.

In the next moment, he found himself standing alone in the middle of the kitchen, as if blown backward by a great wind. Through the open bathroom door, he could see one of his mother's arms propped on the side of the tub. He told Jimbo, 'I went over to the wall phone. It felt like I was swimming underwater. I didn't even know who I was going to call, but I guess I dialed my father's number at Quincy. He told me to call 911 and wait for him outside.'

Mark did exactly that. He called 911, communicated the essential information, and went outside to wait. About five minutes later, his father and the paramedics arrived more or less simultaneously. While he stood on the porch, he felt a numb, suspended clarity that, he thought, must be similar to what ghosts and dead people experienced, watching the living go through their paces.

In Jimbo's opinion, that was the last time Mark had been clear about his own emotions. The next day, he had turned up at Jimbo's back door, his mind focused on an unalterable plan. It was as if he had been considering it for weeks. He wanted to break into the house on Michigan Street, and his friend Jimbo had to come with him. In fact, Jimbo was indispensable. He couldn't do it without him.

He confessed that he had tried to do it by himself and run into some unexpected trouble. His body had gone bananas on him. He'd felt like he couldn't breathe and it was hard to see. All those spider webs, yuck! But none of that would happen if Jimbo went with him, Mark said, he knew they would be able to pass untroubled into the house. And once they got inside, they would be able to check out the strangest part of that building, which Mark had not mentioned to his friend until this very moment, the pup-tent room. Wasn't Jimbo curious about a room like that? Wouldn't he like to get a look at it?

'Not if that guy is in there,' Jimbo said.

'Think back, Jimbo. Are you really sure you saw him? Or did I maybe put the idea in your head?'

'I don't know.'

'It doesn't really matter,' Mark said. 'Because if it's the two of us, we'll be all right.'

'I don't get you.'

'You watch my back, I watch yours,' Mark said. 'I think that house doesn't have anything in it but atmosphere, anyhow.'

'Atmosphere,' Jimbo said. 'Now I really don't get you.'

'Atmosphere makes you see stuff. It made you faint, and it made me feel sick – it felt like spider webs were all over me. But they weren't real spider webs, they were *atmosphere*.'

'Okay,' Jimbo said. 'Maybe I see that, a little bit. But why do you want to go in there again?'

'I *have* to go in there,' Mark said. 'That house killed my mother.'

Silently, Jimbo uttered, *Ooh-kayyy*, startled by an understanding that had come to him as if by angelic messenger: *Mark felt guilty, and he didn't know it*. Jimbo did not have a detailed grasp of his friend's psyche, but he was absolutely certain that Mark would not be ranting in this way if, on the day after he broke his promise to his mother, he had not walked into a bathroom and found her lying dead in the tub. Of that, he would not speak. It was unspeakable by definition. Instead, he could not stop himself from talking about this screwy plan. Jimbo resolved not to give in, to fight Mark on this issue for as long as it took.

Over the following days, Mark tested his resolution so often that Jimbo thought that he had been invited to accompany Mark into the house on Michigan Street on the order of something like once an hour. After the first dozen times, he adopted the approach that he would use on every occasion thereafter, to pretend that Mark's obsessiveness was a joke. Mark might easily have been enraged by this tactic, but he barely noticed it.

One day during that hideous week, Jimbo heard from his father, who had learned of it from an off-duty police officer in a cop bar called the House of Ko-Reck-Shun, that a Los Angeles film crew would be on Jefferson Street early that afternoon, shooting a scene for a gangster movie. He called Mark, and the boys decided to take a bus downtown, an area they did not know as well as they imagined. They knew the number 14 bus would take them past the main library and the county museum, and they assumed that from there they would easily find Jefferson Street in or near the section of downtown located west of the Millhaven River, where theaters, bookstores, specialty shops, and department stores lined Grand Avenue all the way to Lafayette University, west of the library and museum.

They got off the bus too early and wasted twenty minutes wandering north and east before asking directions of a preppy-looking guy who appeared,

Jimbo thought, more than a touch too interested in Mark, although as usual Mark failed to notice that he was being admired. Then they walked an extra block up Orson Street and reached the top of Cathedral Square before looking back to the corner and noticing that they had already gone past Jefferson. To cut off some extra distance, they took one of the paths angling through the square. With a pang, Jimbo realized that earlier in the summer they would never have made such a journey without their skateboards; this time, they had never considered bringing the boards along.

'We have to go in there,' Mark said. 'You know it. You're softening up. Little by little, my logic is wearing away your resistance.'

They reached the bottom of Cathedral Square and turned left on Jefferson. Two blocks ahead, a lot of people were milling around alongside the Pforzheimer Hotel.

Mark jumped ahead and turned around, dancing on the balls of his feet. 'Don't you believe in my stunning logic?' He aimed a fist at Jimbo's left arm and gave him two light blows.

'All right, let's think about it, okay? There's this empty house, except it might not actually be empty.'

'It's empty,' Mark said.

'Be quiet. There's this house, okay? For a long

time you don't really see it, but when you finally do, you want to spend most of your time looking at it. Then your mother makes you promise to leave the place alone. You get spooked out, but you decide to break in anyhow and look around. And the next day, you find out she killed herself. And *then* you lose your mind, you say the house made it happen, and you have to go in and search the place from top to bottom.'

'Sounds logical to me.'

'You know what it sounds like to me?'

'Ah, a great idea?'

'Guilt.'

Mark stared at him, momentarily speechless.

'It *is* guilt, pure guilt. You can't stand it. You're blaming yourself.'

Mark glanced around at the streetlamps, the parked cars, the placards before the buildings on Jefferson Street. He looked almost dazed.

'I swear, no one understands me. Not my father, not even you. My uncle might understand me – he has an imagination. He's coming here today. Maybe he's already in town.'

Mark pointed at the Pforzheimer, unaware that I was looking down at him from a fourth-floor window. 'That's where he's staying, the Pforzheimer. It costs a lot to stay there. For a writer, he makes a lot of money.'

(This was sweet, but not very accurate.)

'Maybe we should go see him right now,' Mark said. 'Wanna do it?'

Jimbo declined. An unpredictable adult stranger from New York could only complicate matters. The two boys continued up the street until they were within about twenty feet of the film crew. A burly man with a ZZ Top beard and a name tag on a string around his neck waved them to a halt.

'It's that dude from *Family Ties*,' Jimbo said.

'Michael J. Fox? You're crazy. Michael J. Fox isn't that old.'

'Not him, the dude who played his father.'

'He must be really old by now. He still looks pretty good, though.'

'No matter how good he looks, that car's going to mess him up,' Mark said, and both boys laughed.

Mark's father spoiled everything, that was the problem. They had seen Timothy Underhill's car pull up in front of the house, and Jimbo could tell that his friend was excited just to see his uncle walk up to the porch. Jimbo thought he looked like an okay kind of guy, kind of big, and comfortable in jeans and a blue blazer. He had a been-around kind of face that made him look easy to get along with.

But when they turned off the boom box and went out of the room, Mark's dad made a dumb, dismissive remark even before they got to the staircase – something about 'the son and heir' and his 'el sidekick-o faithful-o,' making them both sound like fools. When they were being introduced, Mark's dad referred to Jimbo as Mark's 'best buddy-roo' and insisted on treating them as if they were in the second grade, which made it impossible to stay in the house. Then Mark's dad got all anal about what time they had to be back, and Jimbo could see Mark getting jumpier and jumpier. He looked like a guy who had just put down a ticking suitcase and wanted to get the hell out of there before it blew up.

Once they managed to get out, Jimbo followed Mark reluctantly to the sidewalk in front of 3323, where no shadowy nonfigures had not-appeared in the living room window. Jimbo had to agree: whatever might have been true earlier, now the house was as empty as a blown egg. You could tell just by looking at it. The only movement in that place came from the settling of the dust.

'We are going to do this,' Mark said. 'Believe it or not, we are.'

'Do you want me to come along to the thing at the funeral home tonight?'

'If you're not going, I'm not going, and I have to go, so . . .'

'I guess I am el faithful-o sidekick-o,' Jimbo said.

Alone and massive on its little hill, Trott Brothers struck Jimbo as looking like a castle with dungeons and suits of armor. Inside, it was both grand and a little seedy. They were pointed to a small, tired-looking room like a chapel, with four rows of chairs facing an open coffin. To Jimbo, this was terrible, cruel, tasteless: they were forcing Mark to look at his dead mother's face! It was one thing to respect the dead, but how about respecting the living? Jimbo risked a peek at the pale figure in the coffin. The person lying there did not look like Mark's mother, exactly; she looked more like a younger sister of Mrs Underhill's, someone who'd gone off and known a completely different life. Immediately, the men drifted to the back of the little room, and Jimbo and Mark sat down in the last row.

Mark's father handed him a card with a Hawaiian sunset on one side. When he turned it over, Jimbo saw the Lord's Prayer printed beneath Nancy's name and her dates.

'You okay?' he whispered to Mark, who was turning the card over and over in his hands, examining it as if it were a clue to a murder in a mystery novel.

Mark nodded.

A couple of minutes later, he leaned over and whispered, 'Do you think we could sneak out?'

Jimbo shook his head.

Philip ordered his son to get on his feet and pay his respects to his mother. Mark stood up and walked the length of the center aisle until he was in front of the coffin. As Jimbo watched, Philip staged a dramatic moment and put his arm around his son's shoulders, probably the first time he had done that since Mark's tenth birthday. He couldn't help it, Jimbo thought. In fact, he didn't even know that he was putting on a photo op for a nonexistent photographer. He thought he was being genuine. Jimbo could see Mark squirm beneath his father's touch.

As soon as Philip relented and walked away, Jimbo got to his feet and moved up to join his friend. He did not want to look at that cosmeticized not-Nancy in the coffin, so he moved slowly, but he could not bear the thought of Mark standing up there by himself. When he reached Mark's side, he glanced in his direction and saw by a softening in his eyes that Mark was grateful for his presence.

In a voice almost too low to be heard, Mark

said, 'How long do you think I'm supposed to stand here?'

'You could leave now,' Jimbo said.

Mark stared down at the woman in the coffin. His face had settled into an expressionless mask. A single tear leaked from the corner of his left eye, then his right. Startled, Jimbo glanced again at his friend and saw that the mask of his face had begun to tremble. More tears were brimming in his eyes. All at once, Jimbo felt like crying, too.

From the back of the room, Mark's father said in a pompous stage whisper, 'You have to feel sorry for the poor kid,' and Jimbo's tears dried before they were shed. If he'd heard it, so had Mark.

The boys' eyes met. Mark's face had turned violently red. Timothy Underhill said something too soft to be heard, and this time all but forgetting to keep his voice down, Mark's father said, 'Mark found her that afternoon – came home from God knows where . . .'

Jimbo heard Mark gasp.

'By the time I got home,' Philip was saying, 'they were taking her to the ambulance.'

'Oh, no,' said Mark's uncle.

His face rigid but still flushed, Mark stepped back from the coffin and turned around. A few minutes later, all of them were moving back outside into the roaring heat. The huge sun hung too close to the earth, and the light burned Jimbo's eyes. Mark's father buttoned his suit jacket, straightened his tie, and set off down the hill like a salesman off to close a deal. Timothy Underhill gave the boys a look brimming with sympathy, then followed his brother down the descending path. Lines of heat wavered up from the roof of the Volvo.

Mark jammed his hands into the pockets of his jeans and glared at the neat, suspiciously lush grass that ended in a knife edge at the sides of the path. 'I hate my father,' he said in an eerily reasonable voice.

With a brief, electric thrill of panic, Jimbo wondered how Mark was going to get through the funeral.

14

FOR MARK, the day of his mother's funeral revolved around the moment the hard, grayish-brown lump of clay bearing the print of the gravedigger's shovel fell from his right hand into the maw of her grave and struck the top of her coffin. Before that moment, he had wondered if he could make it through everything the day would demand of him, or if he might succumb to various disasters either internal or external in nature. He could see himself fainting, as Jimbo had fainted on the lawn of the house on Michigan Street; far worse, he could also see himself falling down in a frothing, eye-rolling seizure. These humiliations would occur, he thought, in front of the mourners assembled at Sunnyside Cemetery. The minister would be opening his great Bible; the Monaghans, and the Shillingtons, and the Tafts, plus a couple of the goofy ladies from the gas company and maybe a schoolteacher or two would be standing beside the grave, looking sad and dignified; even Jackie Monaghan, who would surely be in a most grievous condition of hangover and therefore in desperate need of a quick, medicinal jolt; and Mark's father would be staring straight ahead, with his hands folded on the mound of his belly in a fury of enraged impatience; and then he would embarrass everyone and disgrace himself by jerking and twitching and drooling into the cemetery's beautifully maintained grass. Or the sky would suddenly darken, abrupt rain would slash down onto the mourners, and a bolt of lightning would slide out of the firmament and fry him where he stood.

The internal catastrophes were far worse, involving as they did a painful death caused by the overheated, untrustworthy physical mechanism that was his body. Because these were worse, they were far more likely. A heart attack, an aneurysm, a brain hemorrhage – common sense told him that he was much likelier to die from a brain hemorrhage than a lightning bolt.

His father's face suggested that he was counting the minutes until he could leave. Mark regarded the stiff, damped-down expression and realized that he was bound to this man for years and years to come.

Standing a bit apart from the rest of the group and wearing a dark blue suit, horn-rimmed sunglasses of an odd, solarized blue, and a dark blue WBGO cap bearing the image of a man playing a tenor saxophone, Uncle Tim looked as though he was checking everybody out. Maybe Mark's father would let him stay with Uncle Tim for a week or two.

He listened to the Rent-a-minister's words, thinking that he seemed like a nice man. He had a slow, pleasant way of speaking, and the sort of rumbling, trustworthy voice that paid off for politicians and voice-over men. Every word the man said seemed to be sensible and carefully chosen. Mark understood each one as it entered his consciousness. The larger verbal units of phrases and sentences, however, made so little sense to Mark that they might as well have been in a foreign language – Basque, maybe, or Atlantean. He was hyperconscious of the breath moving in and out of his throat, the blood traveling through his veins, the sizzle of sunlight on the backs of his hands.

The minister stepped back. A machine like a forklift lowered the coffin into the Astroturf-bedecked grave. The coffin settled on the ground, and two men whisked away the fake grass. Mark's father walked the few steps to the pyramidal heap of earth scooped from the gravesite. He picked up a baseball-sized lump of dirt, leaned over the open grave, and extended his arm. The lump of dirt fell from his hand and struck the lid of the coffin with a reverberant *thunk* that made Mark fear he would be struck deaf and blind. For a second, the world before him faded into hundreds of fast-moving red and white specks like infant comets. The dancing specks resolved into the figure of Philip Underhill wiping his hands as he stepped back from the grave. Mark's head was spinning and the middle of his chest seemed to be filled with effervescent air slightly cooler than the rest of his body. Uncle Tim moved toward the grave. He, too, held a baseball of earth in one hand.

Uncle Tim's rock hit the coffin with the flat, hollow rap of a hand on a massive wooden door.

Still a little disembodied, Mark moved over to the temporary pyramid of grave dirt and pulled from it a lump with long striations on its widest surface. This piece of clay had been through the mill. It had been stabbed in the gut, bitten, and cut in half. The cool gas filling his chest advanced into the bottom of his throat. His feet moved with surprising confidence alongside the deep trench in the ground. He let the hard-edged clod drop from his hand, and it struck the coffin with a high-pitched pinging sound that reminded Mark uncomfortably of a doorbell. A shiver passed through him.

No matter what Jimbo said, Mark suddenly understood that he had *seen* the force that had stopped him inside the back door of the house; he had *seen* the force that had killed his mother. It had been standing at the top of Michigan Street with its back turned to him. Mark remembered the dark, tangled hair, the wide back, the black coat hanging like iron, and the sense of utter wrongness that had flowed out from this figure. That wrongness had seeped into his mother and so poisoned her that she had leaped into her grave.

The day swung around on a pivot, and his fear transformed itself into clarity. Two tasks lay before him. He had to learn whatever he could about the history of 3323 North Michigan Street and those who had lived in it, so that he could put a name to that evil being. And he had, more than ever, to discover its secrets. He could avenge his mother's death in no other way. Images of himself ransacking the closets and ripping up floorboards raced through his mind. According to Jimbo, guilt lay behind these desires, but Jimbo was wrong. What he was feeling was rage.

Like a set of orders, his new clarity accompanied him on the journey back to Superior Street and sent him into the house with the white noise of his purpose humming in his head. The funeral was over, it was time to arrange the next step, hurry hurry the minutes slip away.

Men and women filtered in through the front door, but Jimbo was not among them. Mark's father and Uncle Tim set out the soft drinks and the casseroles and coffee cake brought by the Shillingtons and the Tafts, and soon a crowd as numerous as flies around a bloody corpse had fastened on the dining room table, fracturing and coalescing again as they wandered in and out of the living room holding paper plates and paper cups. The Rochenkos came in hand in hand because they felt shy and ill at ease. A few beats later, Old Man Hillyard eased through the door, not holding hands with anyone, in fact gripping a cane with one hand while the other was deep in a trouser pocket. Annoyingly, Mr Hillyard caught Mark's eye and came limping toward him. On a ninety-degree day, he was wearing a thick plaid shirt, ancient corduroy trousers held up by suspenders, and an incongruous pair of cowboy boots.

'I was very sorry to hear about your mother,' he said. 'You have my condolences, son. If there's anything I can ever do for you, just ask.'

Like that's gonna happen, Mark thought, and thanked the old man.

'See you and the Monaghan boy out on your skateboards almost every day,' Hillyard said. 'Those wheels of yours sure make a hellacious racket.' His face drew itself up into a network of deep corrugations, and Mark realized that he was smiling. 'Looks like you might be improving some. Wish I could get around like the two of you.' He lifted the cane and shook it. 'I was doing all right until my ankle folded right under me when I stepped off my porch the other day. Went down like a sack of potatoes. The way I feel now, I can barely make it to the grocery store.' He leaned forward and whispered, 'Tell you the truth, son, I can barely make it to the can when I have to go wee-wee in the middle of the night.'

'I can't help you with that one,' Mark said, wanting desperately to get away from the old man.

'You and Red spend a heck of a lot of time staring at that empty house across from me,' Old Man Hillyard said, horrifying him. 'The two of you thinking of moving in?'

'Sorry, my dad needs me to do something,' Mark blurted, then backpedaled on an angle that gave him a better view of the front door. His father's boss, Mr Battley, had just appeared at the head of a phalanx of people from the school, all of whom he knew far too well. In their professional costumes of gray suits and white shirts, they resembled FBI agents, but poorly paid ones.

Never before had the house contained so many people. The crowd spilled from the living room into the dining room, where the Quincy people were now single-mindedly headed, and from there into the kitchen. Although most people were speaking quietly, their voices created a noisy Babel in which it was difficult to make out individual words. Ordinarily, this would have resulted in furious eruptions from his father, but Philip seemed more relaxed and at ease than at any time earlier in the day. He looked like a host who had decided to let the party take care of itself. Now his father was following Mr Battley toward the food, and Mark suspected that he would stay by his boss's side until the principal had scarfed down enough free grub and made his good-byes.

When Mark glanced again at the front of the living room, Mr Hillyard was boring the pants off the Rochenkos. The Monaghan family was beginning to come through the door. First Margo, as ever suggesting that some movie star had happened to walk in by mistake; then Jackie, grinning and red-faced, as ever suggesting that he wouldn't at all object were you to offer him a wee dram of pop-skull; and finally Jimbo, who gave him a not-unfriendly glance of inspection.

Before he could signal Jimbo to meet him in the kitchen, his uncle Tim appeared beside him with an unexpected offer. 'I think you should come to New York and stay with me for a week or so. Maybe in August?'

Pleased and surprised, Mark said he would love to do that and asked if Tim had mentioned the visit to his father.

'I will later,' Tim said. He smiled at Mark before cutting through the crowd in search of Philip.

For the next ten minutes, he lost sight of Jimbo as neighbors and coworkers patted his cheek or gripped his upper arm and uttered, over and over again, always with the sense of communicating a great truth, the same useless and depressing remarks. *Must be awfully tough on you, son . . . She's in a better place now . . . God has a reason for everything, you know . . . Gee, I remember when my mom died.*

Finally, he spotted Jimbo eyeing him from just inside the dining room arch and went over to talk to him.

'Are you okay?' Jimbo asked.

'More than you'd think.'

Their fathers stood, conversing quietly, only a few feet away, their backs turned toward the boys.

On the other side of their fathers, Mr Battley was flapping his gums at Uncle Tim.

'Good,' Jimbo said. 'You know . . .' Jimbo's wide mouth turned down at the edges, and his eyes shrank into a look of pure anguish. 'Yo, I'm really sorry about your mom. I should have told you that right away, but I didn't know how.'

Without warning, emotion surged up within Mark, searing everything it touched. For a couple of seconds, an abyss of feeling opened before him, and the sheer weight of the air on his shoulders threatened to push him in. Tears blinded him. He brought a hand up to his eyes; he exhaled and heard himself make a strangled, inarticulate sound of grief.

'Are you sure you're okay?'

Jimbo's voice rescued him.

'I guess,' he said, and wiped his eyes. His body was still reverberating with emotion.

Behind him, Jackie Monaghan said, 'Wasn't Nancy related to this weird guy who used to live around here? Somebody said something about it once, I don't remember who.'

His father said, 'Should have kept his mouth shut, whoever he was.'

'I sort of lost it for a second there,' Mark said, wondering what Jimbo's dad was talking about. Now Jackie was saying that his mother's relative had risked his life to save some children. Mark turned his head just in time to see Jackie tell his father that the kids were black. That would be that, he thought; the conversation would get ugly in a hurry.

'Well, it's no wonder,' said Jimbo.

'No, it's not the funeral,' Mark said. 'I just understood something I should have seen before. Actually, I don't know how I missed it.'

'What?' Jimbo asked.

Mark moved closer to Jimbo and whispered, 'It was *the house*.'

'What do you mean, "the house"?' Comprehension flashed into his eyes. 'Oh, no. No, man. Come on.'

'It's the truth. You didn't hear her chew me out for even thinking about that place. Ask yourself – why would she kill herself?'

'I don't know why,' Jimbo said, miserably.

'Right. I didn't stay far enough away, and something in there killed her. That's what happened, Jimbo. We can't dick around about this anymore. We have to go in there.'

In the silence of Jimbo's inability to respond, both boys clearly heard Philip Underhill say, 'I should have known better than to marry into a bunch of screwballs like that.'

Mark turned pale. Unnoticed by Philip and

Jackie, he moved past them and dodged through the crowd gathered around the table. Jimbo hastened after his friend and caught up with him at the opening into the kitchen, where, surprisingly, Mark had come to a sudden halt.

When Jimbo reached Mark's side, he was struck by the expression on his face. His mouth hung slightly open, and the side of his face visible to Jimbo had gone white. But for a small blue vein beating just above the V of hair at his temple, he might have been carved from marble.

Jimbo did not dare to look into the kitchen. After having glimpsed that being through his father's field glasses, the last thing he wanted to do was to see it in Mark Underhill's kitchen. The thought of that formidable presence standing before him sent fear washing through his stomach.

He had no idea how long he stood beside Mark Underhill, too afraid of what he might see to turn his head. Mark did not move; as far as Jimbo could tell, Mark did not even take a breath. To Jimbo, they seemed to stand, he immobilized by Mark's immobility, for an eternity. Around them, the world, too, had become immobile; yet the blue vein in Mark's temple beat, beat, beat. Jimbo's tongue felt clumsy and enormous in his dry mouth.

Awareness of his own cowardice forced him to turn his head and face what had trespassed into Mark's kitchen. Half the oxygen seemed to leave the space immediately around him, and the light faded as if a subtle rheostat had been more breathed upon than dialed. A faint odor of excrement and corruption, as of a corpse rotting in the distance, tainted the air.

A sound like buzzing, like insects, filtered in through the screen door.

But what he saw after he had turned his head was only Mr Shillington leaning against the sink next to Mrs Taft, who seemed depressed by what her neighbor was saying. When both of them stopped their conversation to stare at the boys, Jimbo saw annoyance in Mr Shillington's eyes, the shine of tears in Mrs Taft's. Two thoughts occurred to him at virtually the same moment: *Mr Shillington and Mrs Taft were having an affair, and he just dumped her* and *For a second or two, time just stopped, so those seconds never happened.*

At the center of his being, Jimbo felt as though some great machine had paused its workings, come to rest, then ponderously swung back into motion.

Beside him, Mark was saying, 'His back is always

turned.' The words reached Jimbo as if through the process of translation from a foreign language. When he had at last absorbed their meaning, he understood Mark's sentence no better. The only man in the kitchen was Mr Shillington, who was pretending to be happy that two teenage boys were staring at him.

'Something in Linda's eye,' he said, and smiled. 'Mrs Taft has something in her eye, and I was trying to get it out.'

'Who?' Jimbo whispered to Mark.

'You didn't see him?' Mark turned upon him in amazed disbelief.

'No, but something happened,' Jimbo said.

'Now, kid,' said Mr Shillington. 'Don't go getting the wrong idea about this.' His long, bony face was undergoing an interesting color shift. Below the cheekbones, he was turning a blotchy red, but from the eyes up, he went white.

'Something happened, all right,' Mark said.

'No, it did *not*,' insisted Mr Shillington. Linda Taft shrank into herself, wrinkling her nose and glancing around.

'Sorry,' Mark said. 'I'm not talking to you.' He looked back at Jimbo. 'You really didn't see him standing between them and the door, with his back turned?'

Jimbo shook his head.

'There was no one in this room but the two of us, Mark, until you and your friend barged in.'

'Well, we're going to barge out now, so you can go back to your eye surgery,' Mark said. 'Come on, Jimbo.'

Their eyes as large and innocent as those of sheep, Linda Taft and Ted Shillington watched Mark drag Jimbo across the room. When he reached the door, Mark pushed it open and shoved Jimbo out into the backyard. The door slammed behind them.

Faintly, Jimbo heard Linda Taft say, 'Did you just smell something funny?'

In the world's loudest whisper, Mark said, 'He – was – there. Standing next to the door. Facing the wall, so all I could see was his back.'

'Yo, I felt something,' Jimbo said, still feeling as though he were mostly asleep.

'Tell me. *Tell* me, Jimbo. I have to know.'

'Something terrible. It was like it was hard to breathe for a while. It sort of got dark, and Mrs Taft was right, I smelled something nasty.'

Mark was nodding his head. His eyes seemed to have retreated far back in his skull, and his mouth was a tight line. 'Damn. I wish you could have seen him, too.'

Jimbo offered his friend the thought that had spoken itself in his mind. 'They would have seen him, too. Mr Shillington and Mrs Taft.'

'I doubt that,' Mark said. A faint smile touched his mouth, then faded. 'But it would have been pretty interesting if they did see him.' He considered that possibility. 'I guess I'm glad they didn't.'

'I'm glad *I* didn't,' Jimbo said.

'He doesn't want you to see him.'

'Who is he?' Jimbo's question came out in a small, strange wail.

'He must be the guy who used to live in that house.' Mark gripped Jimbo's upper arms and for a wild second shook him like a rag doll. His eyes looked enormous and much darker than usual. 'It's obvious. And he's the reason my mother's dead. You know what that means?'

Jimbo knew, but decided to keep his mouth shut.

'It means you and I are for sure going to find out who the son of a bitch was. I want to look at his face. That's what it means. And there won't be any more argument about this, Jimbo.'

Jimbo realized that Mark had him, he was hooked. He was accepting the most outrageous aspect of Mark's theory. He had bought into his friend's crazy theory the moment he'd accepted what Mark told him he had seen in his kitchen. Once you take someone's word about an invisible man, you are playing with his racquet on his court, and it is no use pretending otherwise.

'Aren't you afraid?'

'I don't think anything is going to happen to us if we go in there during the daytime.'

'Even if he is there, I guess I wouldn't be able to see him, anyhow.' He had it in him to giggle, however nervously. 'If I said, Fuck you, you'd do it by yourself, wouldn't you?'

'Of course I would.'

Jimbo sighed as if from the soles of his feet. 'So when are we going to do this thing I said I was never going to do?'

'Tomorrow morning,' Mark said. 'I want us to have plenty of time.'

What do people in Millhaven do at ten o'clock on Sunday mornings in June? Most residents of Millhaven who attend church services are already back home, changed out of the shirts and pants they wore to St Robert's or Mount Zion – almost nobody in Millhaven wears a jacket and tie to church anymore – into T-shirts and shorts, and they're already mowing their lawns or working at the tool bench. Some people are driving across town to see their mother, their brother, or their aunts and uncles. A lot of women are planning meals for the relatives who will show up in a couple of hours, ready for lunch. A lot of men are thinking about piling up the briquettes in the barbecue and wondering if they should drive to the store for some nice juicy pork ribs. A number of people are watching Charles Osgood on CBS's *Sunday Morning*, and a good third of those are still in bed. Hundreds of men and women are dividing their time between reading Sunday's *Ledger* and eating breakfast. Hundreds of others are still asleep, and a few of those, the ones with pasty complexions and foul breath, will wake up hungover. Joggers jog in the parks and along the sides of the roads; shopkeepers open up their shops; young couples awaken beneath rumpled sheets and embrace in shafts of sunlight.

In the Sherman Park area, formerly Pigtown, chambermaids change sheets at the venerable St Alwyn Hotel. Golfers pilot their carts, as happily as is possible for golfers, down the fairways at the Millhaven Country Club, where the grounds-keepers are eyeing the greens. Hardy children thrash around in the big public swimming pools in Hoyt and Pulaski parks, where, at sixty-eight degrees, the water is still a little too cold for most people, no matter how young they are. Pop once took us all the way to Hoyt Park on a morning in June, and the cold water turned Philip's lips cobalt blue.

On Superior Street, the only person left asleep is Jackie Monaghan, who will not slip groaning into a painful wakefulness for another two hours. Margo Monaghan is sliding a tray of cinnamon buns into the oven. In 3324, Philip Underhill sits on the threadbare, sagging green davenport and, ostensibly splitting his attention between the newspaper spread open on his lap and a strutting, roaring evangelist on TV, wonders about the identity of this Sherman Park Killer guy and how many kids he will cause to disappear before being locked up. On either side of brooding Philip, a brittle tranquillity pervades the Taft and Shillington residences. Ted Shillington is standing outside in his backyard, smoking, only half aware that his wife is glaring at him from the window above the kitchen sink. Putting away the breakfast dishes in an identical kitchen two houses south, Linda Taft shocks herself by hoping that Mr Hank Taft might fall down dead of a heart attack before he comes in to ask her what's for lunch.

In his abstracted and melancholy state, Ted Shillington barely registers the firehouse hair and loping gait of Jimbo Monaghan, who glides across his field of vision without saying a word. When Jimbo passes between the ugly eight-foot wall and the Underhills' collapsed fence, Ted registers it not at all, nor the figure of Mark Underhill silently stepping over the fence to join his friend. The boys move quickly southward down the alley to

Townsend Street, entirely unobserved by Ted Shillington, who has become aware that someone is watching him with a quality – to judge by the sensation at the back of his neck – akin to hostility. Unaware of the banality of this desire, he considers how marvelous it would be were his wife, Laura Shillington, and Linda's husband, Hank Taft, to have inaugurated a secret passion so great that the two of them would flee Superior Street hand in hand. That could happen, he and she together, couldn't it? Why should a solution so satisfying, so liberating, so sweet with absolution, be out of court? Why should that automatically be disallowed?

Wordlessly, the boys reach the bottom of the alleyway and begin the turn toward Michigan Street. Mark's intent, fiercely concentrated presence beside him makes Jimbo see everything around him in heightened color: the cobbles at their feet glow a particularly poignant greenish-gray, for which he discovers he feels a kind of premature nostalgia, as if they have been, or are soon to be, lost; the dust at the alley's sunny conclusion burns golden-brown. Jimbo has never seen such beautiful dust – yellow-white light irradiates the floating particles – and a nameless emotion grips his throat.

Around the familiar corner they go, onto dazzled

Michigan Street. The sunlight hangs in a dense, shining curtain, through which they pass like spies, like thieves. It occurs to Jimbo that, unlike Mark, he's pretty frightened, and he cuts the pace in half. Mark rakes him with a glance. 'Keep moving, homey, nothing's going to happen to you.'

'Swell,' Jimbo says.

No one sits on the porches up and down the street, though as far as Jimbo can tell, half the neighborhood might be staring at them through their windows. In front of the second house up on the west side of the street, three giant sunflowers appear to follow him with their single, enormous eyes. Rays of sizzling light surround each sunflower; everything before him, Jimbo notices, is defined by an electric, crackling outline.

Old Skip asleep on his porch is the quietest thing on Michigan Street, Jimbo thinks.

Mark moves up the sidewalk quickly but without obvious haste, and Jimbo does not leave his side. The pavement seems to move up and down with their footsteps, and 3323 breathes in and out, growing with each inhalation.

When Mark's elbow raps against his ribs, Jimbo realizes that he has not been focusing. 'Now we're going to cut across the lawn, and we're not going to run. Okay?'

Without waiting for a reply, Mark swivels off

the pavement and begins walking across the grass at a nice easy pace. His legs swing out before him, his entire body lopes along, Mark's effortless grace carrying him between the houses and out of sight before a casual observer would notice that he had left the sidewalk. Beside him, Jimbo feels that he moves like a mule, a camel, an ungainly beast incapable of picking up speed without redistributing its weight.

At the back of the house, the sheer scale of the disorder makes Jimbo gasp. Some of that stuff is waist-high! What Mark called the 'pup tent' slants downward, heavy as a scar, just past the kitchen door, ending at a stumpy little wall placed about fifteen feet out into the jungly yard. The addition is carelessly built, and although it is the newest part of the house, it will collapse long before the rest of the structure. Jimbo does not care for the look of that slanting roof, no he does not.

'All right,' Mark says, and sets off into the weeds on the suggestion of a path he had made earlier. Walking behind him, Jimbo sees the house inhale and exhale with every step he takes and starts to panic. Mark says, 'For God's sake, calm down,' and Jimbo realizes that the inhalations and exhalations are his.

Mark jumps the steps to the back door. Jimbo trudges behind him. He sees the empty pane in the kitchen door and peers in at what resembles a haze or cloud, then reveals itself as the kitchen's grimy ceiling. Grimly, Mark smiles down at him, tilts to the side, and flattens himself against the door. He thrusts his arm through the empty panel. Mark's smile curdles into a grimace. The knob turns, the door swings open. His mouth now a thin, hard line, Mark gestures for Jimbo to join him. When Jimbo places his feet on the step, Mark clamps a hand on his wrist and without further ceremony propels him into the kitchen.

Part Four

THE RED SKY

15

NOW AND AGAIN during our childhood, Philip and I had the benefit of Pop's discourses on the female gender – never when Mom was within hearing range, of course. Pop gave us the lowdown on women when we accompanied him on his Saturday 'errands,' which involved visits to the houses of his companions Mom disliked or detested. Refreshing stops at local bars and taverns formed the connective tissue between his social calls. Maybe one-third of the time, Philip and I were allowed to come with him into his friends' houses or apartments. We were allowed into the taverns in about the same proportion.

Going with Pop into his friends' places and the bars he frequented on Sherman Boulevard and Burleigh was only slightly more satisfying than having to wait in the car. In the car, we could listen to the radio, and in the taverns we could order Cokes. In both the car and the Saracen Lounge at the St Alwyn Hotel – or Sam n' Aggie's Auer Corner, or Noddy's Sportsmen's Tavern – we were essentially left alone to quarrel with each other while Pop carried on according to the requirements of the moment. Sometimes I saw money changing hands, usually from his pockets to another man's hand, but sometimes the other way around; sometimes he helped one of his friends move boxes or heavy objects like electrical saws or water heaters from one place, say, like a warehouse, to another, say, like a garage. In the bars and taverns he installed us in a booth along the wall, got us set up with Cokes, and left us there for an hour or two while he drank beer or played pool with his buddies. Once he commanded us to stay in the car while he went into the Saracen Lounge to 'have a talk with a guy,' and after half an hour I got out of the car and peered in the window to see Pop nowhere in the room. In the pit of my stomach, I knew he had left us there, really walked away and left us, but I also knew that he would come back. As he eventually did, from around the corner, his eyes filled with handsome apologies.

Pop's theories and opinions about women

seemed not to apply to Mom. Mom was understood to exist in a separate category, distinct from all other females by reason of being beyond criticism, mostly, and anyway too close at hand to be seen whole. When a single tree fills your lens, the rest of the forest takes on a degree of abstraction. By some such process, Pop enabled himself to arrive at a point of view largely hostile to women without including his wife in the general condemnation.

'Boys,' he said (and now we are in the smoky, beer-stained depths of the Saracen Lounge, where two scoundrels named Bisbee and Livernoise lean forward over the table as if they, not we, were the boys being addressed), 'there are two kinds of women, and you better watch out for both of 'em.'

'Thass right,' chimed in Livernoise, commonly called 'Legs.' Mom loathed this guy.

'The first kind acts like you're the feed trough and she's the pony. Everything you've got is fine with her as long as you've got it. Of course, anytime you can do better is aces with her, but she will expect you to stay at that level or higher. The deal with this kind of woman is, you don't go *back*. Once you get up to steaks and onion rings, the peanut butter and hot dogs are gone for good. So there's a strain on you, right away from the start. Unless there's food in that trough, and the food is at least as good as it was the last time, the pony is going out the door. She'll tell you she loves you, but she's leaving anyhow, because self-respect means more to her than love. Get it? What you thought you had with her wasn't what you thought it was, at all. You thought it was about love, or trust, or a good time, or something like that, but all along it was only about her self-respect.

'Now the second kind is like the first, only the part about self-respect is now all about status and possessions. Women like this don't really have brains, they have mental cash registers. Marry one of 'em, and you're so far up shit creek you not only don't have a paddle, you don't have a boat. You're up to your neck, dog-paddling to keep your head above the floating crap. You might as well of joined the army, because all day long you're basically following orders.'

'That's a Jewish woman you're describing,' said Bisbee, or maybe it was Legs Livernoise. 'I went around with a woman like that, and she was one hundred percent Jew, named Tannenbaum.'

'Could be Jewish, could be Baptist, could be anything,' Pop said. 'The Jewish one might be the best at what I told you, but a little Anglo-Saxon bitch with blond hair and no more tits than Legs here can cross her legs and say "diamonds" just as good as if her name was Rachel Goldberg.'

'You just laid it all out, right there,' said Bisbee (I think). 'Your boys should be taking notes, only this discussion is way above their little heads.'

'Now,' Pop said, with an odd look in his eye, 'there is a third kind of woman, but she is extremely hard to find. Which you might or might not care to do, because this kind of woman will Mixmaster your brains a lot faster than those other two.'

'Don't get into that now,' said Legs Livernoise, flapping his hands in the air.

'Spare these boys their precious innocence,' said Bisbee.

Neither one of these dodos had any more idea of what Pop was going to say than we did.

'My boys are old enough to handle this information, besides which it is a father's sacred duty to oversee their education. They should know' – here he looked directly at my brother and myself – 'that although the vast majority of the women they will encounter throughout their lives will fall into the first two categories, once in a blue moon the third kind will cross their path.'

'God's own truth, lads,' Bisbee said.

'The first kind sticks with you as long as the going is good, and the second kind winds up appointing herself president of the corporation of you,' Pop said. 'They both take all they can get with both hands, only the second kind of woman is up-front about it because she's after more than you got right from the start. Now, the third type of woman couldn't care less how much money you got in the bank, and she don't give a shit about what kind of car you drive. And that's what makes her so damn *dangerous*.'

'Pretty in pink, that's what they say,' said Legs Livernoise.

'Egg-zack-tically,' Pop said. 'This is a woman who can think around corners and see you coming before you get there. She's always one step ahead. You're not sure where she's from, but you know for damn sure it's not around here. There's things about her that are *different*. Plus, she's so far ahead you'll never catch up. And believe me, she doesn't want you to catch up. Because if you do, the fun is all over. Her whole game is, keep you guessing. She wants you up on your toes, with your eyes and your mouth wide open. If you should happen to say, 'The sky's a nice blue today,' she will say, 'Oh, blue is just blue. Yesterday, the sky was red.' And you think back, and, you know, yesterday maybe the sky *was* red.'

'And maybe your head was up your ass,' said Bisbee. 'Boys, pardon my French.'

'Up hers, more likely,' said Livernoise.

'That is right,' Pop said. 'You boys are too young to know about sex, but it's never to early to learn a few facts. Sex is an activity shared between men and women, but we enjoy that activity more than they do. It's different with every person. Sometimes it's a lot better than others.' He paused, and his face fell into a pattern of serious reflection. For the first time I realized how drunk he was. 'Don't tell Mom anything about this, or I'll knock your little blocks off. I mean that.' He pointed his finger at us, and left it there until we nodded.

'All right. The point is, with this third woman, the sex is always great. Unless it's really terrible, but that's pretty rare, and for those women, the terrible sex works almost the same way as great sex does for the rest of 'em. Because the point is, either way you're gonna think a lot about that woman. See, these women aren't interested in the stuff the first two are. They don't want to get in your wallet, they want to get into your head. And once they get in there, they send down roots, they throw out grappling hooks, they do everything they can to make sure you can't get them out.

'Remember I said how they don't care about that stuff like jewelry and houses and whatever else money can buy? They want something else instead, and that something is you. They want *you*. Inside and out, but especially in. They don't really want you out in the world, where you can mess around with your friends, they want you in their world, which is a place you never dreamed of before you got there. For all you know, the sky there is red all the livelong day, and up is down, and all the rivers run upstream.'

'Daddy, why is the sky red?' Philip asked, evidently having considered this point for some time.

'To burn the shit out of little knuckleheads like you,' Pop said. His hideous cronies cracked up.

I have often imagined that Philip turned out the way he did because of the kind of person Pop was. Maybe my brother would be the same uptight, ungenerous, cautious prick if Pop had been someone like Dag Hammarskjöld, or even Roy Rogers, but I don't think so.

Sometimes, at odd moments during the day and always completely unexpectedly, I remember the little boy seated next to me in the Saracen's booth asking, 'Daddy, why is the sky red?' He makes me feel like weeping, like battering my fists against the desk.

16

MARK FOLLOWED JIMBO through the door with the sudden and unanticipated sense of having found himself at a hinge moment, from which point everything in his life would divide itself into *before* and *after*. It was a watershed he had passed at the very moment of its observation. He had no idea why he should have the sense that nothing would be quite the same again, but to deny that sense would be like lying to himself. The perception of the watershed moment, with himself at its center, was almost instantly surpassed by the next moment, in which a tremendous tectonic shift had already happened, leaving him with his second great impression of the morning, that the kitchen, and by implication the rest of the house, was far emptier than he had imagined.

Side by side, he and Jimbo took in a perfectly ordinary, empty room that had been left to itself for the past three or four decades. On the floor, the flurry of their footprints carved tracks in the thick carpet of dust. Fox-brown stains blotched the flaking yellow walls. The room felt extraordinarily hot. The air smelled musty and lifeless. The only sound Mark could hear was Jimbo's breathing and his own. So it was true, he thought; in the daytime, they were safe here.

At first glance, the kitchen seemed to be around the same size and shape as the kitchen in Mark's house. The arch to the dining room seemed to replicate its counterpart across the alley. The rooms might have been a bit smaller. Apart from the absence of a stove and the refrigerator, the great difference between this room and the Underhill kitchen lay in the wall to his left, the one that replaced the exterior wall at home. This wall had no window to look out upon the brief length of grass leading to the next house. It seemed never to have held the spice racks and shelves for cookbooks, little figurines of dogs and cats, and china miniatures of shepherds and shepherdesses that stood in that position in the Underhill household. What it had instead was the door, snugly fitted into the frame, he had noticed the last time.

'Well?' Jimbo nodded at the door in a you-first manner.

'We'll get to that,' Mark said. 'First, let's look out the front windows and see if anybody noticed us.'

'Yo, whatever,' Jimbo said, acting cooler than he felt.

Mark moved across the room and discovered, just as he was about to pass through the narrower of the two arches, that the house was not as empty as he had supposed. A shrouded, boxlike object that could only be a table beneath a bedsheet occupied the middle of the dining room. Through the wider arch beyond he could see the shapes of other pieces of furniture draped in sheets. When the owners decamped, they had left behind two good-sized chairs and a long sofa. Why would anyone move out and leave good furniture behind?

With Jimbo breathing noisily in his ear, Mark went through to the living room. Remembering what Jimbo had thought he had seen, and his own vision, or half-vision, of the day before that, Mark looked for footprints in the dust. He saw only tracings, loops and swirls like writing in an unknown alphabet inscribed with the lightest possible pressure of a quill pen. Neither Jimbo's threatening giant, his own monstrous figure of warning, or the girl could have made these faint, delicate patterns. The same hand, that of neglect, had scrawled its ornate but meaningless patterns on the walls. These had faded to the colorlessness of mist – as if you could punch your hands through the unreadable writing and touch nothing more substantial than smoke.

17

Of course nobody saw us, Jimbo thought, *nobody ever really looks at this house. Even when the neighbors get together to mow the lawn, they pretend they're somewhere else. And the last thing they ever do is look in the windows. We could dance naked in here, and they wouldn't see a thing.*

While Mark gazed at the walls and saw God knows what, Jimbo moved toward the big front window without, despite what had just gone through his mind, getting so close to it that he could easily be seen from the street. Deep striations in the film over the glass caught the light and stood out like runes.

With the passing of a cloud, the bright streaks and swirls on the window heightened into beaten gold, a color too rich for late morning in the Midwest. Within Jimbo, something, a particle of his being that felt like remembered pain, moved as if it had been touched. A sense of bereft abandonment passed through him like an X ray, and in sudden confusion he turned from the window. The sheets sagging over the furniture in the living room spoke of a thousand lost things.

Jimbo turned back to the window. The golden runes had faded back into the gaps between smears of dust that offered him an oddly unexpected vision of Michigan Street. Directly opposite stood two houses, the Rochenkos' and Old Man Hillyard's. Although Jimbo knew exactly what these structures looked like, it was as if he had never quite seen them before. From this vantage point, the Rochenko and Hillyard houses seemed subtly different in nature, remote, more mysterious.

A sound like the rustle of fabric over fabric reached Jimbo from somewhere close at hand, and he jerked his head and looked over his shoulder at . . . what? Some white scrap, briefly visible in the murky air? He was spooked enough to ask, 'Did you hear that?'

'You heard something?' Mark took his hand from the wall he had been examining and looked at Jimbo in a manner far too intense for his liking.

'No. Sorry.'

'Let's start upstairs, or down here – with that.' Mark only barely nodded toward the kitchen and the rear of the house. 'Upstairs, what do you say?'

Why ask me? Jimbo wondered, then realized that he was being told, not asked. 'Makes sense to me,' he said. 'And what are we looking for, exactly?'

'Whatever we can find. Especially anything with a name on it – like envelopes. We can always Google a name. Pictures would be good.'

One flight up, the stairs ended at a bleak hallway and the narrow, steeply pitched flight of stairs to the attic. Without a word or a glance, Mark turned to them and went up.

Jimbo came through the attic door and saw that the roof formed an inverted V with its peak about eight feet above the floor. From this peak, the roof slanted steeply down over a hodgepodge of tables, chairs, and dressers.

Ten minutes later, Jimbo wiped sweat from his forehead and looked across the attic to see his friend methodically searching the drawers of a highboy. How many hours would Mark insist spending on this search?

Sweat seemed to leak from Jimbo's every pore. When he leaned over a chest or opened a box, sweat dripped into his eyes and plopped softly onto the surface of whatever he was trying to look at.

Just off to the right, Jimbo thought he saw an upright human body wrapped in a sheet, and fear blasted through his system. With a small cry of shock, he straightened up and turned to face the shrouded figure.

'*What?*' Mark said.

Jimbo was staring at his own pop-eyed, shiny face looking at him from within a full-length mirror in an oval wooden frame. He had turned himself into a horror movie cliché.

'Nothing. Jesus, it just feels creepy, messing around up here.'

'There has to be something,' Mark said, mostly to himself. He wrenched a tiny drawer out of a flimsy-looking lamp table. 'Whoever they were, they left in a hurry. Look at the way this stuff is crammed in here. Even if they were trying to hide shit, probably they got too sloppy to do it right.'

'You know,' Jimbo said, 'I'd just like to get out of this attic.'

Twenty minutes later, they were going back down the narrow staircase. The second floor felt ten degrees cooler than the attic. As a result of having kicked the legs of a little wooden table into splinters, Mark limped slightly during the descent.

Thinking of what waited for them on the ground

floor, Jimbo almost hoped that they would spend a long time upstairs.

The second floor of 3323 North Michigan Street consisted of two bedrooms and a bathroom linked by a common hallway. In the smaller of the bedrooms, two single beds, one with a deeply stained mattress, had been pushed against opposite walls. The bare wooden floor was scuffed, scratched, and dirty. Mark followed Jimbo into the room, frowned at the stained mattress, and flipped it on its side. Dull brown smears in a pattern like paisley covered the bottom of the mattress.

'Ugh, look at that shit.'

'You think it's shit? I don't, I think –'

'You don't know what it is, and neither do I.' Mark lowered the awful mattress back into place. Then he bent down and looked under the bed. He did the same on the other side of the room.

Mark gave the bathroom a desultory once-over. Dead spider webs hung in tatters from the window, and a living spider only slightly smaller than a mouse fought to scale the inner slope of the bathtub. Gritty white powder lay across the floor tiles.

A double bed butted against the inner wall of the larger bedroom. The same gritty white powder covered the floor, and when Jimbo looked up he saw yellow-brown wounds in the ceiling. A wooden crucifix hung over the headboard.

Mark dipped down and looked under the bed. He uttered a sound that combined surprise and disgust and duckwalked backward, trailing his finger along the dusty join between two planks.

Before Jimbo could ask what he was doing, Mark jumped up. He wandered to the opposite wall.

Jimbo went to the window. Again, the unfamiliar angle distorted a well-known landscape. The buildings tilted forward, diminished by perspective and also by what felt like someone else's hatred, suspicion, and fear. He shuddered, and the scene before him snapped back into ordinary reality.

'I have this feeling . . .' Mark was leaning against the inner wall. Slowly, he turned his head and regarded the closet.

'About what?' Jimbo said.

Mark moved along the wall, opened the door, and leaned in.

'Anything there?'

Mark disappeared inside.

Jimbo moved toward the closet and heard a sound as of something sliding off a shelf. Smiling, Mark reappeared through the door. He was holding a dust-covered object Jimbo needed a moment to recognize as an old photo album.

Jimbo had no way of knowing, and Mark had

no intention of telling him, that the smile on his face had been inspired not by the photo album, but by something else altogether – a door set into the back of the closet. A certain theory about the house he was at last exploring had begun to form in his mind, and the door inside the closet seemed to confirm it.

'Bingo!'

'Yeah,' Mark said. 'Let's take a look.' He went to the window and held the album in the light. Dark gray with accumulated dust, it had once been a deep forest green. Quilted plastic rectangles made to resemble cloth surrounded a central plate that read FAVORITE FAMILY PHOTOGRAPHS. Mark opened the cover to the first page of photographs.

A heavy-set young man wearing a long black coat and heavy boots bent sideways on the bumper of an old Ford and shielded his face with a hand. In the second photograph the same young man's face was a stationary blur as he stood with his arm around a smiling girl whose dead-straight hair fell nearly to her waist.

'I don't believe it,' Mark said. 'Look at this.'

Shrouded by his long coat, his back to the camera, the man bent over a table littered with clamps, sanders, and jars of nails.

Then came a photograph taken directly outside

this house. The lawn was barer, the trees looked smaller. Showing only the top of his head, the man held the branchy arms of a small boy of five or six.

As if having a son had released something in him, the three photographs that followed caught him in the midst of a social gathering seemingly located at a lakeside tavern. Wearing his usual garb, the man had been photographed in conversation with other men of his age or older. Here he was standing on a dock next to the tavern, here he perched on an overturned rowboat with two other men and a woman with plucked eyebrows and a cigarette in her mouth. In every photograph, the man's stance made his face unavailable to the camera.

'What's your name, you asshole?' Mark said. 'Don't want to show your face to the camera, do you?'

'I'm sorry, this is creeping me out,' Jimbo said. 'The guy in your kitchen didn't show his face, either.'

'Because this is him, get it? He's *the guy*.'

'This is way too scary for me,' Jimbo said. 'Sorry. We should never have come in here. We should have left the whole thing alone right from the start.'

'Shut up.'

Mark was scowling down at the photographs.

He abruptly bent his neck and lowered his head closer to the page. 'I wonder . . .' He raised his hand and pointed at a rangy, cowpoke-like man also seated on the overturned rowboat. 'Does that guy look familiar to you?'

Mark was never going to let him off the hook. 'Didn't you hear me?'

'Yes, I heard you, but I can't do anything about it. Now look at the guy I'm pointing at.'

Jimbo thought the man looked a little like the Marlboro Man in old advertisements, but he knew better than to say this out loud.

'Come on, look close. Imagine him with a lot of wrinkles.'

'*This* is Old Man Hillyard? I don't believe it.' He looked more closely at the man sitting on the upturned rowboat and almost succeeded in superimposing his features over Mr Hillyard's. 'Maybe it is.'

'Sure, it is. Hillyard knew this guy, see? He's talking to him, they're having a few beers together. We have to talk to Old Man Hillyard.'

'I could do that,' Jimbo said, seeing an excuse for getting out of the house.

'Yeah, he likes you now, doesn't he?' After twisting his ankle the week previous, Mr Hillyard had signaled to Jimbo and asked him to pick up his groceries for him. 'Go see him this afternoon.

In fact, talk to everyone on the block who looks old enough to have known this guy.'

Now Jimbo's gratitude at an honorable reason for escaping the genuinely oppressive atmosphere of the house met the sudden suspicion that Mark seemed to be trying to get rid of him.

'What about you?'

'Are you serious? While you're going around the neighborhood, I'll be here.'

The strange room downstairs, which had never been far from his thoughts, surged fully into Jimbo's consciousness. The farther he could get from that thing, the better he would feel. It was as if it radiated an unnatural heat, or an unwholesome odor.

Mark's eyes were curiously large and bright. 'Both of us don't have to poke around in this place. Anyhow, you don't want to be here, do you?'

Jimbo stepped back, his face filled with suspicion. Contradictory impulses battled in him – Mark really did seem to be putting him on the sidelines. Then he thought again of the man in the photographs and the room downstairs they had yet to enter, and supposed he would be more useful outside the house than in.

'This place doesn't feel right,' he said. 'It's like it's all cramped up, or something. It has this terrible feeling.'

That was the truth. Jimbo felt as though he were wading through some unclean substance that would harden around his ankles if he stood still too long. Mark's ghostly spider webs had been a version of this same feeling.

'You should see where I found the pictures,' Mark said.

No, I shouldn't, Jimbo thought, but he moved forward and went through the door.

There was barely room enough for the two of them in the closet, and the darkness made it difficult to see what Mark was doing. He seemed to be pushing on a high shelf above the clothes rail. The shelf slid up. Mark stepped in closer and opened a panel at the back of the closet.

'Look.'

Jimbo came forward, and Mark leaned to the side and reached into the darkness.

'Can you see?'

'Not really.'

'Come around and stick your hand in.'

They jostled around each other, and Jimbo bent forward and pushed his right hand into a half-visible opening.

'Feel the bottom,' Mark said.

The wooden surface felt furry and scratchy, and softer than it should have been, like the hide of a long-dead bear.

'The wood's a little rotten,' Mark said from behind him.

Jimbo's fingers encountered a raised screw, a small hole, a raised edge. 'I got something.'

'Pull up on it.'

An inner flap detached from the floor of the hidden cabinet. Jimbo probed into the opening and found a sunken compartment about a foot long, two feet wide, and five or six inches deep. 'This is where you found the album?'

'Right in there.'

Jimbo pulled his hand from the secret compartment, and both boys backed out into the room.

'How did you find the flap? How did you know it was there?'

'I guessed.'

Jimbo squinted at him in frustration.

'This place is supposed to be identical to my house, isn't it?'

'I thought so. But the rooms look a little smaller.'

'You got it,' Mark said. 'That's why the rooms seem so cramped to you. Almost all of them are smaller than the rooms in my house. On the outside, though, it's identical. The extra space had to be somewhere.'

'You mean there are hiding places all over this house?'

'That's what I'm thinking,' Mark said, not

saying at least half of what he was thinking.

Without any desire for greater precision, Jimbo immediately understood that hideous possibilities lay in this arrangement.

'Let's say you had someone, a girl, locked in this house,' Mark said. 'She would think she was safe, but . . .'

This was the possibility Jimbo least wished to consider. 'If you were hidden in one of these secret places, you could come out anytime you liked.' Saying it made him feel ill.

'This house *has* to have a really terrible history,' Mark said.

'Its present isn't all that wonderful. I mean, Mark, the place really gives me the creeps. It's almost like there's someone else in here with us.'

'I know what you mean,' Mark said. 'Let's go downstairs and get it over with. I'll do the real searching tomorrow.'

One floor down, the boys roamed through the living room and the dining room, exploring closets and cabinets and examining the floorboards for secret caches. Mark appeared to be observing architectural eccentricities he was not bothering to describe. He lifted his eyebrows, he pushed his lips in and out, he went through all these little gestures of thought and comprehension. Whatever he was comprehending he kept to himself.

Too soon for Jimbo's comfort, they found themselves back in the kitchen. If anything, he felt worse about that extra room than he had earlier. A bad, bad feeling seemed to flow directly from it. As if in response, the door in the wall seemed to have grown larger, taken on increased density.

'I'm not sure I want to see what's in there,' he said.

'Then don't go in.'

Mark went to the door and pulled it open. He stepped back, making it possible for Jimbo, whose heart felt as though it were in free fall, to move up alongside him. Within, the boys could see only a flat sheet of darkness. Mark made a noise low in his throat and went up to the door, and Jimbo trailed a reluctant half step behind.

'We're just going to do this,' Mark said. 'It's only an empty room, that's all.' With a single step, he moved into the dark room. Jimbo hesitated for a moment, swallowed, and went after him into the darkness. Suddenly his face felt hot.

'I should have brought that flashlight,' Mark said.

'Yeah,' Jimbo said, without at all agreeing.

Their eyes began to adjust. Jimbo was reminded of that moment when you walk into a dark theater and pause before moving down the aisle. The featureless darkness faded to a grainy shadowland. Jimbo became aware of a faint but serious odor. Here, something animal and unpleasant had been added to the smell of emptiness and defeat exuded by the rest of the house. He realized that he was looking at a large object with a shape at once familiar and foreign.

'Shit fuck damn. What the hell is *that*?'

'I think it's a bed.'

'That thing can't be a *bed*,' Mark said. They moved closer to the object that dominated the room. It extended sideways under the slanting roofline and bore an initial resemblance to a bed – the bed of a cruel giant who nightly collapsed into it drunk. Thick, crude ten-foot timbers defined the sides, and sloppily assembled planks formed the rough platform on which the giant slept. They moved in closer, and without indicating anything in particular, Mark said, 'Uh-oh.'

'I wouldn't want to spend the night on that thing,' Jimbo said.

'No, look.' Mark pointed at what Jimbo had taken for a darkness in the grain of the long planks. In the center of the darkness, a pair of leather cuffs about three feet apart were fastened to the platform with chains. Another pair of restraints, a little farther apart, had been chained to the platform about four feet beneath them.

'The legs are bolted to the floor,' Mark said. His eyes shone in the darkness.

'Who was this *for*?' Then Jimbo noticed that the series of blotches, which seemed to be black, around and between the restraints were not an element of the grain. 'I'm getting out of here. Sorry, man.'

He was already moving toward the door, holding up his hands as if to ward off an attacker. With a last look at the huge bed, Mark joined him. On the other side of the door, they glanced at each other, and Jimbo was afraid that Mark was going to say something, but he looked away and kept his thoughts to himself.

Feeling as weightless and vague as ghosts, they went out onto the broken little porch. Something had happened to them, Jimbo thought; something had happened to him anyhow, but he could not begin to define what it was. All the breath and most of the life had been driven from his body, as if by a great shock. What was left was just enough to float down the steps into the lush tangle of the backyard.

Jimbo remained silent until they were walking across the mown grass at the side of the house, and then he found he had to speak. 'It was built to hold a kid – that bed-thing.'

Mark stopped moving and looked back.

'He strapped a kid, or maybe even a couple of kids, onto that bed-thing, and he tortured them.' He felt as though he were banging on a bass drum. 'Because those were bloodstains, weren't they? They looked black, but it was blood.'

'I think those stains on the mattress upstairs were blood, too.'

'Good God, Mark, what kind of place *is* that?'

'That's what we're going to find out,' Mark said. 'Unless you changed your mind about helping me. If so, tell me right now. Are you quitting?'

'No, I'll do what you want,' Jimbo said. 'But I still say we should never have gotten involved in this stuff.'

'I didn't have a choice,' Mark said. 'You know what? I feel like I was kind of *selected*. I agree with you, it's terrible and it's scary – but *it killed my mother*!'

'How? Explain it to me, will you?'

'I DON'T KNOW HOW!' Mark yelled. 'What do you think we're DOING here, anyhow?'

Then, for no reason Jimbo could see, Mark's eyes changed. His face went slack and dopey. Mark looked at his empty hands, then at the ground. 'Holy shit.' Still looking at the ground, he went four or five feet back the way they had come. 'Jimbo, what the hell happened to that photograph album?'

Jimbo blinked.

'Did I give it to you?'

'No. You had it when we came down the stairs.'

'I must have left it in the kitchen.' Mark was nodding his head. 'I didn't take it in the room, did I?'

'I don't remember.'

'I must have set it down on a counter so my hands would be free.'

'No,' Jimbo said, knowing what Mark intended to do. 'Leave it. You already saw the pictures.'

But Mark had already set off back toward the undergrowth, and in another second he was following the path they had beaten.

'I don't believe you're doing this.'

'Don't worry, I'll be right back.'

To Jimbo, it was inconceivable that anyone, even Mark, would be willing to expose himself a second time to the interior of 3323. He understood why the neighborhood had silently agreed to forget about the empty house in their midst, to let their eyes go out of focus when they happened accidentally to find themselves looking at it. There were things you *shouldn't* look at, things better not seen.

He sat down and waited. The intense heat amplified the buzzing and clicking of insects hidden in the tall grass. Sweat dripped down the back of his neck and slithered over his ribs, cooling his skin. He kept his eyes on the back door at the top of the broken steps. His shoulders had become uncomfortably hot. He twitched at his T-shirt and rubbed his shoulders, still watching the door.

Jimbo moved around on the grass, searching for a more comfortable place to sit. He wondered if any dead chipmunks or squirrels might be decomposing in his vicinity.

Looking at his watch was a useless gesture, since he had no idea what time it had been when Mark went back into the kitchen. He looked at his watch anyway: 12:30 P.M. Amazing. They must have been in the house for two and a half hours. It had felt much shorter than that. It was almost as if the house had hypnotized him. The thought made him glance again at his watch. Its hands had not moved.

Of course the second hand was in motion, sweeping in its inexorable, clockwise way around the circle of the dial. The little needle darted from 22 to 23, on its way to 30. Jimbo glanced across the top of the grasses at the back door. It looked as though it had never been opened.

The moving needle rolled across the finish line and without hesitation launched into a brand-new minute. Jimbo's eyes lifted to the sinister door, and relief washed through him, followed by an intense flash of anger. Through the opening doorway stepped Mark Underhill, carrying the ugly photo album and signaling apology with his every glance and gesture. Jimbo jumped to his feet. 'What took you so long?'

'I'm sorry, I'm sorry,' Mark said.

'Don't you know how worried I was? Did you forget I was out here waiting for you?'

'Yo, Jimbo, I said I was sorry.'

'Your ass is sorry!'

Mark stared at him with a fixed glare. Jimbo had no idea what he was thinking. His face was still unnaturally pale. Even Mark's lips looked white. 'Didn't you ask what took so much time?'

'Yes. What took so much time?'

'I couldn't find the damn thing anywhere. I looked all around the kitchen, I even looked in the, you know.'

'The room with the bed.'

Mark nodded. 'I went back upstairs. Guess where I found it.'

Jimbo gave him the only possible answer. 'Back in the closet.'

'That's right. It was back in the closet.'

'Well, how did it get there?'

'I want to think about that,' Mark said. 'Don't say anything, okay? Please. Any opinion you have, keep it to yourself.'

'Here's one opinion I'm not keeping to myself – you can't go back inside that place. And you know it! Look how scared you are. Your face is completely white.'

'I think I *could* have left it there, maybe.'

Around and around they went, Mark now claiming to be unable to remember if he had been holding the album as they went downstairs, Jimbo unable to remember if he had seen him carrying it. They were still arguing about it, though less heatedly, when they reached the bottom of Michigan Street. They turned the corner into the alley, and fell silent as if by mutual agreement. Before they parted, Mark asked to borrow the Monaghans' Maglite, and Jimbo ran up the block and got it for him. He handed over the heavy flashlight without asking any questions.

18

From Timothy Underhill's journal, 23 June 2003

It's astounding. Philip had no idea of who used to live in the house across the alley from him. If he ever did know, he made himself forget it. Proximity to the home base of one of the nation's livelier serial killers could induce denial in people a lot less prone to it than Philip. And Philip, of course, had the added incentive of being shamefully aware of being married to the serial killer's first cousin. A share of his blood ran in her veins, a smaller share in their son's. Can that be the reason for Philip's dismissal of the boy? Philip loves Mark, I know that, but his love doesn't stop him from constantly undermining him.

Thanks to Jimbo Monaghan and Omar Hillyard, I know that Philip bought the house directly behind Kalendar's, but the purchase had to have been innocent. I don't think he *could* have bought his place if he had known it was right behind Kalendar's. And of course Philip bought it in a typical rush. He wanted to get out of the suburbs, where his neighbors made him feel outclassed, and he liked the idea of living in the old neighborhood, close to his school. He rushed in, thinking he understood everything, and if he ever picked up a hint about the previous owner of the house across the alley, he closed his mind to it on the spot.

When I learned about Kalendar's house across the alley, I did not say anything to Philip until I showed him the two strange e-mails Mark had sent me before his disappearance, and even then I waited until we were in the police station with Sergeant Pohlhaus. It was quite clear to me that speaking of these matters with Philip alone would be a waste of effort. The first e-mail showed up in my Inbox two days before Mark vanished, the second the day before. Reading the e-mails only cranked up Philip's suspicion that Mark and I had been engaged in some kind of conspiracy. Once Philip read the e-mails, he insisted on showing them to Pohlhaus, which was obviously the right thing to do. Pohlhaus read them, asked both of us a few questions, and put the printouts of the e-mails into a folder he kept in his bottom drawer. 'You never know,' he said, but as he said it, he sighed. I did my best – I told them both about the connection to Joseph Kalendar, but I might as well have been talking to a couple of dogs.

From: munderhill697@aol.com
To: tunderhill@nyc.rr.com
Sent: Monday, June 16, 2003 3:24 PM
Subject: crazy but not that crazy
hi unc

wondering how u r these daze, been thinking abut u. it isn't e z living here after what happened 2 mom. hard 2 concentrate, hard 2 keep myself in focus. now that i'm finally writing, i don't really know what 2 say.

do u ever get some idea u think is totally messed-up mad crazy, and it turns out 2 b right? or good?

b cool
m

'Did you write back?' asked Philip; Sergeant Pohlhaus asked, 'Did you respond to the boy's e-mail?'

'Sure,' I said. 'I wrote that it happens once or twice a week.'

Here is his second e-mail to me:

From: munderhill697@aol.com
To: tunderhill@nyc.rr.com
Sent: Tuesday, June 17, 2003 4:18 PM
Subject: Re: crazy but not that crazy

hi unc t –

deeper & deeper we go, and where we come out nobody knows . . .

so what I want to ask u is . . .

do u ever feel like u r in I of your own books? does the world ever feel that way 2 u? – like a tu book?
thanx,
m

'What did you tell him?' asked Philip and Sergeant Pohlhaus.

'I told him "never" and "all the time,"' I said.

'I'm sorry?' said Sergeant Pohlhaus. He was

a steely, whiplike man, and his question indicated that he was not amused.

So I showed him my e-mail:

From: tunderhill@nyc.rr.com
To: munderhill697@aol.com
Sent: Tuesday, June 17, 2003 7:45 PM
Subject: Re: crazy but not that crazy

Dear Mark,
>do u ever feel like u r in 1 of your own books? does the world
>ever feel that way 2 u? – like a tu book?

Answer:
(1) Never.
(2) All the time.
What the hell is going on out there, anyhow?
Unc T

'He never answered,' I said. 'But don't you think that this mysterious project is probably involved in his disappearance?'

'Maybe,' Philip said.

Both Sergeant Pohlhaus and I looked at him. We were in a room crowded with desks. Plainclothes policemen were talking into their phones and typing up reports. When I asked

Pohlhaus what the room was called, he gave me a funny look and said, 'The bullpen,' as if that was something everyone should know.

'This so-called project obviously had something to do with the Sherman Park Killer,' Philip said.

'I think it was about something else,' I said. 'I just learned that Mark and his friend Jimbo let themselves into that house behind yours, Philip, and after that I think Mark spent a lot of time there by himself. I think the house was his project. Or the project took place in that house. It used to belong to Joseph Kalendar.'

'That's impossible,' Philip said. 'My wife would have told me.' He looked at Pohlhaus. 'This isn't something I want everybody to know, but my wife and Kalendar were cousins.'

'That's interesting,' Pohlhaus said. 'It would have been logical for her to have said something about it at the time.'

'Philip,' I said, 'did you let Nancy see your house before you bought it?'

'Why would I have done that? It was in the right neighborhood, and all the houses are pretty much alike. Besides, I had to act fast.'

'So she didn't know until it was too late to back out. Once she realized where the new house was, I think she wanted to protect you.'

'To *protect* me? That's . . . that's . . .' He fell silent and seemed to ponder the matter.

'Mark was fascinated with that house,' I told Pohlhaus. 'He was obsessed with it.'

'A kid would be,' Pohlhaus said. 'There must be a lot of bloodstains in there. Probably a lot of other stuff, too.'

'Don't you think you ought to go over there and take a look?'

'Hang on, maybe we already did.' Without explaining what he had just said, Pohlhaus took a little notebook from his pocket and flipped through it until he came to the page he wanted. 'Is the address of that house 3323 North Michigan Street?'

I said, 'Yes,' and Philip said, 'How am I supposed to know?'

'It is?' Pohlhaus asked.

'Yes,' I said.

He looked at Philip. 'Your son and his friend called us on the seventh of June. They wanted to inform us of their suspicions that the Sherman Park Killer had been taking refuge in an abandoned residence at 3323 North Michigan.'

'There you are,' Philip said. 'That proves I'm right. Mark and that dummy were snooping around, pretending to be great detectives like your friend Pasmore. I should have known.' He looked as though he were going to spit on the floor.

'Did you know they called the police?'

'What, you think they'd tell me?' Here I got a flat, triumphant glare. 'That's why he was interested in the place. They must have seen someone in there.' He looked at Pohlhaus, whose impervious demeanor had not changed since Philip and I had come into the 'bullpen.' 'You guys checked it out, I'm sure.'

'We went over and had a look. The place was locked up. Had been for years.'

'You never got back in touch with my son?'

'He gave us a tip, we checked it out, and it went nowhere, like most of the tips we get from the public. We don't follow up unless we find something useful.'

'It went nowhere, huh? Is that what you thought after my son disappeared?'

'Mr Underhill, I am very sorry about your son, and we're doing everything we can to find him.'

'You sit here and say that to me. Didn't it occur to you that my son could have drawn attention to himself by his investigative efforts?'

'Not if our bad boy wasn't there,' Pohlhaus said.

My brother looked back at me. 'But that's

what all this garbage in the e-mails is about, isn't it? These crazy ideas, and feeling like he's in one of your books? He wants you to know he's playing detective.'

'He could be talking about something else,' I said.

'I certainly hope you'll let me in on whatever it is you have in mind.'

I glanced at Pohlhaus. 'It seems to me that you should go back to that house and give it a much closer inspection.'

'Another country heard from,' Pohlhaus said.

The day after the break-in, Mark took the photograph album with him when he returned to the empty house. He did not want to leave it at home. His father was getting weird enough to start searching his room, and the album would be impossible to explain. Best to stow the album in its original hiding place, where it would be safe from parental discovery. Also, he wanted to consult the photographs, to go over them many times, dredging for whatever information he could pick up; since he planned to spend most of the day in that house, he more or less had to bring the pictures with him.

Late that morning, he and Jimbo had worked out the day's schedule on their cell phones. They were both basically still in bed. Mark, having showered and dressed, was lying supine on top of the blanket while Jimbo was still prone between his sheets.

'Phase Two, I get it,' Jimbo said. 'Let's get together at the Sherman Diner around lunchtime and compare notes, okay?'

The Sherman Diner, two doors down from the former site of the old Beldame Oriental Theater, was an unofficial hangout for Quincy students. Jimbo's mentioning it meant that he wanted to swap information with Mark but felt like seeing other people afterward. At this time, all the students in the area were constantly gabbing on their cell phones about the local murderer.

Mark said, 'You go, if you want. I don't think I'm going to be very interested in food, and I don't feel like explaining myself to the kids who'll be there. We'll talk later.'

'When, like.'

'Whenever I'm done for the day, Jimbo. You have plenty to keep you busy.'

'I know.' Jimbo sounded a bit aggrieved.

He probably sensed that his best friend was holding out on him. Mark was indeed holding out on him, and he intended to keep on doing just that. While going through the house the day before, Mark had noticed many curiosities that he had not mentioned to Jimbo. In a sense, he had given Jimbo the key to understanding these oddities (if, that is, he was right about them, as he was almost certain he was), so technically perhaps he had withheld nothing. But Mark had known that Jimbo would not understand what to do with the key, or what it meant, or even that it was a key. The house, Mark had concluded, held an immense secret that had been *built into* it by the same madman who had added the ugly little room and created the giant's bed.

After getting off the phone with Jimbo, Mark went downstairs and prowled through the refrigerator. Mark's father shopped only when forced to do so, and he tended to buy unrelated items like bottles of olives, peanut brittle, pickles, lite mayonnaise, and Wonder Bread. On his first foray through the shelves, Mark thought he might have to go over to the 7-Eleven before getting down to business, but his next pass took in the sliding drawer, which yielded cheddar cheese, cream cheese, and some sliced salami that still looked edible. He made a salami and cheddar cheese sandwich with mayo and slid the gooey thing into a plastic bag. Then he put both the sandwich and the photograph album into a paper bag that already held a crowbar, a ripping hammer, and the Maglite, and went outside, rolling down the top of the bag to make it look smaller.

Out into the hot white sunlight he steps, our heroic boy, out into the oven the sun has made of these poor streets, moving like a jockey toward the winner's circle, like a conqueror toward his mistress's tent. For once in his life, he feels *locked in*, prepared for the first stage of whatever destiny will turn out to be destined for him. His fear – for he is actually filled with fear – seems to energize him, to increase his sense of purpose.

Such a manner invites rather than repels notice, and not long after he turns onto Michigan Street and begins his purposeful march toward the fourth house up the block, one Michigan Street resident inclines his head toward his living room window and immediately takes him in.

There's that good-looking Underhill kid, thinks Omar Hillyard, *on his way to the old Kalendar house again, I bet. Where's Sancho Panza, the little Irish bulldog who goes everywhere with him?*

God, what a handsome kid. Bold as brass! Look at him come cutting right up alongside that house . . . he's breaking in, for sure. Little demon! If I were the Irish bulldog, I'd be wildly in love with him.

I bet he finds more than he bargained for inside the Kalendar place.

Enjoying the sensation of light warming his arms and shoulders, Mark moved onto the grass. His legs carried him along, stride after rhythmic stride. If he wanted to, Mark could walk to the Rocky Mountains, jump up one side, down the other, and roll on until he was standing ankle-deep in the Pacific.

He plunged through the tall grasses and parched weeds, bounded up the broken wooden steps, and after the slightest hesitation, opened the back door. Here was the giant's house, and here was he, Mark the giant killer and his little bag of tricks. He had half-expected some form of resistance to his entrance, but his coming alone did not invoke the invisible spider webs and the emotional miasma of his first visit. He passed unimpeded through the door, and without bothering to check out the room containing the obscene bed, carried his laden paper bag up the stairs to the master bedroom.

An excellent carpenter had once lived in this house. The sloppiness of the addition amounted to a deliberate deception: anyone who saw it would be unlikely to guess at the extent of the adjustments its maker had made to the fabric of his house. The sheer monstrosity of the torture bed also had to be deliberate – the carpenter had built an object commensurate with the enormity of his feelings. However, when free to exercise the full extent of his skill, he had set in place a kind of builder's tour de force. This was what Mark had not revealed to his best friend.

Up in the bedroom, he took the crowbar from his bag and used it to pry away a section of the panel in the back of the closet. Plaster and bits of broken lathe rattled to the floor.

He had found the photograph album within a small, square, tablelike construction to the side of the vacancy he had just enlarged. The little table looked as though it had been built to hold a lamp, but Mark knew it had two very different purposes. It provided a perfect place to sit unseen and listen to what was going on in the house. It was a seat for a domestic spy and terrorist, and that it had been built at all demonstrated the extent of the builder's psychosis. By means of a secret, sliding catch, the little box also opened up to become a concealed vault or safe.

Mark stepped into the space he had widened and saw that his secret theory about the house was fact. His heart climbed into his throat, and for a couple of seconds, the sheer weight of his fear made it impossible for him to move forward or back. He wished he hadn't been right: the hiding places that had spooked Jimbo were bad enough, but this was much worse. This was a kind of demented savagery.

He was looking at another wall, separated from the back of the closet by perhaps three feet. After four or five feet, the gap between the inner and outer walls disappeared into darkness. This was a madman's house, and it resembled the workings of his mind, being riddled with unseen, unseeable passageways. Mark would have bet his right arm and leg that this one continued all the way to the other side of the house. He went back into the bedroom for the Maglite.

Once again in the closet, he passed through the opening and turned on the Maglite to send a beam of cool yellow light, wobbling with the trembling of his hand, down a narrow, rubble-strewn corridor. He turned around, and the same thing happened on the other side. His mouth was completely dry. There it was, exactly as he had supposed. Mark was looking at the first few yards of an invented corridor. It proved him right about the nature of the carpenter's modifications. To see if the other part of his theory was correct, he had only to make his way down the narrow passage.

Because what happened at the end of this sadistic secret hallway? Did it just run bang straight into the wall, or did it, as he hoped . . . The narrow beam of light struck a blind wall, and disappointment squeezed his heart. The flashlight drooped in this hand, and the trembling yellow circle of light wavered down over the lifeless plaster and slipped, like a waterfall down the face of a cliff, into a space beneath the level of the floor. Mark heard himself exhale. There was no reason for his having been right to have meant anything more than that he had been clever, but he stepped forward to see the first few steps of the descending staircase with nearly a sense of gratification. The house was a honeycomb.

The man who owned this house had lived alone – he had either killed his family or sent them away. In any case, children had died on the great wooden bed and in the small single bed on the second floor. Once he had eliminated his family, the man had enticed women into this house, or he'd pounced on them in the dark, tied them up, and carried them in. The doors would have been locked, and the windows would have been boarded up. The women had found themselves alone in a house they could not leave. Soon, they would have heard him moving through the house, and they would have tried to run from him, but he would have seemed to rove invisibly from room to room, following their every move. He was like a great spider speeding across his web, and he was capable of appearing anywhere. He liked peering through his peepholes and watching the trapped women. He liked killing them, too, but he loved tormenting them.

Mark felt weak with a mixture of exhilaration, terror, and nausea. He had thrust his way into the evil heart of this poisoned house, and what he saw there sickened him.

Instead of going down the steep stairs, Mark retraced his steps. This time, he saw the drifting tatters of the big spider webs he earlier had failed to notice. Real spider webs did not bother him.

As he had imagined, a second, matching staircase led to the ground floor on the other side of the house. He walked down in the darkness, training the flashlight on the descending steps. At the bottom of the stairs, the Maglite revealed two short corridors branching off to the front and back of the building. Each seemed to end at a door that fit flush into the wall. The monster had wanted to move invisibly around the ground floor of his house, too. What Mark had not expected to find was the yawning mouth of yet a third staircase. He and Jimbo had forgotten all about the basement. An unexpected shiver brushed his lungs with frost.

The basement – why did that sound like a colossally bad idea? You never knew what you might find in a basement, that was one reason.

In spite of these feelings, Mark began moving downstairs through veils of cobwebs. Down, down, down through layers of wickedness, layers of pain and torture, to the cloaca beneath. At the bottom of the steps, the flashlight cast a grainy yellow bull's-eye on a black panel that looked as though it had been pried off a coffin. There seemed to be no doorknob or handle. Experimentally, Mark extended his left arm and prodded the door with his fingers. As if on a great black hinge, the door instantly flew open.

He stepped through the opening and played the flashlight along what looked like a stockade fence. Then he turned around and shone the beam close to the opening in the wall, by reflex looking for a light switch. He found one immediately to the left of the concealed staircase, and before realizing that the power had been cut off years before, flipped it up.

Somewhere near the center of the basement, a single bulb responded, impossibly, and a yellow-gray haze brightened the air. A wave of freezing shock nearly knocked him down. Someone was using this house, someone who paid the electric bills. Mark felt like flattening himself against the wall. He could hear his labored breathing, and a tingle rippled across his face like cold lightning.

The bulb itself was invisible behind the 'stockade fence,' in reality a wall of halved logs, shaggy with bark, that ran the entire length of the basement. At intervals, doors had been sawed into the logs. Mark went to the first of the doors. A minute later, he was vomiting up the breakfast he had not eaten.

19

From Timothy Underhill's journal, 24 June 2003

'So what did he find?' I asked.

Jimbo looked profoundly uncomfortable. I had more or less kidnapped him from the comforts of his living room and driven him downtown to a restaurant that had been hot stuff back in the mid-sixties. The Fireside Lounge had good memories for me, and its steaks were as perfect as any I'd ever eaten in New York. Jimbo had never been there before, and he was unsure of how to respond to its old-fashioned midwestern luxe of dark lighting, red leather booths, and big wooden tables with chairs like thrones. It was a place where you could talk without being overheard, but my plan to get Jimbo loosened up had only half-worked. He was demolishing his steak, which he'd ordered well done and slathered in ketchup, but he still thought he was being disloyal to Mark by talking to me.

'No one's going to be mad at Mark,' I told Jimbo. 'All anybody wants to do is to find out where he is and get him back, if that's possible.'

'I wish we *could* get him back,' Jimbo said.

'Don't you think we can?'

Jimbo pushed a section of overdone meat into a puddle of ketchup.

'I don't want to rush you,' I said.

He nodded, and the slice of steak disappeared into his gullet. Like most teenage boys, Jimbo could eat like a Roman emperor three or four times a day.

'He told you he went down to the basement on this hidden staircase.'

'The third hidden staircase. They were all over that place. And . . .' He stopped talking and his face turned red.

'And what?'

'Nothing.'

I let it go, temporarily. 'What did he find in the basement, Jimbo?'

'It was in the little room, the first one. There were five or six of them, I guess.' Jimbo went inward for a moment, and his forehead wrinkled into creases. He really was a decent boy. 'You know what people used to put their stuff in when they went on boats? Those big boxes like suitcases, only they're not? With padlocks?'

'Steamer trunks,' I said.

'Yeah, a steamer trunk. There was one of those trunks shoved up against a wall. And there was a lock on it, only it was busted open. So he looked inside it. That thing, that trunk, it was full of hair.'

'Hair?'

'Women's hair, all cut off and stuck together. Blond hair, brown hair, red hair.'

'No wonder he threw up.'

Jimbo acted as though I had not spoken. 'Only, he couldn't figure out what it was at first, because it was clumped together. It looked like some kind of big dead animal. So he reached in and took out a clump. It was stuck together with brown stuff that flaked off when he touched it.'

'Oh,' I said.

'That's when he puked,' Jimbo said. 'When he realized he was holding the hair cut off a bunch of women. It was all stuck together with blood.'

'Good God.'

'The police went there, didn't they? Why did they leave that shit behind? They must have taken a ton of crap out of that house.'

'Good question,' I said, though I thought I knew the answer. In those days, there was no DNA evidence. Maybe they had bagged some of the hair and done what they could with it. The police had almost certainly broken the lock.

'You know who used to live there, don't you?' I asked.

Jimbo nodded. 'I do now.'

'From going around the neighborhood, knocking on doors.'

'That was my job. I took the outside, Mark had the inside.'

'And you wound up talking to Mr Hillyard.'

'He's spooky. He wouldn't let me come into his house until he had that accident, and then I saw why. Boo-ya! That's some shit in there, yo.'

'It's not as bad as it looks,' I said, having had my own glimpse into Omar Hillyard's living room. 'Let's go back to Mark.'

'Do I have to do this? You know what that Kalendar guy did, you don't need me to tell you about it.'

I told him that I had known nothing about all that until shortly before Mark's disappearance, when Tom Pasmore had filled me in on some of the details.

'They were related, him and Mark. Because his mother had the same name. I found out from Old Man Hillyard! When I told Mark, he couldn't ask his dad about it since he had hissy fits every time the subject came up. He went on the Internet. And man, was there stuff about Kalendar. These people, they, like, worship serial killers.'

'What did he find on-line about Kalendar?'

'There was a ton of stuff. Then he found a genealogy site put up by a guy in St Louis, and he clicked on it, and he saw a family tree.'

'He was on it, I suppose.'

'His whole family. That was how he found out his mom's dad and Joseph Kalendar's father were brothers. So the two of them, they were cousins. So to Joseph Kalendar, Mark was . . .'

'His first cousin, once removed. Let's get back to Mark inside the house. I don't suppose he stopped looking around after he threw up.'

I had already learned from Omar Hillyard that Mark had gone back to the Kalendar house on every one of the days before his disappearance.

'Yeah, he kept looking. He found a lot of weird stuff in the basement, like a big metal table and this, like, chute that came down from the first floor, and all these old bloodstains. But . . .'

Jimbo stabbed the top end of a French fry into the ketchup. His eyes met mine and slid away. About a third of the red-tipped French fry went into his mouth. He looked around, as if aimlessly, at the businessmen devouring steaks and the suburban ladies working on salads at the big polished tables. Across the room at the long bar, an old man in a wrinkled seersucker suit and a guy in a polo shirt were trying not to ogle the barmaid, who had not been born at the time of my first visits to the Fireside Lounge.

'You keep cutting yourself off at the pass,' I said.

The tip of his tongue slipped between his teeth and curled against his upper lip. His eyes went out of focus an instant before they met mine. 'Do what?'

'Stop yourself from saying something.'

He stared in the general direction of my chin.

'For Mark's sake, you should tell me everything you know. That's why we're here.'

Jimbo nodded, not very persuasively.

'You said he found a chute and a metal table. The Kalendar websites must have told you that he dismembered some of his victims before putting their bodies into his furnace. He ordered the operating table from a medical supply company.'

'We saw, yeah.'

'Then you started to tell me something else, and you cut yourself off at the pass.'

I watched him considering his options. He flicked a glance at me, and the skin over his cheekbones tightened, and I knew he had cleared an internal hurdle.

'Mark went into all those little rooms. There was an operating room, and another room had three or four hampers that were all empty. He thought they were where he put the women's clothes and the cops took it all away.'

'The police didn't search the place nearly as well as Mark did.'

'No, they never found the corridors.' Jimbo chewed the lump of steak in his mouth, swallowed, and took a deep breath. We were about to get closer to the center of what he was hiding from me.

'So he went back upstairs – the normal way. He found the top of the chute in the secret passage between the living room and the dining room. Yo, Kalendar dragged them through the walls and dumped them right onto the table. The first floor was a lot like the other one. From up there, you could take one of the stairs and get everywhere in that house. Mark said before Kalendar killed the women, he tortured them by letting them know he was there, even though they couldn't see him.' He made a sour face. 'In the living room, the opening to the secret corridor was in the coat closet under the regular stairs.' Jimbo hesitated, and now I know exactly why. He had to think about going further.

'A closet,' I said. 'Like the one in the bedroom.'

'Yeah. So he looked.'

He was going to tell me, but not until he absolutely had to. I pushed him to the next square. 'What did he see – another wooden box, like the one upstairs?'

He blinked. I'd gotten it right.

'What was in it? A diary?' I was looking entirely in the wrong direction.

'No, not a diary,' Jimbo mumbled.

A thought came to me. 'Could he open the box up?'

Jimbo nodded. He looked away from me, and his mouth momentarily twitched into something resembling a smile.

'Come on, Jimbo. Stop dancing around. What was in the box? A lot of bones? A skull?'

'Nothing like that.' He *was* smiling. I was so

wide of the mark, it amused him. 'When he opened the box, his paper bag was in it. With the photograph album and his hammer and his crowbar. And his dumb little Wonder Bread sandwich.'

On the other side of the dining room, the barmaid burst into silvery peals of laughter. We turned our heads to see the old man, shaking violently in either humor or agitation. At our distance, he looked like a trembling old skeleton in a suit.

Timothy Underhill, if put to the test, could rattle off, in order, the entire hierarchy of military rank from private to commander in chief. Almost any former soldier could do the same, but Tim's novels had sometimes referred to his experiences in Vietnam, and he had taken pains to get things right. His books also made reference to various police departments here and there, and although every police department in the world acknowledged itself as a paramilitary organization, the meaning of individual rankings varied from place to place. No common standard prevailed.

To take the most immediate case, Tim thought, consider Sergeant Franz Pohlhaus, the grim, authoritative figure at the head of the table around which his audience of six had placed itself. As their little party had proceeded through the station, police officers uniformed and not had visibly deferred to him. Sergeant Pohlhaus was in his early forties, and he wore his handsome blue suit like a supple variety of armor. His biceps filled his sleeves, and his collar met his neck like a tape. Tim supposed that Sergeant Pohlhaus spent a good deal of time at the gym. There were no windows in the room, and the air stank of cigarette smoke. Sergeant Pohlhaus transformed the shabby chamber into a command center.

'Let's go around the table and make sure we know each other's names.'

He looked at the couple nearest him on the left side of the table. A well-padded, pink-faced guy sitting next to a nervous blonde jumped as though he had been jabbed with a pin.

'Uh, we're Flip and Marty Auslander, Shane's parents,' he said. 'Nice to meet you all.'

'Bill Wilk. Trey's dad.'

'Hello, everybody. I'm Jennie Dell, Dewey's mother.'

Bill Wilk's boiled-egg eyes glared out from the close-shaven, bowling-ball head set atop his squat body. Jennie Dell hitched her chair a few more inches away from his.

'I'm Philip Underhill, Mark's father, and this is my brother, Tim. He's from out of town.'

'For starters, I don't think your brother belongs here,' said Wilk, 'but that's the sergeant's call. This was supposed to be just family members, though.'

'I am a family member,' Tim said.

Bill Wilk scowled at him for a moment, then swung his head on his nonexistent neck to glare at the Auslanders. 'One question: which one's Flip and which one's Marty?'

The pink face broke into an embarrassed smile. 'I'm Flip. Marty's my wife.'

'You two ought to switch names, in my opinion.'

Pohlhaus slapped the table with his palm. 'Mr Wilk, cease and desist!'

'I lost my son. What more can you do to me?'

The sergeant smiled at him. It was an extremely disconcerting smile, evoking bolts of lightning and screams of pain. 'Do you want to find out?'

Wilk seemed to lose an inch or two in height. 'Sorry, boss.'

'I want to remind you and everyone else at this table that we are here because of your sons.' The flat blue eyes moved to Tim. 'Or nephew, in your case.' Pohlhaus let everyone inhabit a moment of silence that seemed to increase his own gravity. 'And what I have to tell you represents our first significant break on this case. I wanted to share it with you before it is made public.'

Even Bill Wilk remained silent. Unconsciously, Jennie Dell took in a deep breath and held it.

'You will be pleased to learn that we have a new eyewitness, a Professor Ruth Bellinger, of Madison, Wisconsin. Professor Bellinger is in the Astronomy-Physics Department at the University of Wisconsin. Three weeks ago, Professor Bellinger was in town visiting her sister, and she happened to be seated on a bench near the fountain in Sherman Park when something caught her attention.'

'She saw him?' Marty Auslander leaned past her husband to peer at Pohlhaus. 'She saw the guy?'

'Three weeks ago, the guy hadn't even started yet,' said Bill Wilk.

'This will go faster if you let me proceed without further interruption,' said Pohlhaus. 'Any questions you might have, ask them when I'm done talking.'

Marty Auslander wilted back into her chair.

Pohlhaus swept his gaze around the table, including everyone. 'What caught Professor Bellinger's attention was a conversation between a teenage boy and an adult male, probably in his late thirties. According to the professor, he was an unusually large man, probably six-four or six-five, and solidly built, running to something like two hundred and thirty, two hundred and fifty pounds, black hair. For personal reasons, the professor is very sensitive to the presence of sexual predators. It seemed to her that something of that sort was going on here. The man seemed a little too ingratiating. He kept, in the professor's words, 'moving in on the boy,' and she thought the boy was resisting without wanting to appear rude.

'Professor Bellinger was beginning to wonder if her civic duty – again, I am quoting her – obliged her to interfere when an odd thing happened. The adult male visibly scanned the immediate area. The professor thought he was ascertaining if his actions might be observed. She said that he looked 'feral.' Now comes the part we really like. In the same second, Professor Bellinger stood up and the man spotted her. When she took a step forward, the man said something to the boy and walked off at a rapid rate.'

'She saw his face,' Flip said.

'So did the boy,' said Marty.

'Three weeks ago?' bellowed Bill Wilk. 'Why are we just hearing about this now?'

'Wait your turn, Mr Wilk.' Pohlhaus froze him with a stare. 'Professor Bellinger asked the boy if he knew the name of the man who had been talking to him. All he knew was that his first name was Ronnie, the boy said, and he had upgraded his sound system and wanted to get rid of his old equipment, along with a lot of CDs he didn't play anymore. His first question to the boy had been about the kind of music he liked, and after he heard the answer, he said, 'Great! My car's right over there, and my place is only five minutes away.' Ronnie seemed to want to give away all that stuff a little too much, the kid told her, and he'd been trying to figure out a way to get away from the guy when Ronnie spotted her getting off her bench.'

'Lucky boy,' said Flip Auslander.

'Have you talked to this boy?' his wife asked.

'I'd love to talk to him, but we don't know where he lives, and he never told Professor Bellinger his name.'

'Why did it take so long for her to come forward?' Philip asked.

'Astronomer-physicists don't pay much attention to what's on the news,' Pohlhaus said. 'And the Madison paper didn't give much space to the Sherman Park story. Professor Bellinger became aware of our situation here two days ago, and she called us instantly. The next day, she drove here from Madison. Most of yesterday afternoon, she spent working with our sketch artist. I gather that astronomers are unusually observant, on the whole. The professor remembered many, many more details than the conventional witness.'

Bill Wilk started to stay something, but Pohlhaus shushed him and went around the table to the door. He leaned out and said, 'Stafford, we're ready in here.'

When he turned around, he was holding a small stack of papers. He handed two of them to Philip Underhill, then went to the other side of the table to give papers to the Auslanders, Bill Wilk, and Jennie Dell. He still had two or three pages in his hand when he returned to the head of the table.

'So we are assuming that this is a fairly accurate portrait of Ronnie.' Like the rest of them, Pohlhaus stared down at the picture. 'We think Ronnie is a bad, bad man. We also think that he's been at work here at least five years.'

The man whose face had been drawn by the sketch artist might have been one of those actors like Murray Hamilton or Tim Matheson, actors who appear in one film or television program after another, and whose names you can never remember and probably never knew. His almost-handsome features suggested a salesman's instantaneous affability. That his eyes may have been a fraction of an inch too close together and his nose a millimeter too short only added to his approachability. His minor flaws made him look friendlier.

He probably had some kind of job that put him in contact with people. He was the guy standing next to you at the bar who says, 'So a rabbi, a priest, and a minister walk into a bar.' This man would have little trouble talking gullible teenage boys into his car.

'What do you mean, at least five years?' said Bill Wilk.

'Yes, what makes you say that?' asked Philip.

'When Professor Bellinger pushed our time frame backward, I started to look at other jurisdictions, just to see what turned up. Here's what I found.'

He pulled out the sheet at the bottom of his little stack of papers. It was a typed list.

'August 1998. James Thorn, a sixteen-year-old boy reported missing in Auburn.' Auburn was a little town just south of Millhaven. 'Thorn was a good student who until his disappearance had never so much as stayed out all night.'

He moved his finger down the list. 'Another sixteen-year-old boy, Luther Hardcastle, living with his grandparents in Footeville.' This was an old farming community, now a small town surrounded by suburbs, located about five minutes west of Millhaven. 'He goes missing in July of 1999 and is never seen again. According to his grandmother, Luther was mildly retarded and very obedient.' He looked up. 'Here's the interesting part. The last person reported to have seen Luther Hardcastle was a friend of his, Robert Whittle, who told an officer in Footeville that he ran into Luther on Main Street that afternoon and invited him to listen to some CDs at his house. Luther was a big Billy Joel fan. He told Whittle he'd come by later, but first he was going to Ronnie's house because Ronnie was going to give him a lot of Billy Joel CDs. From the way he said it, Whittle assumed that Ronnie was a friend of Luther's grandparents, or at least someone known to them.'

'Oh, my God,' said Jennie Dell.

'That happened in 1999, and you didn't know about it until today?' Flip Auslander seemed torn between rage and incredulity.

'You'd be amazed by how little communication goes on between departments in different jurisdictions. Anyhow, Luther Hardcastle's story put a lot of things in a different light. Joseph Lilly, for example. He was a seventeen-year-old Laurel Heights boy who disappeared in June of 2000. Then there is Barry Amato, fourteen, disappeared from South Millhaven in July 2001. So we have this pattern of one a year, always in the summer months, when the boys are on vacation and more likely to be outside at night. In 2002, the ante is upped a little. Last year, we had two teenage boys disappear from the Lake Park region, Scott Lebow and Justin Brothers, seventeen years old. Their parents thought that they ran away together, since the Lebow boy had just come out to his mother, and Justin's parents had known he was gay since he went through puberty. Both sets of parents tried to break up the friendship. We thought the boys ran off together, too, but now I believe we must reconsider.'

'The creep got 'em,' said Bill Wilk.

'Here's the situation as I see it,' Pohlhaus said. 'Ronnie has been living in or around this city for years. He has a decent job, and he owns his own house. He is single. He likes to consider himself heterosexual. This man is neat, orderly, and a considerate neighbor. Mainly, he keeps to himself. His neighbors have never been inside his house. Five years ago, something in him snapped, and he could no longer resist the very, very powerful temptation to act on his fantasies. James Thorn fell for his CDs story and wound up buried in a secret location, probably somewhere on Ronnie's property.

'Killing Thorn kept him satisfied for a year, after which time Luther Hardcastle fell into his lap. Luther's probably buried next to or on top of the Thorn boy. I want you to observe that Ronnie went to different parts of the Millhaven area to select his victims, and that he continued to do so until this summer. He keeps to the pattern of one murder a year. In the summer of 2000, he goes hunting again and captures Joseph Lilly. Another body in the backyard, or under his basement floor. In 2001, another body. In 2002, he strikes it rich and gets two victims. His appetite is getting stronger. This year, he bides his time until school gets out, but then loses control completely. He kills four boys in the space of about ten days. My point is, he's getting more and more reckless. Three weeks ago, he approached a boy in broad daylight, and the only thing that stopped him was that our professor scared him off. He laid low for a little while. Then he went into this frenzy.'

Sergeant Pohlhaus's words would have been unbearable but for the almost violently impassive authority with which he delivered them. No one at the table moved.

'This city needs a curfew,' Philip said. His voice sounded as if it were leaking through from the other side of a heavy internal door.

'A curfew is going to be set in place within the next couple of days. Persons sixteen years of age and younger will be required by law to be off the streets by ten P.M. We'll see how effective it is.'

'But what are you going to do?' asked Marty Auslander. 'Wait around hoping you'll catch him before he murders another boy?'

The remainder of the meeting degenerated into a contest of name-calling against stonewalling. As the Underhills left the building, Philip looked so drained and weary that Tim asked if he could drive him home.

'You got it,' Philip said, and tossed him the keys.

Bill Wilk, Jennie Dell, and the Auslanders separated from the brothers and from one another before they reached the sidewalk. All parties went toward their cars without a parting word or a gesture of farewell.

From Timothy Underhill's journal, 25 June 2003

Six o'clock. Without anything to do (maybe without the energy to think of something to do), I sit here on the ugly green sofa of my childhood, scribbling in this journal while pretending not to hear the sounds coming from upstairs. Philip is weeping. Ten minutes ago, he was sobbing, but now he has settled into a soft, steady weep, and I hear sighs instead of groans. I should probably be glad he can cry. Haven't

I been waiting for him to show some genuine emotion?

Now the two of us, along with everyone else in that room, have a name and a face to go with our fears and our grief. Ronnie, what an innocuous-looking fiend. I wonder what Joseph Kalendar looked like. I could Google him on my nephew's computer, but for some reason I feel reluctant to break into Mark's privacy like that. Of course the police felt no such compunction, and they searched his hard disk and his e-mail for clues to what might have happened to him. Since Philip says they returned it without comment, I assume they found nothing relevant.

Which means they ignored the e-mails Mark sent me. If this adventure of his made him feel as though he were inside one of my books, it couldn't be a conventional mystery about a murderer and an empty house. It had to be something about the house itself, and something that was happening to him there. Something he was undergoing. This 'something' both frightened and excited him in a way mere sleuthing could never do. What Jimbo tells me confirms this. Mark's paper bag traveled from the second floor of Kalendar's house to the ground floor through a series of secret corridors between the walls. Earlier, the photo album had traveled from the kitchen to a space hidden behind a panel in an upstairs closet. I don't see how you can avoid the conclusion that someone else was in the house with him.

Part Five

GARDENS AT IMPOSSIBLE DISTANCES

20

IN THE HEAT beneath the stairs, sweat drizzled from his hairline to his eyebrows. For a moment his vision blurred. Through a blanket of humidity, an indistinct hand groped forward in shadows toward a fuzzy shape that two seconds before had been a paper bag. Mark wiped his eyes. The fuzzy shape once again became that of a bag. Even before his fingers closed around its top, he knew it was the bag he had left in the closet upstairs.

He lifted it, and the hammer and the crowbar clunked together. Mark thumped the bag onto the floor. His stomach felt taut, and his eyes hurt. 'Come on,' he said. 'You can't be here.' He unrolled the top and thrust his hand deep inside. The crowbar fell against his wrist, and the hammer tilted into the side of the bag. Here was the album's quilted plastic binding, taking up most of the interior. Behind the album, his sandwich wilted in its smooth container.

Mark's mouth was dry. The little space behind the closet had shrunk around him, crushing him down. Awkwardly, he slid open the panel leading into the closet, trained the light on the inner side of the door, worked the latch, and pushed his way outside. He was sweating furiously.

At the bottom of the staircase, Mark took everything out of the bag and arranged its contents in front of him. The air was a mild gray, brightened by ambient window light to a dusty glow that illuminated the grime on his hands and the dark, embedded layer of grit on the cover of the album.

'How did you . . .'

Mark glanced to both sides, then up the length of the staircase.

Smoky, insubstantial walls: he felt all at once that altogether another world lay on the other side of these vaguenesses, and if he but pushed through the veils of gauze, he could reach that new and infinitely more desirable realm.

'Hello!'

Only silence answered.

'Is anyone here?'

No voice, no footfalls responded.

'I know you're here,' he called in a carrying voice. 'Show yourself!'

His heart thudded. While he was in the basement, someone had slipped out of hiding – this house offered a great many hiding places – gone to the master bedroom, picked up the laden bag, and with it moved through the house on either the visible staircase or a hidden one to the ground floor, where this someone worked the catch on the wooden safe, deposited in it the paper bag, closed the box back up, and thereafter disappeared back into the secret parts of the house. Yesterday, the same person had taken the photo album back to the upstairs closet.

It came to him that everything about the house had changed – changed without transition – and he had only just now registered the difference, which was enormous.

The monstrous snout-being that wished to frighten him away was not interested in playing games. That creature wanted to scare him off, so that it could rejoice in the poisoned atmosphere that it had created. Someone else, someone quick and stealthy as a panther, had shifted the bag from one closet to another. During every moment of Mark's progress through the house's hidden passages, this being had been aware of his exact location. Mark might as well have been blowing a bugle as he worked his way through the house.

Because most of what he knew about this silent someone else was simply that it was present in the house, he thought of it as 'the Presence.' Of course, Mark reminded himself, that the bag and its contents had been moved was all the proof he had of the Presence's existence. That seemed proof enough. The Presence had shifted Mark's things, believing that he would find them in their new hiding place, which meant oho o me-o my-o that it wanted him to know he wasn't alone.

The chill that had moved across his skin receded, and he became aware of the heat of his T-shirt sticking to his skin. Dust swirled in the dim light from the window. The sheets draped over the chairs and the sofa seemed to stir. When he rubbed his eyes and looked again, they hung still as shrouds. A white blur moved across the periphery of his vision. When he turned to look at it, it was gone.

Not long before dusk, the boys sat huddled together on the bench nearest the Sherman Park fountain, conversing intently under the eye of a police officer named Quentin Jester. Patrolman Jester strained to overhear the boys' conversation. The few words he caught were not helpful, nor did they alleviate his boredom, which had returned to him after banishment by a brief and unsettling incident. Along with four strategically placed policemen, plus a homeless man pushing a grocery cart full of empty bottles down a path, the boys were alone in the park.

What Patrolman Jester failed to mention in his report, or at any other opportunity (except for that presented by his fellow officer and academy classmate Louis Easley at the House of Ko-Reck-Shun), was that shortly before the homeless man entered the scene from the east, and first one boy, the red-haired one, then the other, Mark Underhill, entered from the north, a fourth stranger had excited his professional attention not only by his great size and unusual clothing but for another matter as well, one more difficult to put into words. 'He looked like back in the day, he could have played some college ball,' Jester said. 'One thing about this dude, he had some serious size on him. But he never played no ball. He never played anything. This guy never *played*, period, unless it was with a couple of cut-off heads. I got this feeling, like "We got trouble here," okay?'

Patrolman Jester explained that he had at no point seen the man's face. And although he had spent the previous hour and a half monitoring the movements of the few people who entered and left his assigned area of Sherman Park, Jester had failed to observe this gigantic man's appearance until, without any of the usual signals of arrival, the dude had simply come into being in front of him, straight out of nowhere, his back turned to the startled officer. Jester had been following the progress across the grass of a particularly fat and lively squirrel, a squirrel undaunted by the heat that had enervated most of his kind, and upon swinging his gaze back to the broad path and its empty benches, he'd discovered the presence of this massive character, decked out in a long black coat that dropped well past his knees. Huge legs, planted far apart; heavy black boots; massive head held high; and arms folded in front of him. He might have been carved out of half a ton of black marble.

'How could a water buffalo like that sneak up on you?' asked Patrolman Easley.

'I don't know, and I don't care,' Jester told his friend. 'All I knew was, this man is *there*, and he is my problem. Because you know he is a problem.'

'You and me, we haven't been out of the academy long enough to be able to smell the bad guys.'

'You'd know what I'm talking about if you were there. He's one bad mother, is what I'm saying, and there he is in front of me, and I have to deal with him.'

Louis Easley raised both his eyebrows and his beer glass, but he did not drink. 'So this is our man? Mr Sherman Park himself, in person?'

'That's what was going through my mind. I move up on him so I can at least get a look at his face. This rumbling noise is coming toward me from the boulevard entrance, and I look that way, and this red-haired kid is pumping along on a skateboard. When I look back, the big dude is gone. *Gone*, man. Like he fell straight down through a trap door.'

'You, you're some kind of police officer,' Easley told him.

'You wouldn't be laughing, you saw him, too,' Jester said.

A few seconds after Jimbo rolled to the bench and jumped off his board, the policeman who'd been standing on the other side of the walkway gave him a funny look and said, 'Buddy, while you were coming up this path, did you happen to notice a man standing right over here in this position?'

'I didn't see anyone but you,' Jimbo said.

'You had a good view of this area.'

'I guess.'

'Where was I standing when you first saw me?'

'Over there.' Jimbo pointed to a spot on the

edge of the walkway four feet south of the fountain. It was just about where another officer had shown him and Mark the photograph of Shane Auslander.

'And when I was over *there*, no one was over here?'

'Not until you got here.'

'Thank you,' said Officer Jester, retreating.

These guys are losing their minds, Jimbo said to himself.

When he first caught sight of Mark moving empty-handed from the bright sun of Sherman Boulevard into the wavering shade cast by tall lindens on the wide flags of the walkway, he felt a twinge of loss. This time, he had brought his skateboard and Mark had not, which was, he found, worse than the recognition that both of them had left their boards at home. It made him for a moment feel as though Mark had set off on a journey that left him waving from the dock. Mark drew closer, and the urgent expression on his face reminded Jimbo that he, too, had something incredible to announce, although he was not so sure he actually wanted to tell Mark what Mr Hillyard had revealed to him.

Mark suffered from no such scruple. His eyes blazing, he could barely restrain himself from running. Jimbo saw him take in the skateboard and on the spot dismiss it as an irrelevance. The swift, deepening ache this brought Jimbo almost immediately dwindled in the intensity of Mark's eager slide down onto the bench and the swooping tilt of his shieldlike face toward Jimbo's. He was wearing a black T-shirt and black jeans, and his face had a scrubbed, gleaming look. He smelled faintly of soap.

'You just take a shower?'

'You wouldn't believe how dirty I got,' Mark said. He was exulting. 'The bottom of the bathtub was all black.'

'I guess you found something.'

Mark's grin tightened, and his eyes narrowed. Jimbo could not decipher these signals. It looked to him as though what Mark had found was either unspeakably bad or outrageously good.

'How about you?'

'I've got some stuff, yeah, but you go first.'

Mark straightened up on the park bench, placed a hand over his mouth, and looked over his shoulder at Patrolman Jester. Patrolman Jester looked back at him, poker-faced. 'Well, that's a pretty amazing place. Whoever lived there last probably . . . Are you ready for this?'

'I know something about it already. Whoever lived there probably what?'

Another backward glance at Quentin Jester, who

went to visible pains to look elsewhere. 'Probably murdered a lot of people.'

Mark told Jimbo about the hidden corridors, and his exploration of the basement, his discovery of the trunk, and the stains soaked into the concrete floor. 'That's why nobody can stand to look at the place. Something terrible really did happen in there. Maybe he built that big wooden bed so he could torture them before he took them downstairs.'

'You couldn't fit a grown-up woman into those straps,' Jimbo said, knowing more than he was willing to say. He could not understand why Mark seemed to be in such a bubbly mood.

'If they were small, you could.' His all but hidden internal mirth, which would have been visible only to Jimbo and perhaps his father, flickered for a moment into view. 'And how about you, Sherlock. What's this information you said you had?'

Jimbo felt as though he had been pushed to the end of a diving board and ordered to jump. 'Most of the people on Michigan Street don't have a clue about the place. All they know is, some people in the neighborhood got together to keep it from looking like a slum, and they mow the grass on the sides and in front every two weeks. They have a kind of a list, and all these guys take turns. A couple of women told me their husbands hate the place. They hope it'll burn down one night. The

Rochenkos were both home. That was one of the only two places where I got asked why I wanted to know about the house.'

'Where was the other one? Ah. I bet I know. So what did you say?'

Jimbo made a face. 'I said I was thinking up a topic for a research paper I have to do next year. The Rochenkos told me to think about global warming. Mrs Rochenko said she had a bad feeling about 3323, and I shouldn't even look at it if I didn't have to.'

'I bet they don't look at it even when they're mowing the lawn.' Mark stared at Jimbo, and Jimbo braced himself. 'The other guy to ask why you were so curious was Old Man Hillyard, right?'

Jimbo nodded. 'Old Man Hillyard saw us sneaking around the back yesterday, and he saw you going there this morning.'

Alarm bloomed in Mark's eyes. 'He's not going to tell anybody, is he?'

'No, he's not like that. Old Man Hillyard is different from the way we always thought.' Jimbo paused. 'He's pretty off the wall.'

'What did you tell him?'

'Same thing. Research project.'

'Did he believe you?'

'He asked me if I thought he was an idiot. He said, even if high schools assigned research papers in summer, I was the kind of kid who'd put off doing it until the last week of August.'

Mark laughed. After a moment Jimbo laughed, too.

'Okay, okay. So I told him that we were just really interested in the place, that's all. And he said . . .'

'He said . . . ?'

'He said it was interesting that we were interested.'

Mark lifted his chin and opened his mouth just about wide enough to sip the air.

'It was especially interesting that *you* were interested in it.'

Mark's head tilted, and his eyebrows went up. Jimbo had to say it now. It was either that or make up some lie.

'I hope you're going to explain that to me.'

'Naturally, I asked him what he meant.' Jimbo paused again, searching for words.

Mark leaned forward. 'Well?'

Jimbo inhaled. 'The first part, you already know about. The man who lived in that house was a murderer.'

'No shit.'

'And the second part . . . is that he was probably related to your mom. Because they had the same last name. Before your mom married your dad.' Puzzled by the growing recognition visible in his friend's face, Jimbo said, 'Calendar? Like the months and the days, a calendar?'

'Kalendar,' Mark said. He spelled it out for Jimbo. 'You saw it at the funeral home, remember?'

'I guess I didn't really notice. But Old Man Hillyard said the murderer's name was Joseph Kalendar, and he didn't even know it was your mom's maiden name until he went to your house and saw it on those cards. With the sunset and the Lord's Prayer?'

'And?'

'And he was surprised, because Kalendar was such a bad guy. He killed all those women, and he murdered his own son. Old Man Hillyard knew these people!'

'Wow,' Mark said.

'I thought you were going to be upset. But you almost look like you're happy to hear about Kalendar.'

'Of course I'm happy. You just told me what I needed to know. The guy's name, and what he did. He and Mom were related. Maybe he was her brother!'

He gave Jimbo a look of pure wildness, his eyes bulging in their sockets. 'Joseph Kalendar is the Dark Man. And he's the reason my mom killed herself.'

'The Dark Man?'

'The man whose back is always turned. He's the guy I saw at the top of Michigan Street.'

'What? You think he's a ghost?'

Mark shook his head. 'I think he's more like what some people *call* a ghost.' He thought for a moment. 'What happened to Joseph Kalendar?'

'He was sent to a mental hospital, and another inmate killed him.'

'I bet we can find out all about him on the Internet.'

Jimbo nodded, then thought of something else. 'What do you mean, what some people call a ghost?'

Mark laughed and shook his head. 'I mean, like – something left behind. Something real enough so sometimes you can see it.'

'*I* can't see it,' Jimbo said. 'I mean, I couldn't. That day in your kitchen, I didn't see anyone standing with his back to the door.'

'You saw him two nights earlier, and you were so scared you fainted. He was what was left behind of Joseph Kalendar. Maybe I see him more often than you do because I'm related to him. And maybe this Sherman Park Killer is stirring him up.'

'Stuff like that doesn't happen. Parts of people aren't *left behind*. The only person who sees dead people is Haley Joely Osmond, or whatever his name is.'

'Joel Haley Osmond,' Mark said, thinking that did not sound quite right, either. 'Only, you're wrong. A lot of people see dead people – the part left behind. Don't you think? A friend of yours dies, and one day you're walking down the street and you look in a window and just for a second you see him in there. The next day, maybe you see him getting on a bus, or walking across a bridge. That's the part of him that's left behind.'

'Yeah, left behind in you.'

'In you, right. That's what I'm talking about.'

'But you never heard of this guy.'

'My mother knew all about him. She must have worried about him, she must have been afraid of him. This guy had to be a big deal in my mother's life! Don't you think some of that could have passed into me?'

'You're crazy,' Jimbo said.

'No, I'm not. Parents pass things on. Things they have no idea they're passing on, those things especially they pass on to their children.'

As if to put an end to this conversation, Mark stood up and glanced around. A few adults were hurrying homeward through the park. Patrolman Jester stared thoughtfully at an empty place on the other side of the walkway. Together, the boys noticed that the air had begun to darken.

Jimbo stood up, too, looking a bit belligerent. 'That doesn't explain how you can see Joseph Kalendar, who's been dead for twenty-five years!'

Mark and Jimbo walked, their pace slower than usual, down the path to Sherman Boulevard.

'I don't think I actually saw Joseph Kalendar. I think I saw the Dark Man, the part that's left of Joseph Kalendar. Like I said before, maybe the Sherman Park Killer woke him up, and the only person he's visible to is me.'

'Well, maybe the Dark Man is the Sherman Park Killer,' Jimbo said, with the air of one throwing out a random speculation.

'I think it's the other way around, that the Sherman Park Killer is the Dark Man.'

'What's the difference?'

'There's a real killer out there, that's the difference. The Dark Man can't *take* people – he doesn't even have a face. The Sherman Park guy can kill you.'

They strolled across Sherman Boulevard, as usual paying no attention to the traffic lights.

'I wouldn't be surprised if other people saw the Dark Man here and there, you know, in little flashes. Things are getting a little weird in this part of town.'

'You're getting a little weird,' Jimbo said. 'It's

like finding out about this Kalendar, this psycho, cheered you up!' He glanced at Mark's face. 'It did, didn't it? You're all, like, electrified about something.'

'Well,' Mark said.

'A trunk full of hair and a couple of secret passages wouldn't do this to you.'

'Well,' Mark said again, and told Jimbo about finding the paper bag in the downstairs closet after leaving it upstairs. 'Don't you see what happened?'

Jimbo honestly had no idea.

'Somebody moved my bag.' Now Mark's mirth shone from his eyes.

'Kalendar? The Dark Man?'

Mark shook his head. 'This person is playing with me, Jimbo. She's saying, *I'm here, why can't you see me*?'

'It's a she?'

'I think it's that girl, the one I sorta saw through the window that morning. Even back then, I had the feeling she was deliberately showing herself. And this morning, I thought I saw –'

Jimbo stopped moving, then shook his head and resumed walking along the west side of Sherman Boulevard toward West Burleigh Street.

'You just remembered something,' Mark said.

'No, it wasn't anything.'

Mark continued to stare at him.

'When we were in the house together? I thought something moved. I saw this movement, this blur.'

'No kidding,' Mark said. 'There you are. See?'

'Not really.'

'Everything's different in there now. Everything *feels* different.'

Jimbo sighed. 'What do you want me to do tomorrow?'

'See if Old Man Hillyard knows anything about a girl or a young woman.'

'A lot of women died there, did you forget that?'

'Ask anyhow.'

'Kalendar didn't have any daughters.'

'Just ask, okay?'

'If you promise to tell me what happens if she's really there and you meet her.'

'Let's go to your house.'

'Now what do you want to do?'

'Now,' Mark said, 'we are going to Google Joseph Kalendar.'

Patrolman Quentin Jester moved to the far side of an immense clump of dying azaleas growing a few feet from the right side of the walkway. He had already walked once around the periphery of the azaleas, and he felt both discouraged and irritated with himself. It was too hot for a man to spend his working day standing out in the full glare of the sun, waiting for a villain who was never going to show his face. In all that heat and glare, even a trained officer could lose his bearings. Patrolman Jester had let his senses persuade him that he had seen that very same massive, black-haired character dressed in the heavy coat and boots following along behind the red-haired kid and his friend. His professional instincts had come into play, and he'd set off down the big flagstones in pursuit of the mystery man; whereupon the said mystery man peeled off the walkway and stepped behind the long bunch of azaleas. Whereupon, for the second time that day, said mystery man upped and vanished from human view, 'like,' as Patrolman Jester's grandfather used to say, 'the unclean spirit at sparrow fart and cockerel's cry.' Quentin Jester might speak of this enigma to his friend Louis Easley after a couple of beers at the House of Ko-Reck-Shun, but he was never going to put it in a report.

'Yo, ever see one like that before?'

'One what?

'One of those.' Jimbo pointed back across Sherman Boulevard, where eight or nine cars lined up at parking meters stood baking in the sun. Near the center of the row was a red Chevrolet pickup truck, which Mark supposed was the subject of Jimbo's question.

'Yes, odd as it may seem, I have seen a red pickup before.'

Jimbo was shaking his head vehemently and grinning. He was in a good mood, Mark thought, because he had been let off the hook in regard to Joseph Kalendar's house.

'Okay, it's shiny,' he said. 'In fact, it's really shiny. It's the cleanest, brightest pickup I've ever seen. I'd eat a fried egg off its hood.'

'Can't you see?' Jimbo asked. 'It's the only pickup in the world with . . . with . . .'

'Oh,' Mark said, having seen. 'Smoked windows.'

'*Pimp* windows, man. With windows like that, I bet you can hardly see a thing.'

'What kind of guy owns that truck?'

'A rich guy,' Jimbo said. 'That thing never leaves the garage. It's like a toy to the guy who owns it.'

The boys were walking slowly along Sherman Boulevard, watching the truck across the street as they drew parallel to it. 'It's some rich kid,' Mark said. 'Some twenty-year-old guy who lives in his parents' gigantic house on Eastern Shore Drive and who will never, for as long as he lives, ever have to get his hands dirty or work outside and get sweaty.'

'Unlike us,' Jimbo said. 'The sons of the soil.'

Both of them burst into laughter. When they had gone past the pickup truck, what had been a pleasant diversion ceased to exist, and they forgot all about it.

They reached the front of the Sherman Diner, and Jimbo stopped walking and looked in through its long window.

'I'll catch up with you later, okay? I kind of arranged to meet someone here for a Coke or something.'

'I don't believe you,' Mark said, then remembered Jimbo suggesting that they drop in at the diner the day before. 'Who is it?'

'Lee Arlington,' Jimbo said, too quickly.

Lee Arlington was an extremely pretty girl in their class. She was reported to be prone to moods, and she wrote poetry in a big journal she carried everywhere with her in her backpack.

'Come on in, too,' Jimbo said. 'She's with Chloe Manners, and Chloe always liked you.'

Mark wavered. He wanted to go into the diner and see what the girls were talking about and what was on their minds, but he also wanted to see if he could find a full-frontal picture of Joseph Kalendar's face, as well as the details of his crimes.

'You go, have a good time,' he said. 'I want to get some info on this psycho cousin of mine. Come over when you're through here.'

'Half an hour,' Jimbo said. 'I'll be there.'

At the end of the block, Mark remembered the red pickup and glanced back to get another look at it. Jimbo was right: guys who rode around in pickups generally didn't go for tinted windows. Back down the street, a little sky-blue Datsun was reversing into the empty space where the pickup had been. Too bad, he thought, but no major loss – he just wished he could have gotten a glimpse of the lucky son-of-a-bitch kid who owned that truck. Mark swung his head around to look forward again, and bright, gleaming red flashed in the periphery of his vision. He looked to his left and discovered that while he'd been strategizing with Jimbo, the red pickup had done a U-turn and come far enough down his side of the street to arrive at a point immediately behind him. He waited for it to move past him, but it did not.

Curious, he looked over his shoulder again. The dark gray-green panel of the pickup's windshield reflected gold sunlight straight into his eyes. Blinking, Mark shaded his eyes with one hand. All he could see were the windshield and the windows; whatever was inside the cab was invisible. The truck still did not move past him, but kept inching along at exactly his pace.

Mark wished he had gone into the Sherman Diner with Jimbo.

Then he told himself not to worry. He was being silly. The guy hidden behind the slick windshield was a kid from Eastern Shore Drive who had managed to get lost on the decidedly ungridlike streets of the former Pigtown. Getting lost in the Sherman Park area wasn't difficult: Uncle Tim, who had grown up here, had told him that he'd had trouble finding Superior Street on his first day back. The pickup's driver was going to roll down the passenger window and ask for directions. Mark turned around and began walking backward, waiting to be questioned.

The pickup simply trundled along at two, three miles an hour, hanging back at the unvarying distance of eight or nine feet. Seen close up, the vehicle looked amazingly clean and well polished. The curves of the hood and the fenders appeared almost molten. Along the side and the door panel, the red seemed lacquered in layer after layer, so that for all the brilliance of its surface Mark could look down and down, deeper and deeper, as if into a red pool. Completely free of dirt and pebbles, the tires shone a clear, liquid black. Mark had the feeling that this truck had never been driven in the rain, that it had never seen mud or snow, had never been entrusted to a valet or a public parking lot. It was like someone's pet cougar that, after having been pampered and brushed every day of its life, was now at last permitted to explore the outer world. It seemed to Mark like a living thing – a large, dangerous living thing, a real *entity*.

He was letting himself get spooked. Those tinted windows were doing it to him, he knew. If he were able to see the driver, everything about the situation would feel different.

Mark turned his back on the pickup and decided to act as though nothing unusual was going on. In a little while, the truck would drive past him. It had to. And if it did not, he would lose it when he turned onto West Auer, because the red pickup would have no reason to follow him when he left Sherman Boulevard. He moved along the pavement, wondering if anyone in the vicinity thought it was strange that a vehicle should follow along behind a teenage boy, keeping pace as he proceeded down the street. In fact, that was exactly the sort of thing the Sherman Park Killer might do.

The corner of West Auer lay fifteen yards ahead. Mark wanted to look back over his shoulder, but he thought it best to ignore the pickup. In a second, in a couple of seconds, it would pick up speed and move off down Sherman. He quickened his pace, not by much, and the truck clung to him like a shark to its pilot fish. Mark moved along a little faster, but he was still just walking, not jogging or running. He was moving a little faster than usual, that was all. He thought someone watching him would get no special impression of haste.

Ten feet from the corner of West Auer, the pickup moved ahead, advancing into Mark's field of vision, and pulled up level with him. He flicked a glance at it and kept moving. This was getting scary, but he forced himself to keep his pace steady. Out of the side of his eye he checked to see if the passenger window was being lowered. It was not, which helped. Maybe the driver was just trying to frighten him – that almost made sense, if the driver were a rich, bored twenty-year-old from Eastern Shore Drive or Old Point Harbor. Someone like that would get a kick out of throwing a scare into a high school kid from Pigtown.

Pigtown . . . that was a joke, right? Who could take a place seriously if it had a name like Pigtown?

The pickup moved along at exactly his speed. The window did not roll down, but Mark was certain that the driver was looking at him. He could practically feel the driver's gaze on his body. Then he thought he *could* feel it. His stomach turned cold.

He came to Auer and executed a neat, military right-face, hoping to make his getaway before the guy in the pickup realized he was gone. To his dismay, he instantly heard the sound of tires turning in behind him. Mark glanced sideways and saw the hood of the pickup gliding alongside him. When the cab came into view, the passenger window was winding down. *No, no*, he said to himself, *I really don't think I want to have a conversation with you*. Heart pounding, Mark burst into a sprint, thinking that he would run between the houses and make it home through the alley.

The pickup shot ahead and squealed to a halt a little way down the block. The passenger door cracked open. Mark stopped running, unsure of what to do. The driver was not going to come running after him, that was obvious: he wanted to sit behind the wheel and say something to Mark. He had something on his mind, and he wanted to share it. Mark did not want to hear whatever the man had to say. He took a step backward.

The passenger door swung completely open, revealing the dark interior of the pickup's cab and the huddled, massive shape behind the wheel. It was like looking into the back of a cave. The driver was a big, big man, wrapped in a coat that fell around him like a blanket or an opera cape. A squashy, wide-brimmed hat covered his head. He looked mountainous. A big hand fumbled out of the folds of cloth and waved Mark forward.

'No need to be frightened,' said a low, soft voice. 'Aren't you Mark Underhill? I realize this looks a little funny, but I want to pass on a message to your father. It's about your mother.'

'Talk to my father yourself,' Mark said. The man behind the wheel seemed shapeless and without a face – a huge pile of flesh equipped with a hand and a soft voice.

'I'm afraid I don't know him. Come a little closer, will you?'

Somewhere, a door slammed. The shapeless man behind the wheel leaned forward and gestured. Mark looked in the direction of the sound and saw, stepping out onto a porch one house up, the University of Michigan football alum who had called him and Jimbo 'youngbloods.' The pickup had swerved into the curb directly in front of this man's house.

'Pardon me,' the man shouted, 'but could anybody use a little help down there?'

Before Mark could answer, the man slouched behind the wheel had thrust out his arm, yanked his door shut, and spun the gleaming pickup backward into the middle of West Auer. In an instant, the pickup was speeding toward the next intersection; a second later, it skittered around the corner and was gone.

'Holy shit, what was *that*?' the man said. 'Are you okay?'

'That guy said he wanted to tell me something about my mother.'

'No shit.' The man stared at him for a second. 'He knew your name?'

'Yes.'

The man shook his head. 'I didn't get his license number. Did you?'

'No,' Mark said.

'Well, I guess that's that,' the man said. 'But you should probably stay away from red pickup trucks for a while. I'll call the police, tell them what I saw. Just in case.'

Still vibrating, Mark went home to look up Joseph Kalendar on the Internet.

This is how the Sherman Park murders, which were more numerous than even Sergeant Pohlhaus had suspected, were solved. After a wretched lunch with his brother, Timothy Underhill decided to drive around to see Tom Pasmore before returning to his room at the Pforzheimer. Tom welcomed him warmly, poured out a measure of whiskey, and led him to his beautiful old leather sofas and the shelves of sound equipment. For old times' sake, he put on a CD of Glenroy Breakstone's greatest record, *Blue Rose*.

Tom asked, 'Have the police come up with anything new concerning your nephew's disappearance?'

'No,' Tim said. 'But today I discovered that he spent a lot of time fooling around in Joseph Kalendar's old house.'

'Do you think that might be relevant?'

'I'm sure it is,' Tim said. 'Sergeant Pohlhaus said he'd look into it, but I had the impression he was just humoring me.'

'He must like you,' Tom said. 'Sergeant Pohlhaus doesn't have a reputation for humoring people. It might be interesting to learn who owns that house. Who does, do you know?'

'I don't think anyone owns it.'

'Oh, somebody does, you can count on that. Why don't I go upstairs and snoop around on my computer? It's 3323 North Michigan Street, isn't it?'

Tim nodded.

'This won't take more than a couple of minutes.'

And that is how the Sherman Park murders were solved: by a single question and a few keystrokes.

21

From Timothy Underhill's journal, 26 June 2003

This is one of the most remarkable days I've ever lived through, and that includes Vietnam. In the morning, Jimbo finally told me Mark's secret, then Omar Hillyard told me the secret of the secret. In the afternoon, I 'assisted' in the arrest, as the police say, of the Sherman Park Killer. One other remarkable event occurred, and it has kept my spirits afloat ever since. Franz Pohlhaus and Philip believe that the mystery of Mark's disappearance has been almost completely resolved, the final certainty to come with the discovery of his body. (Before that can happen, Ronnie Lloyd-Jones is going to have to admit his guilt and get around to telling Pohlhaus where he buried the rest of the bodies. As of this evening, he shows no interest in doing either.) I don't agree with them, but for once I'm keeping my opinion to myself. And even if Mark's body turns up in Ronnie Lloyd-Jones's backyard, his body is not all that is left of him. Mark said something to Jimbo about the part of Joseph Kalendar that was left behind, and that gives me a way to say what I know: the part of Mark Underhill that was left behind is with *her*.

Jimbo tried to run when he saw me walking up, but the combination of conscience and his mother brought him back. Margo told me he was somewhere in the house, and the slamming of the screen door brought us into the kitchen. I followed her out into the backyard. Bustling down the alley, Jimbo looked over his shoulder and knew instantly that he had been busted. He stopped moving and let his shoulders slump.

'I don't know what's the matter with you,' his mother said.

'Aw, I don't want to talk about Mark anymore.'

'You get back here right now, young man.'

'I wish he'd of stayed in New York,' Jimbo

muttered, already moping back up the alley and into the yard.

'You are going to tell Mr Underhill everything you know,' Margo said. 'Don't you want to help Mark?'

'Help him do what?'

Margo thrust out a handsome arm and pushed him into the house. 'Don't you talk back to me. Don't you remember that those boys *died*?'

Jimbo slouched into the living room and collapsed onto the sofa like a broken marionette. 'Okay, I give up. What do you want to know?'

I told him that he knew what I wanted to know – everything Mark had told him about his experiences in the Kalendar house.

His eyes flared.

'What were you hiding from me in the restaurant, Jimbo?'

He squirmed. 'It's not important.'

'Why isn't it important, Jimbo?'

'Because Mark lied to me,' he said, revealing the core of his reluctance. He felt wounded by what he saw as his friend's mendacity while wishing to keep it out of sight. This was intensely loyal, and in spite of what Philip had said, I thought Mark had been lucky to have had such a friend.

‘Tell me about the lie, then. It won’t make me think any less of my nephew.’

Jimbo stared down into his lap for so long I thought he might have fallen asleep. When he finally spoke, he did not look up until he had come almost to the end of what he had to say.

‘He said he could sort of feel that someone else was in the house with him. He called it the Presence. And he said it was a girl. And he was going to go back there every day and wait for her to show herself.

‘The next day he said he could hear her moving around behind the walls. Hiding from him. Running away whenever he got close. The day after that, according to him, it finally happened. He said she came out through the secret door under the stairs and walked right up to where he was waiting. She took his hand, he said. Her name was Lucy Cleveland, and she was nineteen years old. According to Mark, she was the most totally beautiful girl he’d ever seen. He said it almost hurt to look at her, she was so beautiful.

‘What she said was, she was hiding from her father. Her father did terrible things to her, so she ran away. This was a long time ago. Ever since, she hid out in that house and a few other empty houses in this part of town. Only she called it Pigtown, the way people used to.'

On his third visit after their initial meeting, Mark and Lucy Cleveland had sex together – made love. Jimbo used the word 'screwed.' They screwed – made love – on the giant's bed, Mark told Jimbo. He added that Lucy Cleveland had a way of finding the comfortable places on that ugly bed, and if he positioned himself just as she advised, he could have been lying on his own bed at home.

The second time they made love, Lucy Cleveland told him to put one of his wrists into one of the cuffs on the bed, and when he had done so she fastened the second cuff on her own wrist. Mark said that was fantastic, Jimbo told me. Being bound to the bed that way made the sex even more incredible. Mark said that it was like being carried away on the back of some huge bird, or being swept along by a great river.

'He wanted to spend the whole night with her,' Jimbo said, 'but he knew his father would go crazy if he did. "Tell your dad you're staying with me," I said. "He'll never check." So that's what he did. And the next morning he came over here from her house and my mom made us pancakes. When she left us alone, I asked him if he was bringing Lucy food, and he said, "She doesn't eat."

'"Doesn't eat"? I asked. "Everybody has to eat." "Everybody except her," Mark said. "Don't you get it? She was *left behind*."

'It's all such crap. Last year, Mark told me he had sex with this really hot girl in our class, Molly Witt? Later, he confessed he made it all up. If he did it once, he could do it again. And this time it was a girl I didn't know, and she was older. But he was so happy! He was completely in love with this Lucy Cleveland. He was sort of glowing.'

Jimbo was wild with curiosity. To accept the existence of Lucy Cleveland, he would have to see her, and he was hungry to know if she was as beautiful as Mark claimed. Jimbo knew instinctively that he would not be welcome in the house if Lucy was there. Could she leave the house? Of course she could leave the house, Mark said. Then take her somewhere where I can meet her, or at least see her, Jimbo said. Mark insisted that Lucy Cleveland would refuse to meet him; in fact, she had told Mark that she wanted to know no one in the world but him. Another possibility occurred to Jimbo. He asked Mark to take Lucy Cleveland out for a walk. Unobtrusively, he would appear on the opposite side of the street, say nothing, and melt away again.

But Lucy was afraid to go outside, and when she did leave the house, it was always very late at night. She feared being seen by her father.

They arranged a compromise that satisfied both of them. At noon, Mark would try to get Lucy Cleveland into the living room. He would tell her something about Mr Hillyard or the Rochenkos, and she would come near him, which meant near the window, to look at the place he was talking about. Across the street, Jimbo would do his best to conceal himself somewhere that allowed him a good view of the front window.

'I got there about ten to twelve,' Jimbo told me. 'I got up beside Old Man Hillyard's porch and sort of hunkered down to wait. Old Man Hillyard takes a nap right around then, I knew, and Skip was so used to me by then he didn't pay me any attention at all. A couple of minutes later, I could just barely make out Mark moving around way at the back of the room. He vanished, and he came back again. It looked like he was talking to someone. I assumed he was trying to get Lucy Cleveland to come into the room and look out the window. I really felt relieved. If he was talking to her, then she was there.

'Anyhow, at just about noon on the dot, Mark

came across the room and up to the window. He was talking, but no one was with him. Mark gets this big grin on his face, and he's talking, and he's looking next to him, and waving his hands around, and he looks really happy. Only there isn't anybody standing beside him! This stupid charade goes on for a minute or two, and Mark turns away from the window. Before he disappears again, he looks over his shoulder and gives me a thumbs-up.'

Jimbo at last looked up at me. I saw anger and pain stamped into his good-natured face. 'I pulled out my cell phone and called him, but his was turned off. So I left him this pissed-off message. When he finally did call me back, I was still angry. "Why did you wait so long to call me back?" I said. He said, "I was busy with Lucy." "You're a liar," I said, and he said, "She told me you'd say that." "Say what?" I asked. "That I was lying to you. You can't see her, that's all, not unless she wants you to see her." I told him that was the biggest bunch of bullshit I ever heard and he said no, no, Lucy Cleveland wasn't an ordinary person. "I guess not," I said, and I hung up on him.'

And that night, which was the night before Mark's disappearance, he went to Jimbo's house to try to explain – to give him his story. Lucy

Cleveland *wasn't* an ordinary person, he said. He wasn't really sure what she was. But she had been waiting for him; he had called her into being. All Mark really knew was that Lucy Cleveland was everything to him, and vice versa.

Jimbo couldn't stand listening to this stuff. He yelled at Mark. Mark just wanted him to think he was having sex with a gorgeous nineteen-year-old girl. It was like Molly Witt all over again, only worse, because now he was saying his sex partner could make herself *invisible*! He couldn't dream up a more obvious lie if he worked at it.

Mark said he was sorry Jimbo thought that way, and went back home.

By the next morning, Jimbo regretted yelling at his friend. He'd had a bad night's sleep, and he got out of bed long before the usual hour. After an agreeably surprised Margo had scrambled a couple of eggs for him, he went back to his room and called Mark.

'Good, you decided we're still friends,' Mark said.

'I'm sorry I yelled at you. What do you want to do today?'

'I'm spending most of the day with Lucy Cleveland,' Mark said. 'Sorry. I forgot, you don't think she's real.'

'She's *not* real!' Jimbo shouted, and managed to bring himself back under control. 'All right, let's do it your way. Are you going to spend the entire day hooking up with your imaginary friend, or just part of it?'

'How about we meet around six-thirty at your house?' Mark said.

'If you think you can tear yourself away.'

For the rest of the day, Jimbo wavered between anger and a puzzled variety of forgiveness. He had the idea that Mark's lie had been caused, in some way he did not really grasp, by his mother's suicide. Maybe he was using fantasy to replace her; maybe he was so far gone he believed his own fantasy. Once again Jimbo found himself thinking that it was important for him to take care of Mark, insofar as Mark would permit it. Shortly after Mark turned up at his back door, which was closer to seven o'clock than six-thirty, it became apparent that Mark would allow him only a very little caretaking.

But the first thing Jimbo noticed when he answered his friend's knock was the blissfulness that shone in his face, and the almost alarming degree of contentment and relaxation radiating from him. The second thing he noticed was that if Mark Underhill appeared to be the happiest young man on the face of the earth, his happiness had come at a price. Mark looked subtly older to him, somehow more defined than ever before, and so exhausted he could have fallen asleep leaning against the door.

'How's Lucy Cleveland?' Jimbo asked, unable to keep from sounding sarcastic. But even as he registered his lack of belief in that invisible young woman, he felt jealousy moving through his system. Jimbo would have done anything to know that bliss, to have earned that spectacular exhaustion.

'Lucy Cleveland is extraordinary. Are you going to let me in?'

Jimbo backed away, and Mark entered. Margo Monaghan was out shopping for groceries, so the boys went into the living room, where Mark fell onto the sofa. He drew up his knees and curled around them as comfortably as a cat.

'Was this the last time you saw him?' I asked Jimbo.

He nodded.

'What kind of mood did he seem to be in? Besides happy, I mean. Was there anything more?'

'Yeah. I thought he looked kind of . . . I don't know what the word is. Like he couldn't make up his mind about what he was going to do next. "So how do you feel?" I asked him.

'"Tired, but happy." He uncurled and stretched out. He said, "You'd think I'd be able to sleep at night, but when I get on the bed all I can do is think about her, and I get so excited it's impossible to fall asleep." Then he stared up at the ceiling for a little while. Then he said, "I have to think about something. I came here to think, but I can't really talk about it."

'I said, "Thanks a lot," and he said that Lucy Cleveland had asked him to do something.'

Mark refused to tell Jimbo what Lucy wanted him to do but he had – as do I – the feeling that it would have been on her behalf. According to Jimbo, he refused to say any more, except that he was thinking about the choice she had given him. Jimbo wondered if he was deliberating whether or not to tell him the truth, that he had invented Lucy Cleveland to impress his friend. But when Mark spoke, it was to another purpose entirely.

He chuckled, and Jimbo said, 'Yo, is something funny?'

'I was just remembering something,' Mark said.

'This better be good.'

'When I was sitting in the living room over there, waiting for her to show herself – and I didn't know anything about her then, I didn't even know her name. Back then, she was just the Presence. All I knew was, she was in the house with me, and I knew she was getting closer. I'm sitting on the bottom of the staircase, and all my stupid shit is laid out in front of me. The hammer, the flashlight, that stuff. And I began to smell something really good.'

Mark sensed, knew, understood that the sudden arrival of this delicious odor meant that the presence in the house was on the verge of showing herself to him.

Mark went on: 'I just couldn't believe that I didn't recognize the smell. It was completely familiar, like almost an everyday smell, but really, really good. I heard a footstep behind the closet door, so she had come down those hidden stairs and was about to walk out through the closet. The next thing I heard was the panel opening up and her taking two steps to the closet door.

'And that's when I remembered what that smell was – when she opened the closet door and came out. You won't believe what it was. Chocolate-chip cookies! When they're still in the oven, but almost done. Bubbling up and already that nice brown color.'

To Jimbo, this was a sure sign that Mark had lost his mind. A beautiful woman who smelled like chocolate-chip cookies? How ridiculous could you get?

No, Mark told him, Lucy Cleveland didn't smell like chocolate-chip cookies. Lucy Cleveland smelled sort of like sunlight and fresh grass and fresh bread, things like that, if she smelled like anything. The odor was an announcement, it was like a trumpet fanfare. It meant she was *here*, she was *ready to enter*.

Jimbo could only goggle at him.

Mark pushed himself off the sofa and said his father never noticed he wasn't coming home at night. Philip had stopped attending to his curfew. Actually, he had stopped attending to Mark, and the two of them moved around the house like distant planets, connected by only the vestiges of gravity.

Jimbo asked him where he was going now, and if he wanted company.

No, Mark told him. He was just going out, so he would be able to think a little more. Being able to walk around might help.

Sometime between 7:15 and 7:30 Patrolman Jester observed my nephew seated on one of the benches lining the pathway to the fountain. He appeared to be working out some problem or decision; his lips were moving, though Patrolman Jester had no particular interest in what Mark was saying to himself. In any case, he could not hear it.

By the time Jimbo Monaghan had reached the point in his story where Mark was moving down the walk and waving good-bye, he looked barely capable of going on. He slumped into the back of the sofa like a leaky sack of grain.

'What do you think happened to him after that?' Tim asked.

The boy's eyes found his, flicked away. 'Everybody knows what happened to Mark. He walked into Sherman Park, and the Sherman Park Killer, or the Dark Man, or whatever you call him, grabbed him. Mark wasn't even thinking about his own safety. But don't ask me what he was thinking about, because I couldn't tell you. He was in his own little world.' Again the watery red eyes met Tim's. 'I think that terrible house screwed him up, if you care about what I think. It got to him, right from the start. It changed him.'

'What about Lucy Cleveland?'

'There was no Lucy Cleveland,' Jimbo said. He

seemed amazingly weary. 'A gorgeous nineteen-year-old girl hides out in an empty house and lets a fifteen-year-old boy have sex with her all day long? A gorgeous nineteen-year-old girl that nobody else can see? Yeah, that happens all the time. In books, maybe.'

'Exactly,' Tim said.

Skip poised at the top of the front steps, gazing at Tim while trembling with what looked like the desire to attack. Then it occurred to Tim that the dog was not baring its teeth or snarling, standard behavior for dogs in attack mode. It was trembling with old age, not aggression. The dog was probably cold all the time. Probably Skip spent the whole day on the same few feet of porch because that was where the sunlight fell. Tim extended a hand, and Skip permitted his head to be scratched.

'That poor old animal's so arthritic he doesn't move much anymore. Spends all day sacked out in that one spot of sunlight.'

Tim had not heard the front door open. He looked up to see Omar Hillyard gazing at him through the screen door.

'Sort of like me,' Hillyard said. 'You decided to come back, I see.'

'Yes,' Tim said. 'I hope you don't mind.' He

stepped up beside the dog. Leaning on his cane, Mr Hillyard opened the screen door, awkwardly. 'Just walk around Skip and come on in. He'll move back to his spot, but it'll take him a little while.'

Tim took another step, and Skip either moaned or sighed. Tim looked down at the old dog. When Skip got his front end pointed toward his favorite place, his stiff legs began to carry him toward it.

'He makes a splendid noise when he collapses into the sunlight,' Hillyard said.

Together, they watched Skip hobble across the porch. The old dog moved like a clumsy piece of machinery that had been assembled by someone who had failed to read the manual. He reached the little square of sunlight and fell into it, all at once, and landed with an audible thump. He made a sound of pure contentment, like humming, deep in his chest.

'Know just how he feels,' Hillyard said.

He moved back, and Tim walked through the front door into the living room, which bore a generic resemblance to Philip's, except that the furniture was cleaner and not so old. Stumping in behind him, Hillyard waved toward a brown love seat covered in threadbare corduroy. 'That one's still pretty comfortable. Me, if I sit over here, I can lean my crutch on the footstool, makes it easier to get up.'

He parked himself in a high-backed armchair and propped the cane beside him.

On both sides of the room, framed photographs and drawings of young men, most of them nude, looked out from the walls. Two facing drawings depicted young men in a state of arousal.

'I don't believe I told you this, but the boy on the left is me,' Hillyard said. 'Back in 1946, right after I got out of the army. The other one is my lover, George Olander. He was the artist. George and I bought this house in 1955, when people still used the term "bachelor." We said we were roomies, and nobody bothered us. George died in 1983, exactly twenty years ago. At first your friend Sancho was thrown off course by these pictures, but he decided not to think about it, and pretty soon he was all right.'

'He came over to ask about Joseph Kalendar.'

'Like you. Actually, he came about the house, but pretty soon that brought us to Joseph Kalendar. I've got some iced tea in the kitchen, if you'd care for any.'

'No, thanks.'

'I don't want you to think I'm inhospitable. Truth is, I'm out of practice. For obvious reasons, George and I never had the neighbors in, and I have continued the tradition. Fact is, I went out of my way to discourage visitors. Then I fell down and hurt myself. But am I supposed to take down all my pictures just because the Monaghan boy comes over here?'

'How are you now?'

'Improving. Nothing broke, thank God. Just busted off a few chips, that's all.'

Tim's love seat gave him a perfect view across the street to the Kalendar house. 'I didn't ask you earlier if you ever saw the boys going to that house. It seems they were obsessed with it, my nephew especially.'

'I saw it all,' Hillyard said. 'Either from exactly where you are now, or through my kitchen window. I saw your nephew and his friend stare at that place hour after hour. You could always hear them coming, because of their skateboards. I saw them come over here one night and shine a light on the window. Sancho saw something that knocked him flat on his rear end.'

'He told me about that,' Tim said.

'I always wondered if maybe what he saw was the other fellow.'

'Ah,' Tim said, feeling something hitherto unknown slide into a place exactly its size and shape. 'The other fellow. They called him the Dark Man. My nephew told Jimbo he was something like a ghost.'

'Not unless ghosts are flesh and blood. Man

looked kind of like Joseph Kalendar, except he wasn't quite so huge. He dressed like Kalendar, too. Long black coat.'

'You saw this man? What did he do?'

'He came around at night. Just like the boys, he went to the back of the house and let himself in. I only saw him a couple of times. Even then, I couldn't be sure I wasn't just dreaming.'

'Did you tell Jimbo about this man?'

Hillyard shook his head, looking both fussy and bloated with self-importance. 'Didn't think it was any of his business. Besides, I couldn't be certain I really did see that guy. It was pretty dark out there, and the shadows have a habit of moving around. Anyhow, the boy only wanted to hear about Mr Kalendar, and I gave him an earful, but there's as much of what I didn't tell him as of what I did.'

'Because you didn't think it was any of his business.'

'And one more thing.' He smirked at Tim. 'He didn't ask me the right questions.'

'Are you willing to tell me what you didn't say to Jimbo?'

'If you ask the right questions.'

Tim looked at him in exasperation. 'I'll try. To start with, why don't you fill me in on what you did tell Jimbo?'

'It was pretty much what I told you, the first time you came here. The man was a psycho killer of the first water,' Hillyard said. 'Joseph Kalendar did away with his whole family, and God knows how many women besides. Turned his house into a kind of torture chamber. Brought his own son along with him when he went out raping and murdering, and later on he even murdered the boy! A lunatic, pure and simple. Not that we should have been surprised, mind you. Wouldn't you say there was something wrong with a man that never wants to show his face?'

Tim thought of the snapshots Jimbo had described to him. 'Never? Not just in photographs?'

'The man was extremely uncomfortable showing his face. That's why he eventually grew that big, thick beard. When he lived around here, Kalendar wore a hat, and he turned up the collar of that coat he was always wearing. Sometimes, he went so far as to hold his hands in front of his face. He was always turning his back on you.'

'Did you have much contact with him?'

'Oh, now you're asking better questions. Yes, I did, a bit. The man was a good carpenter, after all. When George and I needed some new shelves, we called Mr Kalendar, and he did a beautiful job. So a few years later, when we found dry rot in some of the timbers and floorboards, we went back to him. Kalendar gave us a good price and replaced all the wood in short order.'

'From what I've been hearing,' Tim said, 'he must have been a great carpenter. I guess you must have liked him, since you hired him twice.'

'Liked him?' Omar Hillyard scowled. 'No one can say I liked Mr Joseph Kalendar.'

'But he spent a lot of time in your house.'

'His prices were low, and the man lived across the street. Otherwise, we would never have spoken to him, much less had him in our house.'

'Ah.' Tim gestured toward the drawings and paintings on the walls. 'He objected to your situation.'

'He hated our situation. The man had religious objections to homosexuality, and no doubt other objections as well. But after he let us know what he thought, and said he was going to pray for us, it wasn't much of a problem anymore. The problem was him. The problem was what he did.'

'Like what?'

'Joseph Kalendar made rooms feel smaller and darker than they were. He had that power. Just by being there. He removed all the extra air from wherever he was. When you were with him, you felt like you were carrying a tremendous weight. Of what, I can hardly say. Hostility. It was like a black cloud surrounded him. When you were with him, it surrounded you, too. You felt all that stifled anger and hostility and depression even when he was telling you that he would pray for you. I've often thought that's what evil feels like. That the evil in him poisoned the atmosphere and made it awful to be around him.'

'I've heard of people like that,' Tim said. 'But only in psychoanalytic case histories.'

'Of course you don't feel it right away. At first, Kalendar seemed like an ordinary, taciturn sort of working man. You had to let him get entangled a bit with you before you got the full effect.'

'Imagine being in the family of a person like that,' Tim said.

'That's why his wife's disappearance never aroused much suspicion. We all thought she ran off to get away from him. And the boy wouldn't have gone with her. He was Kalendar's assistant in the carpentry business ever since he was old enough to pick up a hammer. Dropped out of school. Completely loyal to his father. That's why Kalendar wound up taking him along on his excursions. Naturally, after Myra took off they could bring the bodies home, dispose of them in the furnace. That's where they found what was left of the boy – in the furnace.'

'And here you were,' Tim said. 'Living right

across the street from him. Didn't anything ever strike you as funny? Were you even suspicious? Even if you wouldn't have gone to the police with your suspicions, didn't you have some?'

'*Kalendar* struck me as funny,' Hillyard said. 'Are you kidding? After I knew he was crazy, everything he did seemed wrong to me.'

'You must have been here when he saved the two children from next door.'

'You did some homework, didn't you? But it wasn't next door to *here*, it was 3325, the house just up the street from him. A black family named Watkins lived in that house.'

'Did you see any of what happened?'

'Saw it all, more or less.'

'Just out of curiosity, did this happen before or after he added the strange extra room to his house and built that wall to hide it?'

'That's a very good question,' Hillyard said. 'He rescued the Watkins family only two days before he started working on that big wall at the back of his property. He must have added the room after he finished the wall.'

'How did you know about the extra room if you've never been in the house?'

Hillyard bristled.

'I mow the lawn over there once every couple of months, don't I? Well, I used to, before I got laid up like this, and I'll be doing it again, I can tell you that.'

'Sorry. I didn't mean to imply anything.'

'What could you have implied?'

'Nothing,' Tim said, taken aback. 'I don't know. I just meant, I seemed to have annoyed you with an innocent question.' It occurred to him that Hillyard might have been one of the people who tried to burn down Kalendar's house.

'George used to tell me I sometimes got touchy for no good reason, and I'm probably worse now than I was then. We were talking about Kalendar and the fire. Tell me, Mr Underhill. You're a writer. Doesn't that episode strike you as a little out of character for the man I just described?'

'Wouldn't a very religious man feel it his duty to rescue people from a burning building?'

'Kalendar hated the blacks,' Hillyard said. 'He didn't even think they were people. I had the feeling he'd have been just as happy if the whole Watkins family had burned to a crisp.'

'My brother told me he kept running back in, he was so determined to save them.'

Hillyard gazed at him, looking superior and self-satisfied, like a cat with a bird in its mouth. 'Suppose I tell you what happened, and then see what you think.'

'All right,' Tim said.

'Kalendar was in his backyard when the fire broke out. The flames were mainly at the back of the house, and he had to run around and break down the front door. The whole thing fell down flat. In he charged. Even from my porch, I could hear him yelling, but I couldn't make out the words. In two or three minutes, a long time in a burning house, he came out, carrying one of the Watkins children and holding the other one by the hand. The kids were screaming and wailing. He sure looked like a hero to me, and I couldn't stand the sight of the man.

'I called the fire department as soon as I saw smoke, and I was just hoping the trucks would arrive to save Kalendar and the kids' parents. He dropped the kids down on the front lawn and ran back in. Smoke was pouring out of the side windows, and through the living room window I could see the flames. Right away, he came outside, shoving Mr and Mrs Watkins ahead of him. Then he turned around and ran *back in*. He was yelling a name.'

'A name?'

'"Lily! Lily!"'

'Who was Lily?'

Hillyard shrugged. 'At that point, the fire trucks arrived, and a lot of firefighters ran into the house, and the hoses started up, and in a couple of minutes the firefighters were dragging Kalendar outside and congratulating him for saving the lives of four people. To me, he seemed awfully disoriented, like he wasn't really sure why these people were being so nice to him. He got away as soon as he could. But the *Ledger* and the TV people got hold of the story anyway, and they pushed it as far as Kalendar would let them. A racial harmony story, a feel-good story. This was only a few months after the big riots in Chicago and Milwaukee, remember – 1968, it was. Detroit, too. Black people burned down their own businesses. It was a hideous tragedy. You must remember it.'

'I was out of the country in 1968,' Tim said. 'But you could hardly say that I escaped violence altogether.'

'Do tell.' Hillyard's eyes went flat. 'I went on a lot of marches in 1968. We were marching against racism and against war.'

'Mr Hillyard, you and I were both unhappy with what was going on in Vietnam.'

'All right,' Hillyard said. Tim could tell things were not all right. Omar Hillyard still had all the noblest principles. If he'd had any medals, he had returned them to the government in 1968 or 1969. When he had marched, he'd held up a sign that read VETERANS AGAINST THE WAR. He couldn't get over it. He was still pissed off by people like Tim

Underhill, whom he thought had taken a great army and marched it into a swamp. People like Underhill had tampered with his pride, and he could not forgive them.

'If I hadn't been drafted, I would have been marching right alongside you.'

'All right,' Hillyard said again, meaning *This subject is now officially closed*. 'I was talking about Joseph Kalendar and the press. When he refused to cooperate with them, they called him a modest man, a hero who shunned the spotlight. A nice story, you know? But when the reporters began to ask around about the new hero, it fizzled out in a hurry. The world's most antisocial man wasn't about to invite reporters and photographers into his house. He put up that hideous wall, and we all thought it was to keep the snooping press out of his backyard. At the front of his house, at least he could see the bastards coming.'

'He couldn't have been a hundred percent antisocial,' Tim said.

Mr Hillyard's expression changed to stubborn frustration. He reminded Tim of photographs of Somerset Maugham in old age.

'Jimbo Monaghan saw pictures of you and other people socializing with Kalendar at a lakeside tavern. He said it looked like quite a party.'

Hillyard's face relaxed. 'How in the world did that boy come across those photos, anyhow?'

'He and Mark found them in the house.'

'Those pictures were taken at a neighborhood party, except it was up at Random Lake, not far from Milwaukee. Someone had a cabin up there, near a little tavern with a pier and a beach. That must have been one of the few times Kalendar did something to make his wife happy. He had a good reason to keep her happy, but all the same, he was Joseph Kalendar. He did his best to enjoy himself, but it was all an act. He hated being there. And the feeling was more or less mutual. Kalendar had the power to kill all the pleasure in his vicinity. I actually felt sorry for him. You could see him going up to people and trying to join in the conversation, which meant he just stood there, until one by one the other men peeled away and left him by himself.'

'What do you mean, he had a reason to keep his wife happy?'

'Myra Kalendar had a big, big belly. She must have been seven or eight months pregnant.'

'With their son, the poor devil.'

'I don't think so.' Hillyard seemed irritatingly smug. 'The party at Random Lake was in 1965. In 1965, Billy Kalendar was four years old.'

'I don't get it.'

Omar Hillyard continued to smile at him. 'A month after the party at Random Lake, Kalendar put out the word that his wife had miscarried. They wanted no calls or notes of sympathy, thank you. You can draw your own conclusions.'

22

From Timothy Underhill's journal, 27 June 2003

There he was, Omar Hillyard, annoyed with me but still handing me the secret, the key that unlocked the last, inmost door. I remembered Philip telling me that Myra Kalendar had one day appeared at their house in Carrollton Gardens begging Nancy to do something for her. *Help me save my child's life.* Did she say, *Take her from me?*

I explained all of this to Tom Pasmore shortly after I turned up at the big old house on Eastern Shore Drive, but he refrained from comment until we were climbing the stairs to get to the room that contained his computers and computer paraphernalia. He said, 'In your view, then, your nephew met Joseph Kalendar's daughter in that house. She somehow managed to appear before him in physical form, made love to him day after day, and finally talked him into joining her in a kind of spirit-world?'

'Put that way, it sounds absurd,' I said.

He asked me how I would put it.

'I wouldn't,' I said. 'But remember this sequence. Joseph Kalendar really does have a daughter he conceals from the world. Early one morning when she is three years old, she slips out of the house and hides, probably in the back garden or the alley. Kalendar rushes outside to find her and sees that the house next door is burning. Two little girls live in that house. Isn't it likely that Lily would have watched those girls through the windows, that she would have yearned to play with them? Kalendar thinks so, because he races into the burning house. After rescuing everyone, he charges back in, looking for her. After that, he builds an enormous wall at the back of his garden to hide the next thing he builds, a horrible annex alongside his kitchen. In that room, he tortures his daughter.

'Three years later, his wife makes a desperate

attempt to rescue her daughter, but her husband's cousin, Nancy Underhill, turns her down flat. Philip would never have let her interfere, and he would certainly not have let Kalendar's daughter move into his house.

'Then comes Kalendar's meltdown. He murders a lot of women, undoubtedly including his wife and daughter. In 1980, he is arrested and convicted. Five years later, Kalendar is murdered by a fellow inmate, and the story seems to be over.'

We had reached the computer room. Tom walked around turning on the lights and hearing me out, nodding as he went. I didn't want him to agree with me, I just wanted him to see the pattern.

'This is the interesting part,' I said. 'About three weeks ago, my nephew, who has no conscious knowledge of this story whatsoever, suddenly becomes obsessed with Kalendar's house. His mother forbids him to go near the place. A few days before, a pedophile murderer snatched a boy from Sherman Park.

'My nephew becomes increasingly obsessed with the Kalendar house, and one night he lies to everyone about his plans for the evening and he goes around the block and attempts to break in. He is repulsed by a kind of horrible negative energy. The next day, his mother kills herself.'

'Well, well,' Tom said.

'She's picking up something from her son. Her guilt comes back to her, and what's happening in the neighborhood makes it worse. She can't bear it. The next day, her son finds her body in the bathtub. What do you think that would do to a fifteen-year-old boy, finding his mother's naked corpse in the bathtub?

'Then Mark returns again and again, finding all the creepy modifications Kalendar made to the house. After two days, he tells his best friend that he senses the presence of a young woman, and on the fifth day, she appears, calling herself Lucy Cleveland. Lucy is hiding from her father, a figure Mark has been calling the Dark Man, and whom he has seen on at least two occasions. Mark says Lucy has a plan, she wants him to do something, and he needs time to think about it. He goes off to the park to think, and is never seen again.'

'Very suggestive,' Tom said. 'So you think that while he was in the park, he made up his mind to join Lucy Cleveland and – am I right? – protect her from her father? And after his mind was made up, he went back to 3323 and gave himself to her.'

'Joined her,' I said. 'But gave himself to her, too, yes.'

'Do you think he will ever be seen again?'

'I'm sure of it,' I said. Even then, I could not bear to tell Tom about the e-mail I had found, via a program called Gotomypc.com, on my computer at home. 'Because he isn't dead, he's just elsewhere.'

'You love your nephew, don't you, Tim?'

Suddenly, my eyes burned with tears.

'How much of what you told me do the police know?'

'As much as they could understand. I tried to get them interested in that house, but they blew me off.'

'Well, *I* think it's worth a good, long look. Let's see what we can discover.' Tom had placed himself before a computer wired up to a machine that resembled an enormous toaster equipped with rows of small red lights. It said Vector-Systems on the side, not that I know what that means. Thick cords led from the giant toaster to a number of enigmatic black cubes, some of which clicked and whirred.

'I'll see him again,' I said to Tom Pasmore.

'If she lets him be seen.'

'There's always that,' I said. 'She will, though. I'll never talk to him again, but I'll see him.'

‘And that will be enough?’

‘Almost enough,’ I said.

‘When it happens, will you tell me about it?’

‘I’ll have to tell someone.’

He smiled up at me, glanced at the screen, then back up at me. ‘Do you really want me to do this?’

Of course I wanted him to do it.

‘Then come around behind me, so you can see, too.’

I moved behind him and watched him type *3323 N. Michigan Street* into a blank form he had called up from some municipal office with no idea that Tom Pasmore was roaming through their records. He hit ENTER.

In a nanosecond, these words appeared on his screen:

Ronald Lloyd-Jones
159 Tamarack Way
Old Point Harbor, IL 61725

‘Our Ronnie lives in a pretty nice part of town,’ Tom said.

‘This doesn’t make a lot of sense,’ I said. ‘Millionaires don’t usually mess around in Pigtown . . .’

Old Point Harbor was a long-established

eastern suburb of Millhaven with Tudor mansions, Gothic piles, and huge contemporary houses tucked into wooded landscapes on meandering roads illuminated by imitation gas lamps.

'Wait,' I said. 'What did you say?'

'I think what I said was, "Our Ronnie lives in a pretty nice part of town." Isn't that what we're talking about?'

'You called him Ronnie,' I said. 'It's Ronnie! The guy in the park.'

'What guy in the park?'

I told him about the astronomy professor and the boy and the police sketch.

'Amazing,' Tom said. 'Your friend Sergeant Pohlhaus should have taken that house a little more seriously.' He looked back at the screen.

'When did Ronald Lloyd-Jones buy our little house, I wonder?' Tom pushed a few keys, and the answer appeared in a window on the screen: 1982.

'He's owned that place for twenty-one years,' Tom said. 'In fact, he bought it even before Kalendar was killed. This could . . . hmmm.'

'Why would a guy from Old Point Harbor buy a house on Michigan Street?' I asked.

Some of what Tom did then must have been illegal. Actually, there's no way it could not have been, but I have to say it was amazingly effective. Half an hour later, we knew more about Mr Lloyd-Jones than his parents did.

Ronald Lloyd-Jones was born in Edgerton, Illinois, in 1950. He graduated from Edgerton East High School in 1968. And from the University of Illinois, which he attended on a football scholarship, in 1972. He married pretty Edwina Cass, heiress and orphan, in 1975, and Edwina died in a boating accident in 1978. Lloyd-Jones had inherited approximately twenty million dollars, which matured into something like twice that amount, thanks to the '90s market and other investments. His portfolio was spread across three brokerage houses. An accountant in Chicago handled his bills. He had never remarried and had no children. His garage housed a Jaguar Vanden Plas, a Chevrolet pickup truck, and a Mercedes sedan. A state-of-the-art security system guarded his home and the ten acres surrounding it. Lloyd-Jones had $65,374.08 in his checking account at First Illinois, and his Visa, MasterCard, and American Express accounts were fully paid up. He bought a lot of things on-line, '80s rock music and James Patterson novels in particular. At six foot three and 235 pounds, he was a large man; he had an eighteen-inch neck and a forty-inch waistband, and he wore size thirteen shoes.

Lloyd-Jones drank single-malt Scotch. He visited porn sites and downloaded photographs, which he attempted to delete the next day. His teeth were perfect. He had a gun room with antique pistols and rifles in glass cases, a music room with astonishingly expensive sound equipment, and a screening room with a big flat-screen plasma TV. The screening room speakers had cost him $250,000. He belonged to no club or social organization. No church numbered him in its congregation. He had never voted. This multimillionaire owned the house in Old Point Harbor, a two-bedroom apartment on Park Avenue and East Seventy-eighth Street, a great little farmhouse in Périgord . . . and the house on Michigan Street, the first property he had ever purchased.

The only photograph Tom could find of this man was his high school graduation photo. 'Before it gets dark, I think we should take a little spin out to Old Point Harbor, don't you?' Tom asked.

'He has a great sound system and a mountain of CDs. This guy really *is* the Sherman Park Killer. We have to call the police.'

'First we get a look at Ronnie, then we call the police. I don't want to tell the Millhaven Police Department, especially not Sergeant Franz

Pohlhaus, what I just did here. You remember the police sketch pretty well, I hope?'

'Pretty well,' I said.

'Sounds like probable cause to me,' Tom said.

Ten minutes later, I was driving Tom Pasmore up Eastern Shore Drive in my rented Town Car. Twenty minutes after that we had passed from the farthest outposts of Millhaven into Old Point Harbor. The landscape had opened out into gentle hills sprinkled with a lot of oak trees and tamarack pines. Hidden far back from the road, big houses flickered like mirages among the tree trunks.

[After reading a section of an early journal of mine, Maggie Lah said, 'You write your journal like it was fiction.' I said, 'What makes you think it isn't?']

There were very few street signs. It was one of those communities that do not wish to induce comfort in visitors or deliverypeople. In its mild, slightly wayward northern course, Loblolly Road intersected two apparently anonymous streets before crossing a slightly wider road called Carriage Avenue. Either one of them could have been Tamarack Way.

'Keep going,' Tom said. He had a map of

Old Point Harbor in his head, as he had maps of a hundred different cities and towns, large and small. 'Two streets ahead, you take a left, and Tamarack Way is the first corner you come to.'

'Do I turn right or left?'

'How the hell should I know?' Tom said. 'I don't memorize addresses.'

At the unmarked intersection with what Tom said was Tamarack Way, I turned left and began paying attention to the numbers on the mailboxes. Someone had made a fortune selling rich midwesterners on the idea of over-sized mailboxes painted with New England themes: lighthouses, lobster boats, saltbox houses, beach dunes. We passed 85, 87, 88, 90.

'As the waiters at the Fireside Lounge are fond of saying, good choice,' Tom said.

'You're nice and relaxed.'

'I love this part,' Tom said. 'I get to see if I was right.'

We drifted up Tamarack Way, watching the numbers on the mailboxes get higher.

'Just out of curiosity,' I asked, 'what do you intend to do when we get to 159?'

'I intend to sit in the car. Who knows, maybe we'll get lucky and find him outside, uprooting dandelions.'

He was dressed in one of his typical Tom Pasmore outfits, a light-gray windowpane plaid suit with a dark-blue vest, a forest-green patterned tie, the most beautiful crocodile shoes I'd ever seen in my life, and big round sunglasses. He looked like a Danish count masquerading as an architect.

'What do you envision me doing while you sit in the car?'

'I'll tell you when we get there.'

The number 159 appeared on a standard-fare Old Harbor Point mailbox, an aluminum shell large enough to hold a fleet of toy trucks and embellished with a painting of a steepled old church and a few rows of tilting headstones. Nice touch. A wide black driveway wound in from the road on a long loop toward an immense gray two-story house. Through the trees, we could just make out the glint of a huge circular window set high above the baronial front door. The lawn gleamed an unnatural-looking green.

'Well, he's not doing any yardwork,' Tom said. 'Turn in and drive up to the house.'

I stepped on the brake. 'He's probably watching everything we do. Remember that security system. He's got cameras all along this drive.'

'But you don't know that. You're a tourist

in a rented car, and you got lost looking for your cousin's house on Loblolly Road.'

'You want me to ring his bell?' I was incredulous.

'Can you think of a better way to get a good look at him?'

'Yes. From the other side of a one-way mirror. What if he wants to know my cousin's name?'

'Your cousin's name is Arnold Trueright.'

'Give me a break,' I said.

'Seriously. Arnold Trueright is my accountant and he lives at 304 Loblolly Road.'

Shaking my head, I took my foot off the brake and rolled up the long, curving driveway. Gradually, the house came into view. Half Manderley, half Bill Gates. The enormous round window looked like a well-tended blister.

I got out of the car, knowing that at least one camera, and probably two, were trained on me, and thought of 'Ronnie' scrutinizing my image. It was a deeply uncomfortable moment. When I looked back at Tom Pasmore, he flipped his hand toward the front door. A team of horses could have fit through that thing. The flat gold button of the bell shone from the fluted center of the frame. I pushed it down and heard nothing. I pushed it again.

Without warning, the door swung open. I

found myself looking into the bland face and intense, lively eyes of a large, black-haired man in a blue blazer, a white shirt, and khakis. His nice white smile and nearly snub nose made him appear friendly, harmless, eager to please. Professor Bellinger's description to the police sketch artist had been as accurate as Sergeant Pohlhaus hoped it would be.

'Sir,' he said, and glanced quickly at Tom in the passenger seat, then back to me. Instantly, he noticed something in my face or eyes. 'What? Do we know each other?'

'No,' I said, alarmed. 'For a second I thought you looked familiar. I guess you kind of remind me of Robert Wagner twenty years ago.'

'I'm flattered,' he said. 'Is there some way I can assist you gentlemen? I'm sure you rang my bell for a reason.'

'We got lost,' I said. 'I'm trying to find my cousin's house on Loblolly Road, but I keep driving around and around past the same houses.'

'What part of Loblolly Road?'

'Number 304.'

He *hmmm*ed. His eyes were full of light and amusement. My bowels felt cold and watery. 'What's your cousin's name, by the way? Maybe I know him.'

'Arnold Trueright.'

'Arnold Trueright, the daredevil CPA. Right over on Loblolly, that's correct.' He gave me excellent directions back the way we had come. Then he peered into the car and gave Tom a cheerful little wave. 'Who's your well-dressed friend? Another cousin?'

In my haste to get away from Ronald Lloyd-Jones's chilling force field, I said something stupid. 'Another accountant, actually.'

'Accountants don't look like that. Your friend reminds me of someone . . . someone rather well known who lives in town, I can't think of who it is. Name's right on the tip of my . . .' Still smiling in Tom's direction, he shook his head. His own folly amused him. 'Never mind. Not important. Take care, now.'

'Absolutely,' I said, and moved away as quickly as I could without revealing my alarm.

Lloyd-Jones disappeared behind his fortress door before I got to the car.

'That was him,' I said. 'That's the son of a bitch who tried to pick up the boy in the park.'

'Sometimes,' Tom said, 'I really am forced to admire my genius.'

While we were driving past Arnold Trueright's beautiful imitation Victorian on Loblolly Road, Tom talked to Franz Pohlhaus on his cell phone.

It was simple, he was saying. I'd been so convinced that the Michigan Street house had something to do with Mark's disappearance that we looked up the property records and drove out to see what its owner looked like. What do you know, he looks just like the police sketch of the mysterious Ronnie! Sounded like good probable cause, didn't Sergeant Pohlhaus agree?

Evidently, the sergeant did agree.

'Rich people don't get arrested the way poor people do,' Tom said. 'It's going to take hours to get all their ducks in a row. They'll get him in the end, however. They'll come out with a search warrant and tear that house apart. Lloyd-Jones is going to be taken away in handcuffs. No matter how loudly his lawyer yells, he's going to get arrested, booked, and charged with at least a couple of murders, depending on what and how much they find in his house. He will not get bail. Your Professor Bellinger will positively I.D. him as the man she saw in Sherman Park, and sooner or later, the police will uncover human remains. Just for people like him, I wish this state still had the death penalty. Nevertheless, thanks to you and me, Mr Lloyd-Jones is going to spend the rest of his life alone in a cell. Unless he's killed in prison, which is actually pretty likely.'

'I wish Mark were here to see this,' I said. 'Boy. I feel like I could run a marathon, or jump over a building. What happens now?'

'Pohlhaus promised to keep me in the loop. He'll call me after Lloyd-Jones gets processed through, and he'll let me know if the search of his house turns up anything incriminating. From the look of the guy, they'll find enough to indict him.'

'Why?'

'Because he's so arrogant, that's why. At the very least, I bet we're going to find out that he's obsessed with Joseph Kalendar. That's why he bought that house on Michigan Street. And I bet somewhere in this house, in a closet, an attic room, something like that, he has a little shrine to Joseph Kalendar.'

He took in the expression on my face, leaned toward me, and patted my knee. 'If you don't mind, I'd like to make a stop downtown.'

All the way back to Eastern Shore Drive, I kept seeing Ronald Lloyd-Jones's face in front of me. The impact he had made on me diminished hardly at all as the miles rolled by. He had smiled, he had called me 'Sir' and probed my story. He had been completely accommodating and agreeable. He had frightened me very badly. For far too many people, a number at which I could not even guess, that amused, well-cared-for face had been the last thing they had seen. Ronald Lloyd-Jones had appointed himself the escort to the next world, and he loved his work. After having met him, I was even more grateful that Mark was *elsewhere*.

As proof or reassurance or something of the kind, he wonderfully showed himself to me while I drove Tom to his errand, which turned out to be picking up a Basque beret and a gray homburg hat at one of the few places in America where such things can still be found. Identifying a serial killer, buying two fancy hats, this was a real Tom Pasmore kind of day. We had just pulled up at the light on the corner of Orson and Jefferson streets, directly across from the little pocket park where on my first day back in Millhaven I had seen two boys who turned out to be Mark and Jimbo. At that moment, just before the light changed, there occurred the remarkable event I alluded to earlier, the one that has elevated my spirits from then to now.

Not looking at anything in particular but merely letting my gaze drift across the immediate surroundings, I happened to take in the large plate-glass window of a crowded Starbucks. Young people read newspapers at small tables or picked at the keyboards of their laptops. The first thing that caught my attention was the stunning combination of almost unearthly beauty and real richness and warmth of character shining forth in the face of a young woman at one of the window tables. *No matter how long you live*, said a voice in my head, *you'll never see anything more beautiful than that*.

A kind of electrical tingle ran up my arms. A boy – a young man – was leaning across the table, saying something to the young woman. I noticed that the young man wore layered T-shirts like Mark's before I saw that the young man *was* Mark. He turned his head to the window, to me, and in that half second, two things became radiantly clear: he seemed more adult than he had been, and he was blazingly happy.

It was a gift. Not the only one, but the first. Mark and his 'Lucy Cleveland,' whose real name I knew, had exited their *elsewhere* long enough to display themselves before me in all the fullness of their new lives. After all, the *elsewhere* was right next door.

The light changed. The horns erupted and hallooed behind me, and I made myself accelerate slowly forward, toward the Pforzheimer and Grand Avenue. A big loop onto Prospect Avenue, then Eastern Shore Drive would bring us home. A share of that blazing joy resided in me now, and I thought it would be mine for eternity. *It partook of* eternity. What I had seen, that glory, burned in my memory. What I saw there and then, on Jefferson Street at approximately four-thirty in the afternoon, burns in me still, as I sit here in Tom Pasmore's vast, eccentric living room waiting to hear from Sergeant Pohlhaus or one of his juniors.

God bless Mark Underhill, I say within the resounding chambers of my heart and mind, *God bless Lucy Cleveland, too, though already they are so blessed, they have the power to bless me.*

This, too, was a blessing, and I had kept it a secret since the day Philip called to accuse me of hiding his son in my loft. I could have said, 'Actually, Philip, two days after he vanished, Mark sent me an e-mail,' but certain things about the e-mail made me decide to keep it to myself, at least until I got to Millhaven. The 'Subject' and 'From' lines would have raised questions I could not have answered, and they might even have led Philip and the authorities to question its authenticity. Certain *other* things about the e-mail, sitting ever at the back of my mind, had given direction to my search. Philip and Sergeant Pohlhaus would have dismissed it as a fraud, so I had kept it to myself until this moment. But after that incredible gift, I could not resist; I had to share what I knew. So I showed Mark's 'posthumous' e-mail to Tom.

He had made our drinks. We were sprawled on the sofas in the section of the big, mazy room where the sound equipment lives. Tom was tilted back like Henry Higgins, his eyes closed, listening to whatever he'd put in the CD player. Mozart piano sonatas, maybe, Mitsuko Uchida or Alfred Brendel, I don't know which – I wasn't paying attention to either the music or what he told me about it. *Little Richard* could have been playing Mozart. I could barely hear. The roaring of angels' wings filled my ears.

'This is going to sound pretty crazy to you,' I said.

Tom opened his eyes.

'When we were stopped at Cathedral Square, I saw Mark through the Starbucks window. He was with Lucy Cleveland.'

'You mean Lily Kalendar?' Tom said.

'What she calls herself doesn't matter,' I said. 'You should have seen her.'

'As beautiful as Mark told his friend.'

'You have no idea.'

'If you'd said something at the time, I could have seen them, too.'

'I don't think I could have said anything. I was so stunned, and then so grateful.'

'You're sure it was Mark?'

'I couldn't be wrong about this, Tom.'

'How did he look?'

'A little older. More experienced. Very, very happy.'

'I take it this – *sighting* – was not an accident.'

'He wanted me to see them. He wanted me to know he was all right.'

Tom said a strange thing then. 'Maybe you think he's all right because the Sherman Park Killer is being arrested this evening.' When it became clear that I had not understood his remark, he added, 'Because he can tell us where he put the bodies.'

'Sorry,' I said. 'I don't really get you.'

'Final resting places and all that. Decent burials. No more speculation on the part of the families. Everybody can get down to the business of grief.'

'I don't have to grieve for Mark,' I insisted. 'I'll see him again, here and there. Maybe I won't see him now for years, but I will see him again.

He can show himself to me anywhere. And he will always be with Lucy Cleveland.'

'I suppose that's true,' Tom said. 'You might see him anywhere.'

'Which means, Tom, that he was not a victim of that monster I talked to today. He was not mistreated and tortured. He was not subject to the desires of that psychotic creep. What happened to Shane Auslander and Dewey Dell and all the others did not happen to Mark Underhill. His name is not on that list.'

'I see,' Tom said, meaning that he didn't.

'You will,' I said. 'I want to show you something. Would you mind going back up to the computer room?'

'You want to show me something on a computer?' He was already standing up.

'I want to show you something on my computer.'

He led me up the stairs. Inside the room, he went around turning on the lights.

'Should I use a specific machine, or doesn't it matter?' I asked.

'Use the one I used to look up the address.'

I sat down in front of the keyboard and typed in Gotomypc.com, a site that lets me connect to the monitor of my own computer from the keyboard of a remote machine.

I got to the website and put in my user name and password. Much faster on Tom's T1 line than on Mark's computer, the screen changed and asked me for my access code. I tapped it in.

On Tom's beautiful nineteen-inch screen, my seventeen-inch screen appeared, a little smaller and muddier than in reality, but my screen all the same.

'Fascinating,' Tom said. 'Do you use all those programs?'

'Of course not,' I said, and clicked on the envelope that stood for Outlook Express.

Three-fourths of the headings in boldface were spam. **Size Does Matter, Earn $50,000 in Three Days at Home, Other Singles in Your Area, Free Viagra Pak.** I took a moment to delete them.

'Now look at this one.' I clicked on **Subject: lost boy lost girl; From: munderhill.** 'Do you see that date?'

'Um,' Tom said. 'Looks like it was sent on Sunday, the twentieth of June.'

'That was two days after Mark's disappearance.'

'My goodness.' Tom put a hand to his mouth and bent toward the screen. 'Right you are. Extraordinary.'

This e-mail appeared on my screen and Tom's.

From: munderhill

To: tunderhill@nyc.rr.com

Sent: Friday, June 20, 2003 4:32 AM

Subject: lost boy lost girl

u know u have done work enuf

u can rest old writer

we r 2gether

in this other world
rite next door

m

'Print that out,' Tom said.

'If I did, it would use my printer, not yours.'

He grimaced. Nice as he is, Tom likes getting his own way. '"u can rest old writer"?'

'He's telling me not to worry about him.'

'"u know u have done work enuf"? What does that mean? He wants you to stop writing?'

'I've done enough for him,' I said. 'I've done all I have to do.'

'There's no domain name,' Tom said. 'Where did he send it from?'

'From wherever they are.'

'This is astonishing – two days *after* . . .'

'Back in New York,' I said, 'before I knew that Mark's mother had killed herself and I would have to come here, I saw *lost boy lost girl* stenciled on the sidewalk. In black paint. The next time I looked, it was gone.'

'They do that to advertise things.'

'I know, Tom. I'm just telling you what I saw. I never even mentioned it to Mark.'

'I think you liked the phrase,' Tom said. 'I think you saw it on the sidewalk, and it stuck in your head. Somehow or other, you told Mark about it. That's the way you work. It's the way all writers work.'

'You don't know everything,' I said.

Tom put his hands in his jacket pockets and bent his neck. He frowned at his shoes. 'Tim,' he said. His voice was as relaxed and soft as an old glove. 'Is this thing real?'

'As real as it can be,' I said.

On a humid, sunny afternoon in June, Mark Underhill sat at the bottom of the stairs in an empty house he knew not to be empty. It never had been, he thought. A presence had inhabited it from the first. The presence was female, and she had come for him. Her arrival in the house, which once had been a stage for the enactment of unspeakable and sacred horrors, had tumbled him off his skateboard and rooted him to the middle of Michigan Street. In what now seemed the last days of his childhood, she had stopped him cold. She had whispered to his mind, to his heart, and without hearing he had heard.

A light footstep sounded from somewhere above him. Successive footsteps proceeded softly overhead, he thought either in the bedroom or the corridor hidden behind it.

Above, a door opened or closed. Mark's body tightened, then relaxed. He thought he heard faraway laughter.

When he thought of the giant's bed two rooms away, the entire house filled with heat and light. The ugly added room that contained the bed rang and vibrated with a deep, resonant note that only a second before had melted into the material of the floor and walls. A great tuning fork had been struck. This was what he had been called to witness, Mark thought – this enormous thing that had already passed from view. The great feathers of its mighty wings beat the air, and in the tumult of its wake rode endless loss. His heart filled.

Mark listened to the small, light footsteps

descending a staircase parallel to his, but narrower, steeper, and enclosed. When she at last showed herself, if this time she did, she would emerge through the closet door ten feet to his left. The footsteps chimed like brush strokes. It was like hearing someone stepping down a passage within his own head.

As though it shared his substance, 3323 North Michigan contracted, and he felt himself contract around his excitement. The little brush strokes descended another few steps and drew level.

That sound of wing beats; blood rushing through his ears. No, he thought, actual wing beats, those of birds that were not there and, to begin with, were not even birds.

He had no idea what was going to happen to him. He had put himself here, and now he would have to accept what occurred. If there was any comfort in the sudden chill awareness that everything was about to be immeasurably different, it was that he had not been placed in this moment randomly, by luck or chance. It had been waiting for him ever since the house had risen up before him like a castle rising from a plain.

Trembling, he shifted, drew up his knees, and fixed his eyes on the closet door. There came the pad of a soft footfall, the first faint click of a doorknob gripped and revolved. In the quarter second before the door began to swing open, time stopped for Mark Underhill.

Dust motes hung unmoving in the still air.

There came a sound, quiet at first, not to be identified. As it grew, he thought it was the overtone of a note from an upright bass, hanging in the air after the note itself had faded –

Then he thought he heard the hot buzzing metallic hum of a thousand cicadas. A mindless drone, greedy, intrusive . . . were there cicadas in Millhaven?

Cicadas? he thought. *I don't even know what a cicada looks like!*

Ten feet to his left, the door opened on its hinges, and unlocked from some old chamber in his memory, the smell of chocolate-chip cookies drifted toward him – his mother had been baking cookies, and now they were swelling swelling swelling on the baking pan, melting beyond their boundaries, pushing up and forward and out. A slight figure slipped into the room.

That day, she told him her name.

The next, she threw off the simple things she had been wearing, then undressed him, and led him to the sheet-covered sofa. After that, Mark felt as if branded. She brought him hand in hand to the giant's terrible bed and taught him to arrange his limbs in its grooves and hollows, which received her as well as him, so that they seemed almost to remake the giant's bed beneath them as they moved.

He could not say to Jimbo: *I wore her body like a second skin.*

Is this real? he asked.

As real as it can be, she said. *As real as I can make it.*

Time changed its old, old nature and gave them its first, primal face. A single hour rocketed by in a lazy month. There was no time.

Go now and think, she said. *Do you leave your world with me or in some lesser way? For all in your world must in their own time leave it.*

She said, *Make haste make haste the sun swims round the Dark Man cometh. But you may come with me.*

Mark met his dearest friend and knew he would do so no more. He walked into the park on a summer evening and sat on a familiar bench. The first faint coolness of the coming night touched his cheek. The breeze said, *Make haste make haste*. Soon he rose and walked.

23

'APPARENTLY HE WANTS to talk to you,' Philip said. 'You know that. I already told you.'

'It would be nice to know why.'

Philip pulled into a parking lot a block away from police headquarters, where some nineteen hours earlier Ronald Lloyd-Jones had been fingerprinted, photographed, stripped of his valuables and personal items, and formally charged with multiple homicides. The attending officers considered that he had endured these humiliations with an unsettling degree of good humor. He had refused to make a statement until his lawyer was present, but guess what? His lawyer was on a golfing vacation in St Croix and would not be returning for another two or three days. Under the circumstances, he requested the dignity of a private cell, regular meals, and the use of legal pads and writing implements with which he could, as he said, 'begin to organize my defense.' And, oh, by the way – did his arrest have any connection to the two gentlemen who had driven up to his house that afternoon, asking directions to Loblolly Road? The first half dozen officers he encountered knew nothing and, repulsed by their big, smiling captive, would have remained silent even if they had been able to answer his question. The seventh officer Lloyd-Jones met in the course of his busy afternoon was Sergeant Franz Pohlhaus. Pohlhaus informed Lloyd-Jones that he could not go into that matter.

– Then tell me, Lloyd-Jones said, since you must feel you have grounds for my arrest, were you acting on the basis of an identification made from a sketch?

Franz Pohlhaus allowed that a police sketch had played a role in the events of the afternoon.

– Was your witness the strange old lady who approached me in Sherman Park while I was engaged in an innocent conversation?

– Anything is possible, sir.

– Sounds like a yes to me. And the man who came to my front door was checking out my resemblance to the sketch made from that woman's description?

– I cannot really tell you that, sir.

– This man came accompanied by someone else. If I am not mistaken, the gentleman accompanying him was Mr Thomas Pasmore.

– You are not mistaken, Pohlhaus said.

– I *am* honored.

That was it for the rest of the evening. Ronald Lloyd-Jones was granted his single-occupancy cell, a dinner he declined to eat, and writing implements. The following morning the sergeant once again met Lloyd-Jones in an interrogation room. Lloyd-Jones complained of being unable to bathe himself, and Pohlhaus explained that he would not be able to shower until the initial proceedings had been completed. Unless he wanted to give a full confession at that moment, his shower would have to be delayed until the arrival of his attorney.

– If that's how you want to play it, Lloyd-Jones said. But in your position, I would do everything in my power to make me a comfortable prisoner.

– You seem pretty comfortable to me, Mr Lloyd-Jones, Pohlhaus said.

Lloyd-Jones said he had been doing some thinking, primarily about Thomas Pasmore. – I read the papers like everyone else, you know, and I have some idea how Mr Pasmore works his miracles. Uses public documents and public records a good deal, doesn't he?

– That is well known, Pohlhaus said.

– Sounds to me like a fellow who's good with computers and codes and passwords could get into a lot of trouble that way. If he were to step outside of the legal limits, all sorts of evidence would be inadmissible, wouldn't it?

This gave Sergeant Pohlhaus an uneasy moment. He had no idea how many legal boundaries Tom Pasmore might have stepped over.

– Would you be willing to tell me who the other man was, the one I actually spoke to?

– You're going to find that out anyhow, as soon as your lawyer shows up, so I might as well tell you. His name is Timothy Underhill.

– Timothy Underhill the writer?

– That's right, yes.

– You're kidding me.

Pohlhaus gave him a glare that would have burned the eyelashes off an ordinary man.

– Forget everything I told you, Lloyd-Jones said. Get Tim Underhill to come down here, because I want to talk to him. I want to talk to him now. I'm not talking to anyone else until that happens.

'I think he knows you,' Pohlhaus told Tim as the three of them went through the maze of corridors. 'Your books, I mean.'

'What gives you that idea?'

'His reaction to your name.'

Tim was a little winded from their race through the hallways. In the rush, he had been able to take in only Pohlhaus's excitement and, pinned to the message boards they passed, the usual business cards offering the services of lawyers specializing in divorce. Pohlhaus came to a stop in front of a green door marked B.

'He wants to talk to you alone,' he said. 'Your brother and I, along with the lieutenant from the Homicide Squad, will be watching through a one-way mirror. A voice-activated machine will record everything the two of you say.'

'What do you want me to do?' Tim asked.

'Let him talk. See if you can get him to say anything about your nephew. You could ask him about Joseph Kalendar. With luck, maybe he'll divulge where he hid the bodies. What can I tell you? The more he says, the better.'

'Is he in there now?' Tim felt a moment of irrational terror. Despite his curiosity, walking into that room was the last thing he wanted to do.

Pohlhaus nodded. 'Let me give you a proper introduction.'

He opened the door, and for a second Tim thought he smelled something acrid, smoky, and bitter. Then Pohlhaus walked into the room, and the odor disappeared. Fighting the impulse to turn around and walk away, Tim followed the sergeant's tall, slender back, straight as a plumb line, into the interrogation room. The man at the far side of a wide green metal table had already risen to his feet, and was staring at him with an expectant smile. Apart from the light in his eyes and his expression of comic chagrin, he could have been a fan waiting in an autograph line.

'You two have met before,' Pohlhaus said. 'Tim Underhill, Ronald Lloyd-Jones.'

Lloyd-Jones grinned and held out a firm, pink hand, which Tim reluctantly shook.

'Mr Lloyd-Jones, you may wish to remember that you are being observed, and that your conversation will be recorded. Once again, anything you say may be used against you. And I would like you to verify that you have declined to have your attorney present for this interview.'

'Bobby will get his turn later,' Lloyd-Jones said.

'Then I will leave you to it.'

As soon as Pohlhaus had left, Lloyd-Jones gestured to the chair on the other side of the table and said, 'We might as well make ourselves comfortable.'

Unwilling to surrender control so quickly, Tim said, 'Satisfy my curiosity. Why did you ask to see me?'

'I like your books – what other reason could I have? You're one of my favorite writers. Have a seat, please.'

They lowered themselves to their chairs.

'My friend, you need a new author photo,' Lloyd-Jones said. 'If the sergeant hadn't told me who you were, I'd never had recognized you. How old is that picture, anyhow?'

'Too old, I gather.'

'Make your publisher pay for someone good, someone with style. You have a nice face, you know, you should make the most of it.'

The way you made the most of yours, Tim said to himself.

Which was exactly what Lloyd-Jones wanted him to think, he realized. He had no real interest in Timothy Underhill; he wanted to amuse himself. No mere incarceration could keep him from playing his games.

'I'm sorry I failed to recognize Tom Pasmore before you drove away. One of Millhaven's most famous residents, wouldn't you say?'

Tim nodded. This encounter was beginning to make him feel as though soon he would have to lie down.

'I suppose Mr Pasmore was the one who thought I was worth a visit. To compare with the sketch, I mean.'

'Yes,' Tim said.

'What exactly was his basis for focusing on me?'

'Your name came up.'

Lloyd-Jones gave him a smile of pure sympathy. Light danced in his slightly close-set eyes. 'Let's think about that a little more. I understand from reading about your friend that he gets many of his – shall we say, inspirations? – from public records. So clever, I've always thought. If you can remember, I'd be very interested to know if it was something in the public records that brought my name to Mr Pasmore's attention. And to yours, of course.'

'It was, yes.'

'Tom Pasmore, true to form. And what sort of records were they, Tim? Tax records, something of that sort?'

'We wanted to find out who owned Joseph Kalendar's old house,' Tim said. 'And there you were.'

Lloyd-Jones blinked, and some of the suppressed glee drained from his face. He recovered almost instantaneously. 'Oh, yes, of course. I bought that little place as an investment, then never did anything with it. Let's go on to something a great deal more important to me.

'Here I am, identified by you as the person some

elderly female described to a police sketch artist after something silly brought him to her attention. She objected to a harmless chat I was having with a delightful young man in Sherman Park. I freely admit to being the man in the sketch, for I certainly am the man who was chatting with the boy. But I believe that is about as far as you can go, isn't it?'

The room seemed to be a degree or two warmer and a bit darker and dimmer, as if the overhead lights were failing.

'Go with what?'

'The identification. A woman sees me in the park, a police artist draws up a sketch, you see a resemblance between me and the sketch . . .' He looked up at the mirror behind Tim's head. 'And what does that prove, Sergeant? Nothing at all. It certainly is not the basis for an arrest, is it, unless talking to people in the park has suddenly become a crime.'

'I suppose they must have more to go on.'

Lloyd-Jones regarded Tim as he would a charming though backward pupil. 'Why in the world should you and Mr Pasmore have been interested in that little house on Michigan Street?'

Tim took a photograph Philip had given him from his pocket and slid it across the table toward Lloyd-Jones, who raised his expressive eyebrows and gazed blandly down at it. 'Nice-looking boy. Your son?'

'My nephew, Mark Underhill. Does he look familiar to you? Have you ever seen him before?'

'Let me see.' He drew the photograph toward him and bent over it. The thought that he might touch it made Tim feel ill.

Lloyd-Jones smiled at him and deliberately, using only the tips of his fingers, slid the photograph back across the table. 'I don't think he looks familiar, but it's hard to be sure. Especially with an old photograph like that one.'

'Mark was fascinated with what you called that little house on Michigan Street. According to his best friend, he went so far as to break in and look around. He found all kinds of interesting things. It didn't take him long to learn its history.'

'That's really too bad. I'm sorry to hear it.'

'Why is that, Mr Lloyd-Jones?'

'Please – call me Ronnie. I insist.'

The thought of Franz Pohlhaus watching from the other side of the mirror made Tim acquiesce. 'If you like.'

'Good. Of course, what I find regrettable is that your nephew trespassed on my property. And since you have told me that he did, I must tell you that although I could not recognize him from that picture, I did in fact notice a teenage boy lurking around that house from time to time.'

'How did you happen to notice him, Ronnie?'

'From inside, how else? Through the window. Now and again, I used the place as a getaway. I liked to go over there and collect my thoughts. It was extraordinarily peaceful. I'd just sit in the dark and, I suppose you could say, meditate. Your nephew's persistent attentions were a terrible distraction. One night he and his friend went so far as to shine a light in the window. I was in there at the time, and I sort of *showed* myself. Scared the hell out of the little snoops.'

'Were there other times when you deliberately *showed* yourself to my nephew?'

A smile tucked the corners of Ronnie's mouth. 'Yes, a few. Once, I stood up the hill with my back turned to him. I did things like that a couple of times. I was hoping it might frighten him off, just a bit.'

'Did you ever go into his house? On the day of his mother's funeral, did you let yourself into his kitchen?'

Ronnie looked shocked. 'Please let me express my sympathy for the loss of your sister-in-law. But no, of course not. I'd never do a thing like that.'

'Why did you think standing with your back to him would be frightening?'

'Because of Joseph Kalendar, of course. Kalendar was in the habit of turning his back on photographers. He did it as often as possible. I assume that Kalendar was the reason for the boys' fixation on my property.'

'You were interested in Kalendar yourself, weren't you?'

'Most people in this city were interested in Joseph Kalendar, at one time.'

'In 1980, maybe. Not now.'

'I wouldn't be so sure of that, Tim. Have people forgotten about Jack the Ripper? Men of colorful accomplishments tend to be remembered long after their deaths. Wouldn't you agree?'

The walls seemed to have drawn in, the air become foul. The rage and depression streaming from smiling Ronnie Lloyd-Jones made Tim feel as though he were trapped in a cave with him. It was as if Ronnie were standing on his chest.

'Up to a point, I agree with you.'

'I am very, very happy to hear that, Tim. I have a proposition to make to you.'

Tim knew what the 'proposition' was going to be, and the thought of it made him feel sick.

'Can I be frank, Tim? I'd like nothing better than to be frank with you.'

'Sure, you be Frank. I'll be Dino.'

Tim was looking hard at a spot on the table between his spreadout hands. The muscles in his neck and upper arms had begun to ache. A long time ago, someone had used a pocketknife to scratch a slogan into the top of the table. THEEZ COPPS SUK.

'You're a brilliant writer, Tim. You understand things. You're insightful. And you're a great story-teller.'

'Don't do this,' Tim said.

'We could do an enormous amount of good for each other. I want it to be a partnership. The second I heard that you were the man who came to my door yesterday, I understood why you'd come. You're the only person in the world who could do justice to my story.'

Before Tim had time to react, Ronnie Lloyd-Jones leaned across the table and forced him, as if by black art, to meet his eyes.

'Please understand me – I'm not confessing to anything. I say this to you personally and for the record. I am completely innocent of these Sherman Park murders, so of course I can't confess to them. What I can do, however, and this might be helpful to everyone, is to describe a certain hypothetical situation. Shall we consider this hypothetical situation?'

'I don't think I could stop you,' Tim said.

'I'm going to pretend that I am the Sherman Park Killer. *If* I were guilty of his crimes, I would be able to give you complete details of every murder, going back to before people knew there *was* a Sherman Park Killer. *If* I were guilty of those crimes, I would give you access to every aspect of my life. Still speaking hypothetically, I would tell you exactly where to find the bodies. All of them. I assure you, there would be a tidy little number.'

'Impossible,' Tim said.

'All I'd expect is an account that presented my hypothetical point of view. Fair-mindedness is what we're looking for here. Joseph Kalendar would have to be a part of it. The spiritual rapport, the scale of his achievement. The scale of *mine*, plus a close look at the workings of my psyche.

'Let me make it easy for you, Tim. If you accept, I'll guarantee you compensation in the amount of one million dollars. I'll give you twice that if the book turns out as well as it should. This is irrespective of whatever advance you get from publishers. Your publishers are going to do cartwheels. Remember Mailer and *The Executioner's Song*? I can do wonders for your career.'

'I can't stand this horrible bullshit anymore,' Tim said, looking over his shoulder at the mirror behind him. 'I'm getting out of here.'

Seconds later, Sergeant Pohlhaus strode into the room and said, 'This conversation is now at an end.'

When Pohlhaus led Tim out of the interrogation room, Philip surged forward. 'What's wrong with you? He was going to tell you where he buried my son!'

'Mr Underhill,' Pohlhaus said. The authority of his tone instantly silenced Philip. 'It is extremely unlikely that Lloyd-Jones would have told your brother the truth. He would have fed him one story after another, having the time of his life.'

'I'm sorry to let you down,' Tim said, 'but I couldn't agree to work with him. I couldn't even lie about it.'

'You did a fine job,' Pohlhaus said. 'I'm very happy with what happened in there.'

'I never saw anyone turn down two million dollars before,' Philip said. 'Did you enjoy throwing all that money away?'

Unable to help himself, Tim burst into laughter.

'There isn't any two million dollars,' Pohlhaus said. 'The money was bait, like the CDs he promised to give the boys. Mr Lloyd-Jones is aware that he's going to spend the rest of his life in jail, and he was trying to arrange a hobby for himself. Plus whatever else he could get out of having your brother write about him. Let's duck in here, okay?' He opened the door to the room in which he had met the parents of the missing boys.

'I think we're done here, Sergeant,' Philip said.

'Indulge me, Mr Underhill.'

Once inside, they took their old places at the table, with Pohlhaus at the head and Philip and Tim seated on his right side.

Pohlhaus leaned forward to look at Tim. 'Did you notice when Ronnie lost his composure?'

'When I asked if he'd ever gone into Philip's house?'

'And what was the purpose of that?' Philip roared.

Pohlhaus ignored him. 'It happened when you told him that Tom Pasmore discovered that he owned Joseph Kalendar's old house.'

'What did your men find at his house?' Tim asked. 'Pictures of Kalendar?'

'Pictures, articles, clippings, even clothes like Kalendar's . . . One of his rooms is like a Kalendar museum.'

'You can't convict someone on those grounds,' Philip snapped.

'Conviction won't be a problem,' Pohlhaus said. 'We found photographs of boys who looked drugged, photos of boys tied up, and photos of boys who were obviously dead. It's clear that Mr Lloyd-Jones assumed his house would never be searched. He kept wallets and watches, articles of clothing.'

'Did you find Mark's clothes?' Philip asked.

'At this point, we haven't identified any of the clothing,' Pohlhaus said. 'We will, and we'll do it before long. It isn't just clothing and photographs, either. Ronnie had the fanciest stereo system you ever saw in your life, and yes, he owned a thousand CDs. But the ones he kept next to his CD player had all been burned on a laptop equipped with a camera. They're like home movies. The one I looked at showed boys pleading for their lives.'

'Did he kill them at the house in Old Point Harbor?' Tim asked.

'Yes. It's nice and secluded.'

'Which leaves the question, What made him so uneasy about our knowing he owned Kalendar's house?'

'Exactly,' Pohlhaus said. 'I want to go over there and poke around. If you promise to behave, you can join me. Just don't touch anything or get in the way.'

'Now?' Tim asked. 'Well, why not?'

'You can't be serious,' Philip said.

'You're invited, too, Mr Underhill, under the same conditions.'

'The whole idea is ridiculous.'

'All right, then,' Pohlhaus said. 'Drive yourself home. Your brother can drop in on you later, if there's anything to report.'

'Philip?' Tim said.

'I don't care what you do,' Philip said, already bolting from the room.

From Timothy Underhill's journal, 28 June 2003

One of the strangest trips of my life, that drive to Michigan Street with Sergeant Pohlhaus. Ronnie Lloyd-Jones's toxins had not yet fully left me, and I kept having the fantasy that the unmarked car was the size of a gocart, and that Pohlhaus and I were like a pair of dwarfs hurtling through an underground tunnel. The man made me feel depressed and unclean, blocked in every way. I suppose that's one way to define evil: as the capacity to make other people feel unclean and stifled. Philip scarcely made me feel much better, although then more than ever I saw him as the clueless little boy paralyzed by Pop's aimless brutality.

Pohlhaus pulled into the little half-drive, and we got out and walked around to the back. I thought of Omar Hillyard perched on his love seat, watching everything we did. His eyes were practically drilling into my back.

Like Mark, we went in through the back door, but I felt nothing of what he had on first going into Kalendar's house. It was almost disappointing. I had been half-expecting the ecto-plasmic spider webs, the terrible smell, and the rejecting force field. Instead, all that happened was that the sergeant and I walked into an empty kitchen.

'Ronnie didn't spend a lot of time in this place,' Pohlhaus said. 'He said he tried to scare the boys away, didn't he? Why should he bother?'

'Maybe there was something he didn't want them to see,' I said.

'That's what I think.'

'But Mark went all through the house,' I told him. 'And he didn't find anything except what Joseph Kalendar left behind.'

'So let's *look* at what Kalendar left behind,' Pohlhaus said.

Unlike the boys, we began with the added room and what Mark had called 'the giant's bed.'

'God, that's nasty,' Pohlhaus said.

'Kalendar had a daughter,' I said. 'He told everyone his wife had miscarried, and he kept the child a secret from everyone outside the house. When she was three or four, she tried to escape, and he added this room and slapped this so-called bed together so he could torture her on it.'

'Where does this stuff come from? There was no daughter.'

'Not officially, no. But she existed.'

'And we never knew anything about this daughter? That's hard to believe.'

'If you want to hear the story, talk to a man named Omar Hillyard. He's lived across the street since 1955.'

Pohlhaus gave me an interrogative glance. 'I think I'll do that.' He prodded the straps with a ballpoint pen.

Mark and 'Lucy Cleveland' came vividly to mind: they had coupled here to vanquish the memory of her torture; or to accomplish some darker, still restorative purpose. What you can't convert, you can sometimes incorporate exactly as is, or so I found myself thinking. Either way, you make it yours.

Together, we walked through every inch of that place. I saw exactly where Mark had been when he found the photograph album; I saw the hole in the plaster he made with his crowbar; like him I moved down the narrow secret corridors and staircases between the walls. In the living room, I saw their footprints in the dust, Mark's and Jimbo's, and some that must have been Ronnie Lloyd-Jones's. I also thought I saw the small, high-arched traces of Lucy Cleveland's lovely naked foot.

Sergeant Pohlhaus was astonished by the hidden passages. All of this was new to him. The peculiarities Kalendar had added to his house had never figured in the official accounts of his crime, because they had remained undiscovered until Mark opened them up.

In the basement, a real warren, the old coal-burning furnace that had been original to the house stood next to an oil burner installed sometime in the fifties. The newer heating system was piped into the old flues.

Here were the chute and the metal 'operating table' Mark had described to Jimbo, the empty hampers and the trunk filled with women's hair – the legacy of Joseph Kalendar's insanity.

'This is what turned Ronnie on,' I said.

Pohlhaus nodded. He was moving carefully around the furnace, picking his way through the old stains as he stared down at the floor. I watched him bend down on a clear spot and look at a blackened feather of blood as if he expected it to sit up and talk. When he had enough of the old stains, he stood up again and went around to the front of the older of the two furnaces. He swung open its heavy door.

From a jacket pocket he pulled out a flashlight the size of a ballpoint pen and shone it into the furnace's maw.

'Pretty clean,' he said.

I thought he was acting exactly like a civil servant. I did my best to play along. 'Didn't Kalendar burn some of his victims in there?'

'That he did.' Pohlhaus swung shut the furnace door and began to do his tiptoeing-through-the-tulips act again with the antique bloodstains. He turned his little pocket flashlight on the floor, and when the narrow beam of light fell on the stains, they seemed to turn purple, as if they were molten at the core.

I said, 'You wouldn't think there'd be color like that in thirty-year-old bloodstains.'

'They aren't that old,' he said. 'Some of them might be ten years old, but most of them were deposited more recently.'

'How could that be?' I asked, still not getting it.

'Joseph Kalendar didn't spill this blood,' Pohlhaus said. 'Your friend Ronnie did. This is where he brought some of the boys he abducted. Your brother suspected that we would find something like this. That's why he couldn't face the idea of coming along.'

I looked at the floor in horror.

'The next question is, Where did he bury the bodies?'

The faces of dead boys stared up at me from a few inches beneath the concrete.

'Not down here,' he said. 'This whole surface is uniform and intact. We have to check outside.'

I must have looked stunned, because he asked me if I was all right.

we r 2gether, I remembered.

He pulled out his cell phone as we walked up the stairs. Half of what he said into it was code, but I understood that he was asking for a crime-scene unit to be detailed to Michigan Street, along with two pairs of officers.

'You look a little off your feed,' Pohlhaus said. 'If you'd like to go to your brother's house while I do this, I'd understand. Or if you'd like to go back to the Pforzheimer, I'll have one of my officers take you there.'

I told him I was fine, which was stretching a point beyond recognition.

'I won't send you away if you still want to help out here,' Pohlhaus said. 'But your family was involved, and this might be hard for you.'

'My nephew is okay.'

'Your brother doesn't seem to share your opinion.' Pohlhaus scanned me with his hunter's eyes. I was sure that he had no doubt as to Mark's fate.

'Philip gave up as soon as Mark vanished. He couldn't bear the anxiety of wondering if his son was still alive. So he quit wondering.'

'I see.'

'He buried his own son. I'll never forgive him for it.'

'If your nephew is okay, where is he?'

'I have no idea,' I said.

We were standing at the top of the basement stairs, just inside the door to the kitchen. Some of those footprints in the dust were Mark's, and some of them were another's.

Pohlhaus said, 'Let's go out in back.'

We went outside onto the broken steps. Insects buzzed in the tall grass. 'We have dogs that can sniff out bodies, but for the moment let's see what we can do by ourselves, all right?'

'Look at those weeds,' I said. 'Nobody's been buried back here, at least not recently.'

'You could be right, Mr Underhill.' He stepped down into the waist-high tangle of weeds and grasses. 'But he did kill his victims here, at least some of them. And given his reverence for Joseph Kalendar, I think this yard is still a good bet.'

I stepped down beside him and pretended to know what I was looking for.

The trail beaten down by Mark and Jimbo, then by Mark alone, straggled toward the wooden steps and the kitchen door from the lawn on the south side of the house. There were no other signs of passage through the backyard.

'If he carried the bodies out here, there'd be beatendown grass, there'd be some kind of trail.'

'Don't give up so soon,' Pohlhaus said. He loosened his tie and wiped his handkerchief across his forehead. In spite of this gesture he still looked impervious to the heat. My hair was glued to my head with perspiration.

'Do you know how you can always tell if you've found a place where someone stashed a corpse?'

I looked at him.

'Push in a shovel. A stick does just as well. All you need is an opening. The smell builds up underground, waiting to jump out at you.'

'Swell,' I said. 'I still say he couldn't have buried anything back here. We'd be able to see his tracks.'

Pohlhaus began ambling along toward the back of the yard and the big fence. He was moving slowly and keeping his eyes on the ground. I shuffled here and there, positive I would find nothing. After a little while, I realized that Pohlhaus was moving in a straight line for about six feet, then turning on his heel and reversing himself along the path he had just taken. In effect, he was creating a grid, which then could be linked to other grids until every inch of the weedy ground had been inspected.

'You can leave, if you want to. In another couple of minutes, we're going to be drowning in cops here.'

I said if he wasn't going to give up, neither was I.

The forensic team showed up, and after introducing me, Pohlhaus went inside to show them the basement and the bloodstains. The patrolmen rolled up and were organized to put up crime-scene tape and keep civilians away.

'At this point, you'd better stand down, Mr Underhill,' he told me.

Two uniformed men I remembered seeing in Sherman Park divided the front half of the yard between them. They were wasting their time, I knew. I wanted to see Pohlhaus admit he'd been wrong.

A criminalist named Gary Sung, who had been introduced to me as a trainee from Singapore, popped out of the back door, waved Pohlhaus toward him, and engaged in a brief conversation that required his pointing several times toward the wall. I had no idea what they were talking about, so I ignored it. I was leaning against the side of the house, just at the edge of the overgrown yard.

The two officers I had seen in the park, Rote and Selwidge, looked at something and called for Pohlhaus. He walked up to them and stared down at whatever they had discovered. He waved me toward them. When I got there, I saw what the height of the grasses had until then kept from view. Someone, having decided to clear a long strip of ground about three feet wide and running the length of the property from fence to fence, had overturned the earth in that strip a thousand times, breaking up the surface, softening the ground, and leaving a nice fat stripe of brown earth, through which only a few weeds had begun to protrude. It had been cultivated, that little strip of land.

'I wonder,' I said. 'If that's it, how did he . . . ?'

'If I'm right about what Gary Sung told me, any minute now we're going to see him pop up out of the ground right over . . . *there*.'

He had just spotted exactly what he had been hoping to see.

'Out of the ground?' I asked. Then I understood: I knew what he had known for the previous twenty minutes or so.

There came a groaning noise, and the sound of earth and pebbles clattering into a hole. Exactly at the few square feet of ground where the sergeant was pointing, a panel of weeds and grass swung up into the air and fell away, revealing the sweaty, smiling face of Gary Sung.

'It's *dahk* in there!' Sung crowed.

I moved toward his head, which by stages rose out of the ground as he climbed up the steps built into the earth.

'Do you believe this madman?' Sung sprang out of the hole, waving an entrenching tool. 'He dug a tunnel and hid it behind a door you can't see!'

Mark had not noticed the door in the basement wall; Sergeant Pohlhaus and I had failed to see it; only Gary Sung had seen it, and he was transported with pleasure. 'So now we know,' he said. 'Gotta be careful.'

'Very careful,' Pohlhaus agreed. He looked at me. 'Our Dangerous Materials Squad handles this kind of thing. I'll get them out here. We'll probably want to pull down that miserable wall, give us some room to maneuver.'

He went up to the strip of ground that looked like temporarily neglected farmland. 'Gary, give me that tool, please.'

Gary Sung went across eight feet of ground and passed it to him, handle first.

'Come over here,' Pohlhaus said to me.

I moved up beside him. He hunkered down next to the wide brown stripe on the ground, slid the entrenching tool into the soft earth, and scooped away some dirt, then a little more. 'Ah,' he said. I bent over and caught the stench drifting out of the little opening Pohlhaus had made; death and rot and ammonia, a smell of primal process. In a second, it seemed to coat my skin.

I've been writing for more than an hour, and I can't go on. Anyhow, some kind of earthmoving machine is coming up the alley, making a noise like a motorcycle gang.

Tim put down his pen and thought about what he was going to do next. Dressed in his Principal Battley costume of gray suit, white shirt, and necktie, Philip had announced that he had no interest in 'standing around' in his backyard and 'gawking at' the police while they leveled the cement wall and excavated for bodies. While Tim had occupied himself with his journal, Philip had wandered around the house, snapping the television on and off, picking up magazines and putting them down again. Around three P.M., Philip clumped up the steps; he reappeared downstairs ten minutes later minus the necktie.

'I hope you're not going to stand out there and watch,' he said. Without his necktie, he looked oddly naked, like a man seen for the first time without his glasses.

'They're just going to knock down a wall,' Tim said.

'I mean after that.' He was obviously in anguish, and just as obviously had no idea of how to cope with it. 'Anybody can knock down a wall. I could knock down a wall. Even you could knock down a wall. It's the part that comes after. You might want to spectate, but not me. I'm serious.'

'Spectate?' Tim said.

'Frivolity is par for the course with you, isn't it?' He charged into his den.

'I never heard the word before,' Tim said to himself. 'Spectate. Philip chooses not to spectate.'

The living room seemed to retain some of the tension of Philip's little speech and annoyed departure. Tim felt like moving around, going somewhere, yet he did not want to leave Philip alone, if only because it would be counted against him later. Then he remembered that Mark's computer – the very computer from which he had e-mailed his Uncle Tim – was still upstairs, waiting to be used. With the help of good old Gotomypc.com and Mark's laptop, he could spectate his e-mail, see if anyone interesting had written to him, and clean out the spam before it became overwhelming. It would be a way to fill the time: spam as distraction.

'Philip,' he said to the obdurate door, 'I'm going upstairs to look at my e-mail on Mark's computer. Do you mind?'

Philip said he could do whatever he liked.

Upstairs, Tim sat in Mark's desk chair and clicked open the lid of the laptop. He felt slightly guilty, as if he were trespassing on his nephew's privacy. Instantly, the computer screen sprang to life. Icons in neat rows arranged themselves across a charcoal-green field. Tim clicked an icon and waded through the inevitable commands and delays before he managed to get connected.

On a dial-up modem, his program moved with excruciating sluggishness, and the server was having a grouchy, error-ridden day. After three tries, Tim finally succeeded in linking up with his computer at home. Using Mark's mouse, he moved his cursor to the Outlook Express icon on his screen and clicked once. It was like watching the Mississippi River drift around a wide bend: everything swam along in a brown, sleepy current. The boldface of the new e-mails came to life on his screen. Five and six appeared, then a rapid, ascending column that even at one remove hit the screen with the rapidity of microwave popcorn exploding in a bag. The number at the bottom of Tim's screen rose from 24 to 30 to 45 to 67. There it stayed, all the popcorn having popped.

He read wearily down the From list, bypassing **Depraved** and **PC Doctor** and **Virtual Deals** and the first names of women he did not know because they did not exist, and was then all but levitated out of the chair by the familiar but entirely unexpected name **munderhill. munderhill** had e-mailed his old adviser and confidante tunderhill a message bearing the subject line **4 u 2 c**. There was no date.

Tim selected this heading with a click and cursed the draggy modem, the draggy server, and the sluggish program.

At length, the message appeared in the wide lower-left-hand box.

From: munderhill

To: tunderhill@nyc.rr.com

Sent:

Subject: 4 u 2 c

deer :) my unk

old writer

try this link

lostboylostgirl.com

it is

4 u 1 nce 2 c

so u know

u have & hold our luv

m & lc

Did he hesitate, did he think about it? He rammed the cursor over the blue underlined text and double-clicked, double-clicked, double-clicked.

Another brown, blurry Mississippi episode overtook both monitors, his on Grand Street and Mark's in Millhaven, and while it lasted, Tim Underhill, otherwise known as tunderhill, leaned forward far enough to breathe on the screen were he breathing. Onto his screen, then Mark's, appeared the ordinary Explorer window bearing the link's URL.

Across the top of the larger interior window scrolled the words BROUGHT TO YOU BY lostboylostgirl.com. Beneath that was: 1-Time Only Showing! The Windows Media Player's rectangle opened beneath the caution, if that was what it was and, without the conventional delay for buffering, filled immediately with light and color. So Tim was to see a film clip. The line on the bottom of the rectangle told him that the clip ran for one minute and twenty-two seconds, one of which had already slipped into oblivion. A golden beach ornamented with arching palm trees, a long blue ocean, occupied the little window. A movie, a webcam? A webcam, Tim thought, broadcasting to an audience of one from a world where there were no webcameras. Faintly, he heard the sound of gentle surf and wind rustling the palm fronds. His heart tightened.

The bright sky darkened above the water. First a blond head, then a dark, entered the screen from the bottom left-hand corner. 'Lucy,' *lc*, and Mark, moving hand in hand into the frame, leaving the prints of their bare feet on the sand beneath them as they went. There was the faintest suggestion of haste. A rattle of palm came from the speakers. From the left, heavy dark clouds swam in above the sea; a branching reddish light irradiated the open sky. Hasten hasten the globe revolves. Wind rustled and stirred their scant garments, little better than rags, though beautiful rags. Moving quickly but without running, they briefly occupied the dead center of the Windows Media rectangle, then moved rightward toward the margin. Boiling darkness occupied the distant reaches of the sky, and a harsh illuminated red forked above, distant but traveling forward. The timer showed one minute and two seconds to go.

They paused, the lovers, mid-beach and looked toward the turmoil over the darkening water, which rolled toward them. Oh stay; oh hurry.

b safe my deers:)

Their beautiful poised slim legs lifted into a sprint; their rags flew.

Tim could not see the faces turned from him, but he knew them. They were unforgettable. Through the Starbucks window, indelible, that staggering goddess-visage: he did not have to see it again to remember it.

Now the whole sky grew dark, ripped through with dark, dark red. Thirty-two seconds remained. It seemed an eternity. These luxurious thirty-two, now thirty-one seconds, would last him the rest of his life. But the timer sped up, cruelly, and the lost boy and lost girl sprinted toward the margin of the little frame. Tim Underhill sent himself *toward* them, as if he could, poor bereft old man, to absorb every particle, mote, and cell of their departing seconds, which numbered fourteen, thirteen, ten, six. Mark's head turned, and his upper body twisted not even a quarter turn, sufficient for his smile to shine forth and his eyes to meet tunderhill's with the force of a soft, underground explosion – four seconds, rain sluiced over their heads, two, they flew into the not-to-be-seen, none, they were gone utterly.

It was to gasp, it was to tremble.

The Media Player rectangle with its buttons and keys vanished into the gray beneath Mark's charcoal-green. Tim clicked the little x on the top right-hand corner of both screens. The linked website should have zipped away and revealed his e-mail window. Instead, it collapsed into itself to leave no more than an impression of broken glass shattering inward. His screen flashed the flat deadly blue of hard-disk crashes and visits from or to the local computer wizard; it hung there for perhaps another second, then faded away to nothing, to disengaged gray, as if a fuse had blown.

For a while, Tim kept hitting the return key and double-clicking on everything in sight. Then he noticed that the green strip of Gotomypc.com still ran across the top and bottom of Mark's screen. Trying to control his panic, he managed to back out of the program and get Mark's computer off-line.

Through the bedroom's closed window came the sounds of metal scraping on stone and the whining of gears. He groaned, clutched his head, bent over the keyboard, groaned again. His need for drama satisfied, Tim unfurled from the chair and went to the window. Just beyond the flattened wooden fence, a yellow earth-moving machine nearly the width of the alley was pushing its enormous blade into what remained of Joseph Kalendar's rear wall. The concrete blocks at the edge of the blade shattered into chunks of powder, and the rows above them swooned outward, bulging before they separated, and crashed down into the blade and the alley. Through the dust, a portion of the wide brown strip of exposed earth became visible.

Tim fished his cell phone from his jacket pocket and dialed a number at 55 Grand Street. Since all there were close friends of his, and everybody spent hours in one another's lofts, it almost didn't matter who answered. As it happened, he had dialed Vinh's number, and Maggie Lah answered. He told her to go upstairs and look at his computer, then call him back on his desk telephone. When Maggie called back, it was to say that his computer appeared to be deceased. Expired. Not a single vital sign. He asked Maggie to call Myron, the wizard next door, and tell him he was having an emergency caused by Gotomypc.com, which Myron had installed on his computer.

Down in the alley, the bulldozer was collecting broken concrete blocks in its bucket and depositing them into the back of a pickup truck dropping progressively lower on its wheels. Uniformed policemen, four men in yellow space suits, and detectives in sports jackets milled around in

Kalendar's backyard and the alley. Sergeant Franz Pohlhaus was watching the wall removal from just inside Philip's ruined fence. To Tim's amazement, Philip stood next to him.

Myron called to say he was walking up the stairs at 55 Grand.

'You're the man,' Tim said.

'You're still out of town, huh?'

'That's right.'

'Okay, I'm in your apartment,' Myron said. 'Here we are. Are you sure this thing is plugged in? . . . Okay, it's plugged in. You were using that program I installed?'

'Yes,' Tim said. 'I want to return to the last website I was on. I want to go back to where I was when the computer crashed.'

'Nothin's shakin',' Myron said. 'Let me undress this thing, see what I can see.'

For a minute and a half, Myron wielded his screwdriver and removed the case. 'Now, let me get it turned around . . . Holy shit. Maggie, look at this.'

Tim heard Maggie giggle.

'What's so funny?'

'Your hard disk, man. It like . . . squirted out. I can just about wiggle it free, but it's, like, misshapen. And it's hot! What did this? The program didn't do it.'

‘I know,’ Tim said. ‘I just said that to get you over to my apartment in a hurry.’

Myron agreed to set up a new hard disk before Tim returned to New York the next day.

‘What was that website you wanted to get back to?’

‘It’s not important. I’ll talk to you tomorrow, all right?’

Tim hung up and returned to the window. He felt shaken and oddly dispossessed by what had just happened. Mark, Lucy: running barely covered from the storm, like Adam and Eve. Even, it seemed, in that world, safety was fragile and came at a price. Yet their joy had burned through the image on his commandeered monitor, along with their absolute connection. *Red sky at night, sailor’s delight*, Tim remembered, *red sky at morning, sailor take warning*. The *Old Farmer’s Almanac* neglected to consider the case of red sky at midafternoon, when ragged beautiful Adam and ragged beautiful Eve made haste, made haste.

He watched the bulldozer scrape away and decant into the laden pickup the last of Joseph Kalendar’s eight-foot wall. As docile as a probationer, Philip Underhill had not strayed from Franz Pohlhaus’s side.

Tim let the screen door bang behind him. Philip turned his head to give his brother the glance of a captain to a platoon leader who had arrived late for a briefing. What he had seen must stay with him, Tim realized.

The fat, red-haired man in the cab of the bulldozer shouted, 'Excuse me, Sergeant. Sergeant! Excuse me.'

'Sorry,' Pohlhaus said. 'Yes?'

'Should I start on the ground now? We got a good clear shot.'

'Nice and slow,' Pohlhaus said. 'Plus I want a DM man. Thompson! Pick up a shovel and work alongside Dozier here, will you?' One of the men in yellow space suits and clumsy boots trotted forward.

'The rest of you guys, move in as soon as we find something,' Pohlhaus said.

He gave Tim an unreadable glance. 'Little news flash.' He seemed entirely gathered into himself, like a creature enfolded within its own wings. 'Lloyd-Jones took himself out.' Anger surrounded him like a red mist. 'Out of the game.'

'Oh, no,' Tim said. In his brother's grim satisfaction, he saw that Philip already knew.

'About an hour ago, Lloyd-Jones killed himself in his cell. He ripped his shirt in half, tied one end around his neck and the other around one of his bars, and he rolled off the bed. You wouldn't think it would work, but it did.'

'He got off so, so easy,' Philip said. 'That sick bastard.'

'I guess he realized your brother wasn't going to write a book about him,' Pohlhaus said.

The bulldozer snorted and jerked to a halt, rocking on its treads. Thompson, who had been treading backward in front of the machine as it delicately sliced away a thin layer of earth, shouted, 'Sergeant! We got one!'

All three men at the bottom of Philip Underhill's backyard walked over the defeated fence and into the alley. Officer Thompson scraped the blade of his shovel across the strip of earth, then bent down. Using one of his space gloves, he tugged into view a gray-green human hand, then an entire forearm, encased in a white sleeve.

'That's not Mark's arm,' Philip said.

Pohlhaus waved them back. The brothers retreated to Philip's lot line and looked on as the first of the adolescent dead began his journey upward into daylight.

Acknowledgements

For professional assistance in the writing of this novel, thanks go to Visconti pens (Van Gogh and Kaleido), Boorum & Pease journals (900–3 R), and Kathy Kinsner (eighty words a minute); for moral and emotional support during the writing of this novel, grateful thanks to Lila Kalinich and Susan Straub; for her inspired editing, profound thanks to extraordinary Lee Boudreaux.